Jan 2013

299 Days: The Preparation

by

Glen Tate

D1328060

PrepperPress

Your Survival Library

www.PrepperPress.com

299 Days: The Preparation

ISBN 978-0615680682

Copyright © 2012 by Glen Tate

All rights reserved.

Printed in the United States of America.

Prepper Press Trade Paperback Edition: September 2012

Prepper Press is a division of Northern House Media, LLC

- To the outside thought Who made all of this possible.

From Chapter One to Chapter 299, this 10-book series follows Grant Matson and others as they navigate through a partial collapse of society. Set in Washington State, this series depicts the conflicting worlds of preppers, those who don't understand them, and those who fear and resent them.

Book One, THE PREPARATION, introduces Grant as a young boy and describes the life events that shaped him into becoming the average suburban man who can no longer ignore the voice telling him to get prepared for what is to come. This first book in the 299 Days series provides a front row seat to what happens to people who are mentally and physically prepared for a collapse, and what happens to those who are not.

For more about this series, free chapters, and to be notified about future releases, please visit **www.299days.com**.

About the Author:

Glen Tate has a front row seat to the corruption in government and writes the *299 Days* series from his first-hand observations of why a collapse is coming and predictions on how it will unfold. Much like the main character in the series, Grant Matson, the author grew up in a rural and remote part of Washington State. He is now a forty-something resident of Olympia, Washington, and is a very active prepper. "Glen" keeps his real identity a secret so he won't lose his job because, in his line of work, being a prepper and questioning the motives of the government is not appreciated.

Prologue

(February 24, year after Collapse)

His pants were falling down. Damn it. Stay up.

Grant Matson hated wearing a suit, and he hated a tuxedo even more. A tuxedo that was too big was even worse. His pants were several inches too big and his shirt was baggy and had about two inches too much collar. His bowtie looked silly cinched up in an attempt to hide the fact that the collar was too big. Oh well. Almost everyone else was in the same boat.

No one had clothes that fit anymore. It was a mixed blessing. Everyone lost some weight they probably didn't need. The old way of living, like having plenty of food to make those clothes fit, was a thing of the past. But, things were getting back to a new kind of normal and there was enough to eat now. Things were getting better. Much better than they had been 299 days ago.

Two hundred ninety-nine days. His son, who loved to count days and could tell anyone how many were between any two given dates like he was a computer, told him earlier today that it had been 299 days since May 1. That was the day it all started. And now, just 299 days later, it was wrapping up, as symbolized by the event he was attending tonight. Thank God it hadn't lasted longer.

There he was in their new house. "New house" used to be a happy term as in "we just bought a new house and it's great." It used to mean the fun of moving up and getting something better. That was the old America.

This new house, a "guesthouse", wasn't like that. It was a fine house; in fact, it was a little nicer than his old one. But it wasn't his. It wasn't the house his kids spent most of their childhood in. His wife didn't like it. She missed the old house, but understood why they had the new one. Tonight, she was dropping the kids off at her parents' who would be babysitting while they were out. He was all alone. He chuckled at how lucky he had been throughout this whole thing. He had almost been alone forever. In fact, twice he had almost been alone forever.

Tonight, Grant wasn't alone. There were some plainclothes soldiers outside the guesthouse in inconspicuous places, guarding him. But no one was inside the house. Just him. It was so quiet. He felt alone.

In the downstairs bathroom of the guesthouse, Grant looked in the mirror to adjust his bowtie. He was the same guy in his mid-forties with brown hair. But wow. Look at that. His face looked so much thinner than just a few months ago. Grant barely recognized himself because he had finally shaved. He hardly recognized himself without that military "contractor" beard.

Grant had aged quite a bit in the past 299 days. His face was toughened, and he looked confident. Deadly confident; the kind of confidence that it takes to stand up to bullies and help people. His eyes were different than before the Collapse. There was a hint of loss in them. Not a cry-at-the-drop-of-a-hat kind of loss. His eyes showed that there was less of him now, that something had been lost. Taken from him.

Staring at the new him in the mirror, Grant got lost in memories. That was happening a lot lately. He would just lose his train of thought and drift into heavy thoughts, usually triggered by remembering someone or some event. Extremely vivid memories like waking from a realistic dream, in that first moment when the dream is so vivid it feels real, despite it being a crazy and unrealistic dream. The memories he was having were real, however. That's why they were so vivid. And, in this case, reality had been crazy and unrealistic.

Grant looked again in the mirror and examined his tuxedo. It was symbolic of so much going on that night. He bought it about five years ago when he was climbing the ladder of law and politics in Olympia, the capitol of Washington State, and occasionally had to attend formal events. He would have fit in it just fine 299 days ago.

On this night, Grant was wearing a tuxedo to an event that warranted a tuxedo. It was the kind of night that only happens once in a lifetime, and never happens at all in the lifetimes of most people. Dinner tonight was a victory celebration. It was a victory in the biggest thing in his life or the lives of almost any American. He would be remembered throughout state history, at least as a small figure. He would have a school or something named after him. He should be happy, shouldn't he?

This victory came at an enormous price. "Bittersweet" is a

cliché, but it was true in this instance. Bitter because a lot of people died and suffered. Not billions of people like in some over-the-top apocalypse movie, but plenty of people. People Grant knew, some of them very well. Everyone knew many people who were killed, widowed, maimed, went crazy, were ruined, or had their families broken up. Grant thought about sweet Kellie. All she had ever wanted was a good man. He died in the war.

Almost everyone had been hungry and afraid. Grant didn't lose his wife, but they weren't nearly as close as before the Collapse and it would probably stay that way for the rest of their lives. His daughter was no longer the bubbly outgoing teenage girl she had been; now she was quiet and deadly serious most of the time. She had seen and done things that no teenage girl, or anyone for that matter, should have to experience. His son had faired okay as far as Grant knew.

His old home was trashed so he was borrowing this new one, the "guesthouse," from someone who was now in jail. Grant would rebuild his real home but it would take a while. Things like police protection, farming, and rebuilding roads were a higher priority than remodeling. His old home was a symbol of what everyone was going through. It would take years of hard work to rebuild his town, state, and his country. Actually, the countries.

The "sweet" part of bittersweet was that some very bad things ended. Some wrongs were made right, and some guilty people paid for what they did. They couldn't hurt people anymore. Some people who thought they were losers found out they were heroes. People came together and really lived for the first time in their lives. Lifelong friendships were formed between people who just 299 days ago wouldn't have talked to each other. And, Grant felt guilty for thinking about himself, he was absolutely certain that he'd made the most out of his life. He saw dozens of "coincidences" in his life that were planted years ago and then sprang up at just the right time so some absolutely amazing things could be accomplished. He was being used to do great things. Grant was just a guy with no particular skills who didn't exactly lead the perfect life.

All Grant did right was have a little faith and listen to the outside thoughts, even when they said things that seemed crazy at the time. There was no denying that, for nearly forty years, the "coincidences" had been pointing him in the direction of helping people and fixing a bunch of really terrible things that needed to be fixed. He was here for a reason.

Snapping out of the vivid memories and back into getting

dressed for the big event, Grant realized that all the bad things that had been fixed were what he needed to focus on tonight. Measures would be put in place to prevent the bad things from happening again, he hoped. That was his new job and the reason for the dinner tonight. I have to get this right, Grant thought. I can't screw this up. Please help me, he thought. Actually, he prayed that.

Grant looked at the invitation on the sink in the bathroom of the guesthouse. The invitation was beautiful, made of parchment paper and written in calligraphy. That was a rare sight nowadays, something ornate like that. He picked it up and soaked it all in. He was holding an invitation to dinner with the Interim Governor before the Inaugural Ball. It was a very select group; just a handful of the Governor's oldest friends and closest advisors. It was a dinner to chart out the future of New Washington State. The inauguration was for "Governor Benjamin Trenton." Ben's name looked so funny like that. More of those vivid memories were coming back.

Like when, years ago, Grant and Ben got drunk at a Super Bowl party and had the half serious, half joking talk about Ben being the Governor someday, and then laughed because that could never happen. But it had actually happened. What a crazy world.

There was a knock at the front door downstairs. Grant grabbed his Glock and carefully poked his head out the bathroom door down the short hall toward the front door. He wasn't alarmed enough to aim his pistol at the door, but he was alarmed enough to have it in his hand.

"Yes. Who is it?" Grant said loudly enough to be heard through the door. There was that command voice he had developed in the past few months. It was not his peacetime voice.

"Sgt. Vasquez and Trooper Timmons," a male voice said. Grant was expecting them. He laughed at himself for having the habit, acquired only recently, of always having his gun with him and assuming every knock on the door could be someone trying to take him away. He put his Glock down on the sink, not wanting the troopers to shoot him by mistake if he were waving it at them. He'd come this far, with so many guns pointed at him recently and was about to be the Governor's dinner guest before the Inaugural Ball; he would be too embarrassed to get shot now by friendly fire.

"Be right there, gentlemen," Grant said casually. He looked at his Glock again. The memories started flooding back like they had been all evening. He knew every detail of that gun. Nothing was more comforting than holding it in his hand. It had comforted him through the absolute worst things in his life. He'd carried it almost constantly the past 299 days, and had used it several times to save his life or the lives of others. There had been that terrifying night in the neighborhood when everything changed forever. There had been that other time...

Grant realized he was keeping the gentlemen at the door waiting while he was remembering all those things. It was impolite to leave people waiting. He wanted to grab his pistol again when he headed toward the door. No. He forced himself to put it down on the sink.

He needed to get his head into the new normal, and the new normal was that he didn't need a gun all the time. In fact, other people had guns and were protecting him. That was such a weird thought. But, so was everything that was happening, so why not throw this weird thing into the big pile of weirdness. Roll with it, Grant thought. He looked at his Glock on the sink and took a deep breath. He could do this without his gun. He put his beloved pistol in the locking carry case he had intentionally placed in the bathroom because he knew he'd have to stow it there before leaving. He took a deep breath and walked out of the bathroom, unarmed and feeling naked.

Grant opened the door and saw the two plainclothes State Police troopers. They looked so young. Much to Grant's delight, their suits didn't fit too well, either. He didn't feel so poorly dressed now. "Come on in, guys."

"Thank you, Colonel," one of them said to Grant.

That sounded so strange: "Colonel." Grant had acquired that title only a few days ago. His first reaction to hearing people call him "Colonel" was always a little guilt because he hadn't really done anything to get that title. Well, he thought, maybe he did do something but he couldn't get past the feeling that having that title was a little disrespectful to real military men who did real military things to earn their titles. But he knew that "Colonel" was not strictly a military recognition now.

The New Washington Legislature recognized forty-three people from the war who had done various helpful things of a military nature and awarded them the honorary title of "Colonel." Grant was one of them. He chuckled to himself. I'm more like Colonel Sanders, he thought. Except I don't know how to make fried chicken.

The troopers were standing in the entryway with him. Grant still wanted his pistol. He pointed to the bathroom down the hall and said to the troopers, "Let me guess, guys, I can't bring my pistol with me to the Governor's Mansion."

"Correct, sir," the older one said.

"That's cool. I have you two," Grant said. He started to get a tear in his eye for no apparent reason, which was happening a lot lately. He tried to control his emotions by distracting them with some conversation.

"Hey," Grant said to the troopers, "I really appreciate what you guys are doing for me. I know the odds of a gunfight are pretty low, but I appreciate…" Grant wanted to say "you risking your lives" but didn't. "I appreciate what you're doing," is all he could get out. The troopers could sense that Grant was seeing in them other young men and women who had volunteered for things and who were no longer with them. Or, they were alive, but messed up.

"No problem, sir," the younger one said.

The older one checked his watch and said, "We need to get going, Colonel."

Grant composed himself again. He was getting better at that as time went on. He was decompressing from the events of the past few weeks and slowly getting his emotions under control. Most of the time.

"Is a separate detail getting Dr. Matson and my daughter?" Grant asked. He knew the answer. He knew the plan well because it involved his wife's and daughter's safety. He always knew where his wife and kids were because there were still isolated instances of Loyalist violence. And given his new job, he and his family would be a juicy prime target.

"Yes, sir," the older trooper said. "At Dr. Matson's parents' house. Another detail will be there at 18:45 to take them to the ball." Grant nodded to them.

Grant's daughter, Manda, was coming, too. Grant had pulled a few strings and got a nice Inaugural Prom for the young people who had been cheated out of their high school proms by the Collapse. Ben, "Governor Trenton" Grant forced himself to call him, had made that happen. Manda was the Queen of the Inaugural Prom.

As they were going out the door, Grant said to the troopers, "Did I ever tell you guys about how Governor Trenton and I got really drunk when the Seahawks were in the Super Bowl and talked about how a guy like him would never be Governor?"

It was going to be a great night.

- Book 1 -

Chapter 1

A Forks Loser

It wasn't supposed to happen. Grant Wallace Matson was born on a cold day. He had multiple complications, and the doctors told his mother and father that he would probably not live through the birth. They had assembled all the equipment and nurses for a troubled birth; all the equipment they had back then.

Well, there he was, crying. He was rushed straight into the incubator and what passed for a rural hospital's intensive care unit in those days. He actually lived, and everyone was so happy, except for his dad.

Oh, sure, things were great for the first week or two because they had expected the worst and it didn't happen. But a needy crying baby soon started cutting into his dad's recreational time, which was drinking with his buddies.

Grant's father, Larry Matson, liked to drink. He was an injured logger in Forks, Washington. Forks was an isolated timber town on the extreme northwest corner of Washington State. It was a rough town, but people basically kept each other in check. It was "rough" in the sense of people being tough and occasionally violent, but not raving maniacs. It was like lots of small rural towns in the 1960s, 1970s, and into the 1980s.

Many people thought Larry was faking his "injury" to get out of working, and there was some evidence of that, although his back did seem to hurt a lot. That wasn't surprising, considering how hard the work was out in the woods. Setting choker line — the wire around a downed log to be picked up by a giant log boom tower — killed and injured loggers on a pretty regular basis.

To supplement their limited workers' compensation income, Grant's mom, Patty, worked hard as a waitress in one of the two coffee shops in Forks. She was taking a little time off for the new baby but she

1

went back to waiting tables within a few weeks. Larry, who no longer worked, would take care of Grant and, later, Grant's sister Carol. Larry hated that he had to stay home with the kids. And he let them know it.

Patty Matson was a tough bird. Because she was determined to be a proper woman with a family, she would suffer in silence her whole life. That meant making sure Larry was a husband and a father. Without that, the whole thing would fall apart. She needed him, so she would put up with a lot, which included letting him treat the kids like crap.

Grant had a relatively normal first few years. Carol was born two years later. Other than the abusive father and co-dependent mother, things were pretty normal in the Matson house. They had a little house on a five-acre country lot, a car, and a TV. They got by. One of the main ways they got by on such a small income was to have a few cattle and pigs and a garden. Everyone in Forks canned food, hunted, fished, cut their own firewood, and knew how to fix things. The Matsons were no exception, and Grant learned how to do all these things, just like everyone else in Forks.

Gardening was hard, given the climate. Forks was near an actual rain forest. It rained so much in Forks that, by measured rainfall, Forks was technically a "rain forest," receiving 120 or more inches of precipitation a year. The moisture blew in from the nearby ocean, and then hit the Olympic Mountains and came down for months every year. This meant gardening in Forks wasn't too productive, but was possible.

Grant would go out in the summer and pick berries for jam. They had several apple trees that led to more than enough canned pie filling and applesauce to last all winter. In fact, applesauce was at every meal from about fall to early summer. Deer meat was the norm. Grant's dad never took him out hunting, though, because his back always hurt. Grant had to go out with friends and their dads, but he learned to hunt. He remembered getting his first deer as a freshman in high school with a 30-30. He was so proud when it went into the freezer. He, at age 14, was providing for the family. That meant everything.

When Grant and Carol were young, Larry was a raging alcoholic. Over time, Larry quit drinking as much and was getting acclimated to being a "house husband," which was so contrary to his tough-guy logger personality. Larry kind of loved his kids; he would be nice to them from time to time. But, his life wasn't going the way it was supposed to, and he felt trapped with the kids in the house all day. He couldn't stand that a woman was the breadwinner in the family.

2

That would get him drinking and hanging out with his friends to get back to what life was supposed to be in Forks: a logger drinking with his logging buddies.

Larry smacked his kids around. It wasn't vicious bone-breaking beatings; just a lot of slaps, sometimes in public. Screaming at the kids was common for Larry. Grant assumed all of this was normal.

One time when Grant was in the sixth grade, he forgot to feed the family's pig. His dad exploded and just started kicking him, really hard, knocking Grant to the ground. His dad kept kicking him, even when he was down. The kicks kept coming one after the other. Grant had the wind knocked out of him and thought he was dying. It was terrifying. It was like his dad went from being normal to some kind of animal who couldn't stop hurting him.

Grant could barely move after that and spent a few days recovering in bed. His mom said there was no need to go to the doctor's office for Grant's "fall." Grant assumed it was because they didn't have any money for the doctor. Later he would realize it was because of the shame that his mom would have felt if the doctor knew what had happened. Grant was bewildered that his mom wouldn't protect him. He realized early on that he couldn't count on others to protect him. He had to take care of himself in this world.

His dad would go a few months without hitting the kids. He would be a pissed-off jerk for those months and still yell at them, but he wouldn't hit the kids unless they did something wrong. The anger was sudden, vicious, and uncontrollable, and then it went away. It never ended with an apology. It was always the kids' fault for whatever happened to them.

His little sister, Carol, was a good sister. They had to band together to fight the "ogre" as they called their dad. Later in life, Grant could see how he naturally rallied people together to fight off threats. He had lots of practice from an early age.

Grant and Carol would cover for each other and standardize their stories so they could stay out of trouble. Carol was a quiet girl, and she was very smart. She would stay out of the fights between Grant and their dad except when she just had to help her big brother. However, Grant thought Carol was a little too much like his mom by staying out of most of the fights. One day he said so. Carol shot back, "What am I supposed to do? Fight him with my fists?" She had a point. A person had to have the ability to fight, or people would pick on them. That's just how it was.

Grant had to protect his sister. When his dad was hitting her or screaming at her, Grant would lunge at him and try to help. He usually got his ass beat, but he couldn't stand by and watch an innocent person be hurt. He just couldn't.

Grant was drawn to helping people in danger. From an early age, he would rush in and help people. His willingness to leap into danger made people think there was something wrong with him. Grant thought just the opposite; there was something wrong with everyone else for not helping. But he got it; they were weak. They didn't want to rock the boat. They would let people be mistreated as long as they were left alone.

Grant remembered when he was eight years old and riding his bike with some friends in Forks. An old man in the neighborhood was walking and fell to the ground. The man was holding his chest like he was having a heart attack. The other kids were scared. Grant went right over and tried to help. He didn't know what to do. The man was turning blue and having seizures. Even at that young age, Grant knew the man was dying. There was no 911 back then, so no help was coming. The other kids scattered, especially when the seizures started. Not Grant. He stayed there with the man and held his hand. That's all he knew how to do. Grant told the man that everything would be fine. When the seizures stopped, the man smiled at Grant. It was a peaceful smile. The man knew he was dying and that some nice boy came to comfort him. Grant smiled back, knowing that the man was going somewhere better. The man died with Grant holding his hand. It was the least Grant could do. He sat there holding the man's hand until a police officer and ambulance arrived to take him away.

Later, the kids playing with Grant wouldn't have anything to do with him. "Grant touched a dead dude," they said. They said Grant was weird for touching a dead person. They were probably ashamed that they hadn't done anything, but they took it out on Grant by shunning him. Grant couldn't understand why people hated him for doing the right thing.

Decades later, Grant would understand what was going on when he learned the term "sheepdog." Sheep are blissfully ignorant and peacefully graze on grass while wolves are lurking in the shadows, planning their attack. Farms with sheep always had sheepdogs to guard the sheep. The sheepdogs can't stand to see a sheep in danger so they rush in to help, putting themselves in danger. To a sheepdog, the thought of seeing a sheep hurt is worse than having the wolf attack the sheepdog. The sheepdog can't help rushing into danger; it is innate.

The other reason Grant would later understand that the

4

sheepdog analogy was so fitting was that sheep are scared of the sheepdogs trying to protect them. After all, a sheepdog looks a little bit like a wolf to a sheep. They're both in the dog family. The sheep can't understand that a sheepdog would rush in to protect them because they wouldn't protect each other. The sheep view the wolf-looking sheepdogs with suspicion.

The sheepdogs, like Grant, accept that the sheep didn't appreciate them, but they still can't stand to see the suffering so they jump in to help. They can't help it. It's just how they are.

Grant and his sister would escape the ogre Larry and the dreary Forks house by reading. The Matson kids were frequent visitors to the library in town. It was a pretty decent one. The local logging company that ran the town donated all the books. The great thing about the library was that their dad wasn't there. Grant remembered his dad's attitude about the library. One time Carol said, "Dad, we're going to the library." Their dad answered, "Good. You can bother the people there and leave me alone." That about summed it up.

There was a whole world in that library, a world outside of Forks and the ogre. It was full of stories from all over the world and from different time periods. Grant especially liked to read about the American Revolution. A small band of underdogs take on the most powerful people on earth and win! What a story. Grant could relate. These stories made a big impact on Grant as he grew up.

One of Grant's strongest memories of his childhood was his mom sitting at the dining table with bills and a checkbook and crying uncontrollably. They "got by," but it was really a struggle. He would watch her cry and think about being rich. Not millionaire rich. Just rich enough so he wouldn't have to cry when he paid the bills. That seemed impossible there in Forks, but Grant could sense that what he was thinking about would happen later.

Grant got those feelings sometimes when it came to big things like what he would be when he grew up. It was hard to explain, but what he thought was going to happen in the future was just going to happen. He knew it was unlikely that a person could actually tell what was going to happen, but it seemed like there was a path to what he saw happening in the future. He couldn't actually see the exact contours of the path. But it was there; someone couldn't see it unless they were looking for it. Like a deer path in the woods. It's there if a person is looking for it. Grant knew the path was taking him somewhere good—out of Forks. It was just going to happen. Maybe he would do all the work to make it happen, or maybe it just would happen. Or maybe it was a combination of both. He got used to this feeling.

One day when Grant was about nine, his dad seemed mad. This sometimes meant Grant was going to get hit. He would walk on eggshells and avoid his dad, which worked part of the time.

"Come here!" Grant's dad yelled. Oh crap. Grant walked into the kitchen not knowing what was coming. His dad looked at him and, like he was talking to an adult, said to Grant, "You ruined my life." Grant's dad then explained how he could have been a photographer if he didn't have to stay home, "and take care of you little brats." Grant waited to see if he was going to get hit. After a few seconds of silence, Grant just left.

It was weird. Grant, at the ripe old age of nine, thought what his dad had just said was so absurd. A photographer? His dad didn't even own a camera. Grant knew he should be devastated that he was just told that he had ruined his dad's life, but for some reason Grant couldn't take it seriously. He just thought about how he was going to get out of there when he graduated from high school. He wondered how many nine year-olds were calmly making escape plans. He even felt sorry for his dad.

But, Grant still hated his dad. Being told you ruined your dad's life was actually a pretty good day compared to others. Getting beat up is no fun. Grant felt helpless, being so small and unable to fight back.

The worst part was the time he had to go to school with a black eye. Everyone knew what had happened. It was the most humiliating experience in his life. Words couldn't describe how embarrassing it was. People, especially kids, treated someone differently when they knew that person was getting their ass beat at home. The bullies at school would pick on that person more. They sensed the weakness and wanted to get in on the fun. The decent kids would pity that kid, though. When he had the black eye, Grant got physically ill before going to school. He threw up and tried to stay home claiming he was sick.

Grant's mom wouldn't let him stay home. She didn't want to make Larry mad. In her mind, there was some sort of disagreement between Larry and her son that led to the black eye. It was their business, and she wasn't going to get involved.

Grant could never understand why his mom didn't stick up for him. Actually, he could. She had the self-esteem of a turnip. But that didn't excuse it. Mothers were supposed to protect their children, weren't they?

It was particularly hard for a sheepdog like Grant to understand how a mother could let this happen to her kids. People were supposed to protect the weak. All she had to do was tell Larry to stop or call the police, but she wouldn't.

Grant developed a strong dislike for people who could stop bullies but didn't almost as much as he hated the bullies themselves. He and his sister would talk about why their mom wasn't doing anything. Was it because they were bad kids? One time they both went to their mom and told her to divorce their dad. She cried for days.

Larry Matson was a socialist. Grant remembered his dad always talking about "corporations" and the "proletariat." Every bad thing that had happened to their dad was caused by corporations, like the logging company. By about middle school, Grant knew more about Lenin and Marx from listening to his dad than most adults would ever know.

There was a little church across the street from Grant's house. He noticed that every Sunday nice people who were dressed up went there. They seemed happy. Something good must be happening in that building, Grant thought.

"Hey, Dad, can I go to the church?" Grant asked, one day. Of course it would be OK to go to church.

"Hell no," his dad said. A speech on how Christianity is used to oppress workers followed. Grant's mother just sat there quietly, listening idly by while her husband basically set Grant on a course that could prevent him from ever going to church.

One Sunday when his dad was out of the house, Grant snuck over to the church. It was a great place. It was full of normal people were who were so glad to have him there. After that day, Grant snuck over whenever he could. He felt like such a rebel going to church.

It was hard to say how often he got beat up by his dad. Entire segments of Grant's childhood were a blur to him; he just erased it from his memory. But Grant did remember one thing clearly; the day the beatings changed.

A sophomore in high school, Grant was now over six feet tall. He came home from school one day and his dad was in the kitchen. His dad started yelling at him about some chore that hadn't been done, and then started coming at him. Grant planted his feet, clenched his fist, and punched his dad right in the face. It hurt Grant's hand, but it hurt his dad more. For a split second, the look on his dad's face was total surprise. It was like he was saying, "You... just hit... me?" In that moment, it was obvious his dad had realized that Grant was now big enough to fight back. The bastard was scared.

Grant loved it. The bully was getting hit for a change! Grant felt a surge of adrenaline. It was like he was fully alive and invincible. That felt really good (despite the throbbing pain in his fist). He wanted to do it again. Grant started chasing his dad through the house. He loved to see the ogre run like a scared little girl. This was for all the times his dad had hurt him and his sister. Hurt defenseless innocent little kids. Grant didn't want to hurt the guy as much as he wanted the guy to quit hurting him. But, yeah, Grant did want to hurt him, at least a little.

After showing the old man what a pussy he was, Grant waited for the inevitable retaliation. Sure enough, the next day he was home from school in the kitchen cutting a block of (government) cheese with a big knife. His dad came into the kitchen looking like he was going to kill Grant. Like he was going to actually kill him. It was a look Grant never forgot.

Grant was terrified. He dropped the big knife and started to run. As he got out of the kitchen, he looked back to see his dad picking up the knife and starting to chase after him, with the huge butcher knife. Grant saw everything in slow motion. He was focused on the blade and couldn't really see anything else. He couldn't hear anything. All he could see was the knife in slow motion. The fear gave him super human strength.

Grant ran, faster than ever, through the dining room and living room and out the front door. The ogre was a few seconds behind him. Grant had the strangest thought as he was running down the porch and into the street; hopefully no neighbors would see this. Oh, how the town would talk. That was actually running through his mind as he was running for his life.

Grant kept running for blocks. He was amazed at how fast he'd run and how far. That fat old bastard couldn't keep up. Grant was several blocks from his house.

And then he stopped. Now what would he do? He had to come back home at some point. Would that knife be waiting for him? Would his dad wait until Grant fell asleep and slit his throat at night?

Grant walked around the neighborhood for a few hours. It was getting dark. What would he do? As he was deciding to go back home, his dog, Buttons, came running up to him. Grant was glad to see him and noticed Buttons' collar chain. Grant loosened the chain and swung 't a couple of times in the air as a weapon. It was a pretty decent ghting tool.

"Thanks, Buttons," Grant said as he gripped onto his

improvised weapon. "Might as well get this over with," he said to Buttons. He walked toward home. Every step was terrifying. Each step brought him closer to the house where the ogre and the knife were. The lights were on in his house. His dad was waiting for him.

Be a man and get it over with, Grant thought. It never occurred to him to go for help. Who would help him? He couldn't think of a single person who could help him. He needed to do this himself. No one was ever around to help. You had to do things like this on your own. It's just how the world was.

Grant walked in the front door with the chain out as a weapon. The old man saw him with the chain. The bastard decided that his boy was getting big enough and smart enough to whip him.

"It's dinner time," his dad said to Grant.

That's it? Grant thought. The rest of the night, his dad didn't say anything to Grant, which was fine with him. Grant couldn't sleep that night. He kept the dog chain under his pillow. He also loaded his .22 rifle and put it by the bed.

Grant woke up the next morning, and was genuinely surprised that he was alive. He got ready for school.

School sucked. It was so stupid. Grant was an extremely good student; straight As when he tried. School was so easy that he was bored. Except for history, especially American History.

Grant loved the Revolutionary War. He read every book in the library about George Washington. His hero was Marion Fox, the "Swamp Fox" who fought a guerilla war in South Carolina against the British. Grant was fascinated about how a small band of farmers and other average men and women could tie up a sizable chunk of the most powerful army in the world at the time. Fascinated; and he wondered why he was so drawn to this subject.

Grant could get along with anyone (except Larry, apparently). He was the one kid who could hang out with just about every clique: preppies, stoners, rednecks, Mexicans, the town's one black kid — anyone. Grant found it easy to move from one kind of person to another for two reasons. First, he didn't care about a person's status or social standing. If a person's social standing mattered then, by definition, Grant was worthless. So this wasn't a way for him to measure people because he would fail that test.

Second, Grant had a strong innate political sense. Not "politics" like the obnoxious "vote for me!" student body candidate. That was "retail" politics; shaking hands, figuring who could help you, and promising things you couldn't ever deliver. That wasn't Grant at all.

Grant was a master of "wholesale" politics. Figuring out what motivates people to do things they wouldn't normally do, how to make people feel comfortable, how to explain a complicated problem facing them by relating it to something in their everyday lives so they understood that their little problem is part of something bigger. Grant knew exactly how far the other person could go towards doing what Grant wanted and when it was time to stop asking for more. He understood how vanity and ego were tools to get people to do what he wanted. He figured out a lot about institutions — teachers, bureaucracies, businesses — and how they made decisions, which allowed him to tailor a plan toward getting that institution to decide the issue his way. This skill can't be taught; Grant was born with it.

While Grant downplayed his intelligence as much as possible, other kids could tell that he was smart — but that didn't help him in high school social circles where conformity was more important than merit. On the positive side, Grant was fairly good looking so that helped. But no girls really took him seriously since he was… well, a loser.

He did have one weapon that no one in his class could match. He was funny; hilarious, in fact. He could turn a phrase, make a play on words, recall lines from movies, and do amazing impressions. His impressions of teachers and other kids had people rolling on the floor. Even if they thought he was a loser, they laughed at his jokes and were entertained by him. Grant was the most well liked loser at Forks High School.

Since he was a loser, he could instantly identify with other losers. This would have a major impact on his life. He knew what it was like to be humiliated and he hated it. So Grant helped other losers whenever he could. It was more than just being a sheepdog and helping people who happened to be losers. Grant had a loser bond with all fellow losers. They were all in a club, The Loser Club. But, hey, it was still a club.

Grant's best friend in high school, Steve Briggs, was a lot like Grant — except Steve wasn't a loser. Steve was the typical Forks redneck kid. He wore flannel shirts with red logger suspenders. He always wore a baseball hat with the Stihl chainsaw logo like most other males in Forks. Steve's dad was a logger, like everyone else.

Steve was one of the most outgoing guys Grant had ever met. He loved Grant's sense of humor. He was a truly tough guy and was extremely confident. So he didn't care if other people thought Grant was a loser; Grant was his friend, so everyone else could screw off if they didn't like that. This was just what Grant needed in a friend. The two were inseparable.

People find escapes in many different ways. Many kids in Forks did drugs and everyone drank (except the handful of Mormon kids). Grant did his share of drinking. Quite a bit, actually. But his real escape was something no one expected him to do.

Chapter 2

What a Beret Can Do for a Loser

Civil Air Patrol (CAP) was the Air Force auxiliary. They had a cadet program for high school kids. Back in those days, CAP was responsible for much of the search and rescue for small civilian planes. With all the mountains around Forks and the rest of western Washington, they had plenty of work. CAP also provided military training like drilling and basic Junior ROTC kinds of things. The Air Force and the other military branches got a lot of recruits out of CAP. It was the best way a high school kid could see if the military life was for him or her.

And, for a sheepdog like Grant, CAP was heaven. They actually went out and rescued people in plane crashes. What could be better for a sheepdog than that?

Steve Briggs joined the tiny Forks squadron of CAP because he wanted to go into the military when he graduated from high school. Steve told Grant all about how cool it was: getting to fly in planes and occasionally helicopters, wearing military uniforms, saluting, getting to go out in the woods and looking for crashed airplanes.

"We spend almost every weekend training," Steve told Grant. Weekends away from home—Grant was in.

Grant learned the basics of military culture. He learned how to salute and how rank worked. He learned about uniforms. He also learned the bare basics of how a military unit operated, which would be very valuable later.

Pretty quickly, Grant became the cadet squadron commander of the Forks squadron. He was really good at motivating people and making them want to be around him. He treated each and every cadet like a valued member of the team. Fellow "losers" felt especially at ease around him because he could see their potential and figure out a way for each of them to shine. Grant managed to get the very best out of people.

His first role in search and rescue was "base support." CAP operated out of little air civilian airfields where their small Cessna search planes would go out and look for the crashed plane. Cadets couldn't fly the planes; adult CAP volunteers did that. Since CAP was so small, every search team member needed to know just about every role. This included fueling small planes and taxiing them. Grant learned this quickly.

Base support also included making sure the aircrews had food and a place to sleep. Grant was an organizational whiz. He would get local restaurants and hotels to donate to the search effort. Another task at the search base was dealing with the press when they were covering a story about an airplane crash. He first got noticed by the CAP leadership for his ability to handle the press at age sixteen. He was a fresh-faced teen in a uniform who would keep the newspaper and occasional TV reporters updated on the status of the search. He artfully dodged questions asking for information that wasn't public. He was amazingly articulate and mature for a kid.

That was great, but what Grant really wanted was to go out into the woods and actually do the searching. Grant, being a hillbilly kid, was good at the outdoorsy search and rescue parts of CAP. They learned how to survive in the woods, navigate with a compass, use radios, climb rocks and repel down cliffs. Out in the woods, Grant wasn't a loser. He was a leader. He was rescuing people. He was in his element. His guys loved him.

The CAP cadets were the junior, extremely junior, civilian version of the Air Force pararescue special operations squadrons who would search for crashed military aircraft and crews behind enemy lines. The Air Force searchers were called "PJs" which stood for "parajumpers." One of the adult CAP officers, Capt. Smithson, was a PJ in Vietnam. Grant and all the other cadets idolized him. CAP cadet searchers were about 1/1,000th as tough or skilled as the Air Force PJs but the fifteen to seventeen year-old CAP cadets convinced themselves they were "just about" PJ material, which was laughable, but harmless.

Grant planned on joining the military. He wanted to try out for the PJs. While that would be very cool, he would be happy doing just about anything as long as it was far from Forks. He went to the nearest "big" town, Port Angeles, and talked to the Air Force recruiter.

He learned that one of the complications from his birth prevented him from joining. He was born without pectoral muscles on the left side of his chest. The pectoral muscle locks the arm in place when it's lifting or holding a lot of weight. The lack of a pectoral muscle didn't affect anything in everyday life except that he couldn't hold heavy things up easily with his left arm, or do pushups or pull ups.

Grant was disappointed that he couldn't join the military, but he would be fine with just going to college far away so he could become a white collar guy living in a nice house. Anything as long as it wasn't in Forks.

Another CAP experience shaped Grant and directly contributed to how he handled future big events. During Grant's senior year of high school, he earned his way, along with Steve, onto the elite statewide CAP search team called Squadron 3. There were six cadets on the team out of the 1,000 or so in the state, although only about a hundred tried out for the team. But still, they were elite. A loser like Grant had never been "elite" before. It was awesome.

While he was pretty good at the search and rescue things like land navigation, he wondered why he got into Squadron 3. There were guys in Squadron 3 who were way better than him at the technical aspects of search and rescue. He asked their commander, the former PJ, Capt. Smithson, what Grant did to get selected for the Squadron 3.

"You remember," Capt. Smithson asked Grant, "the land navigation final course where your team carried a team member in a stretcher for six miles through the woods?" Capt. Smithson was smiling.

"Yes, sir," Grant said. He thought for a while but was embarrassed to say what was true. Finally, Grant said, "I was leading the team but I made a wrong turn at the ridge and we came in second. I thought I wouldn't make the team for that."

"Oh, yeah, that wasn't good," Capt. Smithson said. "I'd forgotten about the wrong turn. But do you remember what you did when you got back to base, Matson?"

"Not really, sir," Grant said. Then he thought some more. "Well, I went back out, linked up with the teams that were still running the course and encouraged them."

Capt. Smithson was smiling even wider then. "Exactly," he said. "You went back out and motivated the others. You were cracking jokes and getting them focused on getting the job done. That's why you're in Squadron 3. You're a born leader, Matson."

Later in life, Grant would understand why he went back out to motivate the stragglers. He knew what it was like to come in last and he felt for the guys who didn't come in first. He wanted all of them to make it across the finish line with their chins up high.

As members of the Squadron 3, they were the only CAP cadets who got to wear a beret and jungle fatigues (like the PJs). At age seventeen, Squadron 3 thought they were the baddest asses on the planet. That beret was the second most important thing to him. The first was his team members.

Grant would do anything for his team members. They would do anything for him. The team was like a gang; one that saves people's lives, not one that hurts people. It was hard to get in, but once they were in, the teammates had each other's back. The team would go through a lot together, and they got through it because they helped each other. They shared scarce food out in the woods. They would carry a guy's gear when he was hurt. Their life was literally in each other's hands, like when one is climbing a cliff and another teammate has the safety line. They shared victories together like rescuing someone in a plane crash, which Squadron 3 did on more than one occasion. They would do anything—absolutely anything—for their team members. Grant would never forget that feeling. He would have that same feeling decades later with another team.

CAP Squadron 3 was the best thing to happen to Grant up to that point in his life. He was confident. He knew he was good—really good—at something important. He was "elite." He had respect from his CAP peers. It was the exact opposite of being a loser at Forks High School. Squadron 3 was precisely what Grant needed.

Chapter 3

Oklahoma

Another much needed escape, and good influence for Grant, was his grandparents' ranch in Oklahoma. He was named after his grandfather, Wallace Grant. Grandpa was a real live Indian; a Creek (sometimes called the Muscogee Creek Indians) to be exact. He lived on a ranch, and owned horses, guns, and everything cool. On his ranch in the South, there was no talk of corporations and imperialism. His grandparents even went to church. Grandma and Grandpa were nice to each other. They didn't hit each other or scream. They were happy. They were "normal." They were the complete opposite of what Grant knew in Forks, Washington.

From elementary school through high school, Grant and Carol spent every other summer in Oklahoma. Grant grew very close to his grandpa. Grandpa didn't like Larry for the obvious reasons. Grandpa didn't like it one bit that that lazy communist Larry married his daughter and was poisoning his grandchildren's minds with all that socialist stuff. So Grandma and Grandpa tried to show Grant and Carol everything they could about how decent people lived. They prayed a lot that their grandkids would turn out decent, given the strikes they had against them.

Grandpa was a war hero, but he wouldn't talk about it. Grant learned that Grandpa was in the Army Air Corps in World War II. His plane got shot up over Northern Germany and they managed to limp it over to Sweden. They bailed out over Sweden and landed safely. The Germans couldn't touch him in Sweden because it was a neutral country.

Grandpa got to the U.S. Embassy in Stockholm and spent the war working there. He would never say, but everyone knew he was spying there. Grant thought this was the coolest thing ever.

Grant asked Grandma about it one day. "Isn't it great that Grandpa was a spy during the war?" He expected Grandma to be so proud.

She wasn't. She acted like she hadn't heard him.

"Grandma," Grant asked again, "isn't it great what Grandpa did during the war?

She looked right at Grant; anger filled her eyes. He had never seen her that way. "No, it isn't," she said and walked out of the room.

What was that all about? Grant asked Grandpa why Grandma was so mad about him being a hero.

Grandpa didn't want to talk about it, either. Finally, he said, "Grandma didn't want me to go off to war. She wanted me to stay in the states and be safe. She felt…," he was getting teary, which Grant had never seen, "that I was going off on some big adventure and leaving her at home. We love each other very much, but I must admit, Grant, that Grandma and I were never the same after I left for the war. She wouldn't even come to greet me when I got back home after the war. It took her several years to get over it." Grandpa smiled and said, "Things are fine now. But she still gets a little mad when people bring it up."

"Sorry, Grandpa," Grant said. "I didn't know."

"That's OK," Grandpa said. "She'll be fine in a few minutes. But do me a favor; never go off to a war that you don't have to."

Never go off to a war that you don't have to?

That sounded odd. Why would someone do that? Decades later, Grant would remember this conversation vividly, and understand it fully.

One of the best parts about going to Grandpa's ranch was his guns. Specifically, his cowboy guns, which are a big deal to a boy. Grandpa and Grant went shooting all the time during Grant's visits. Grandpa taught Grant how to shoot properly and safely, and how to clean and maintain a gun. Grandpa gave Grant a .22 and he took it back home to Forks where he shot it all the time. He earned money for .22 shells with his paper route and lawn-mowing business. At the hardware store, Grant could get a box of fifty shells for $0.99, which was a lot of money to him, but worth every penny.

Guns became a powerful symbol to Grant. A symbol of how normal, decent people lived, like in Oklahoma. More importantly, guns meant safety to Grant. He understood that having a gun meant people couldn't hurt him. He could use a gun to make a bad person go away, like when he had the .22 by his bed back in Forks after the knife incident. Grant loved to hold a gun just because he instantly felt safe with one in his hand. He couldn't explain the feeling but that was it: he felt safe with a gun. He felt instantly calm and able to handle any bad situation.

Grandpa noticed that Grant was good with words. There was a lawyer in the family, Uncle Mike. Grant reminded Grandpa of Uncle Mike.

One day, out of the blue, Grandpa said to Grant, "You should think about being a lawyer." That was the most preposterous thing Grant had ever heard.

"Ah, Grandpa," Grant said with a shrug, "only rich people can be a lawyer."

Grandpa said, "Not in America. You can do anything you set your mind to."

Grant didn't take it seriously. Grant, a lawyer? That would never happen. He didn't want to let down his Grandpa so he said, "I'll think about it." But to be a lawyer, you had to go to college and how would he pay for that?

Chapter 4

"You Gonna Eat That Pickle?"

Grant wanted to go to the University of Washington in Seattle. The SAT college entrance test was on a Saturday morning. For some stupid reason they never would understand, the Friday night before the test, Grant and Steve got very drunk. Steve wasn't taking the SAT, but Grant was. He got up after about two hours sleep and drove (still drunk) to Port Angeles and made it to the test on time. By the time the test was over, Grant had gone from drunk to hung over. Taking the SAT drunk? Oh well, no college for him. He figured he'd take the test again.

Except that Grant got a great score, one that would easily get him in to the UW. Boy, that was lucky. It was like he was supposed to go there despite the stupidity of getting drunk before the SATs.

Grant loved watching the UW football team on TV, and the thought of living in a big city like Seattle would be the perfect escape from crappy little Forks. Plus, a UW degree meant that he could have a professional job and finally be a "normal" American. He didn't really care what job he got, just that it wouldn't be in Forks and that he would earn enough money to live in the suburbs. He felt this slight but discernible attraction to the UW as if he was supposed to go there. He couldn't explain it except that it was like that feeling he would get that something was just going to happen. It was that path that he could barely see. Just the faint outlines of it, but it was there. There was no question that he needed to go down that path.

Not only did Grant get accepted to the UW, but he also got a scholarship. Him? Accepted into the UW? With a scholarship? His mom wanted him to use the Indian thing to get some more tuition money, but Grant thought that real Indians should get the money. Grant didn't really look like an Indian, not like Grandpa did. Besides, the idea of giving things to people based on their race seemed wrong. So Grant checked "white" on the application, and never told his mom.

Grant could feel that he was on the cusp of his great escape. It started to sink in during the winter of his senior year of high school.

The path out of Forks he saw back when he was nine years old was actually happening. Just like he knew it would, despite how hard it still was for him to believe.

Steve was staying in Forks. Steve was considering joining the military too, probably the Air Force to try out for the PJs. However, the spring of his senior year, his dad got him a job on a logging crew. Steve was fine with that; he would be a regular Forks guy.

Grant wanted to hurry up and get to the UW. He couldn't wait to get out of Forks. He always worked in the summer for a small company related to the paper products plant in town. The little company, Olympic Paper Products, was run by a nice old man, Mr. Reynolds. Olympic took the abundant sawdust from the mill and put it into a very loud (and dangerous) machine that turned it into a finer grade product that was shipped to the paper mill. Grant cleaned the machines, shoveling and sweeping out the sawdust and finer dust. It was pretty miserable. He learned how to work, though, and the $4.00 per hour wage was a pretty big deal in the Matson family budget. He had to pay for all his school clothes and anything else he wanted other than room and board.

One time, Grant saved up $100 and went to the bank to get a hundred dollar bill. That $100 bill was amazing. It looked like all the money in the world. He had worked extremely hard for it and that $100 bill was a symbol of his hard work and achievement.

Until his dad stole it. Grant kept it in an old bread pan in his dresser. One day it was gone. Only people in his family knew where the $100 bill was. Grant's dad actually mocked him, asking, "Where's your $100 bill, Grant?" and laughing. Grant couldn't believe it—well, actually, he could. He hated working so hard just to have a bully steal something. It was more than just the money. It was wrong. Grant instantly developed an almost irrational hatred of bullies. But given what happened to him, it made sense.

That summer after graduation but before leaving for college, Grant's dad had been virtually silent to him. His dad knew that Grant had just accomplished more at by age eighteen than he ever would. Grant could clearly sense his dad's jealousy, anger, and resentment. But Larry knew that Grant was even bigger and in better shape than when he was a sophomore and whipped his ass. Larry wouldn't even think about hitting Grant now. Grant knew it. Just about every time Grant saw his dad that summer he thought to himself that the only thing keeping him from getting hit was that Grant could hit harder.

Grant understood violence. And he understood what it took to stop violence—the threat of superior violence. Yet another life lesson Grant learned during his childhood. It was a lesson that most other people would never understand.

In late August, it was finally time to go. Grant would be staying in the dorms. He didn't even try to get into a fraternity; poor kids from Forks wouldn't be welcomed there, he figured. His dad drove Grant the four hours to Seattle, virtually without speaking a word. It was a very long trip.

When they got to the UW, his dad did something unusual. He smiled. He looked Grant in the eye and said, "I'm proud of you, son." Grant was stunned.

"Thanks, Dad," Grant said. That was it. Grant was now a college student.

He loved college life. He loved the drinking and the huge library full of books on the Revolutionary War. And the girls. He loved the girls. They were gorgeous. These weren't like the girls in Forks. They would actually go out with him, because they didn't know he was a loser. Yet. He had to keep his past under wraps.

Grant made a complete transformation of himself when he got to the UW. He spent the money he made from working his ass off over the summer on decent clothes. He looked entirely different. He fit in. He was a new person.

Grant got invited to a fraternity party. What the hell, Grant thought, this is part of the college experience, right? Grant went to the party. There were lots of really beautiful girls there. Sorority girls.

Everyone was drinking beer. Grant went up to the keg and poured a cup like the experienced drinker he was. That was a thing that kids from Forks knew how to do well.

And then, there she was. Coming in the door. A beautiful girl, with a beautiful smile. Amazingly beautiful. Like an "I have to spend my life with her" kind of amazing. A great song was playing, "Lips like Sugar" by Echo and the Bunnymen. Grant would never forget that song. It seemed to fit the scene perfectly.

Grant was decent looking, so he had a chance with this girl, but it would still be a long shot. He needed to use his secret weapon: humor.

The party was a barbeque, so this girl had a paper plate with a hamburger and a pickle spear on it. Grant was keeping an eye on her in between chats with other people. He was waiting for her to finish eating; there was no use trying to get her attention when she's trying to eat. When the hamburger was gone and only the pickle spear was left,

Grant decided to take a risk. He walked up, smiled his big country boy smile, looked at her and gave it his best shot.

"You gonna eat that pickle?" he asked.

She started laughing.

"Oh, you can have it if you'd like," she said, smiling. That was a good sign. So far, so good.

"Nah, I don't want the pickle," Grant said very confidently. "I just wanted to introduce myself. I'm Grant."

"I'm Lisa and I knew you didn't want the pickle," she said with yet another smile. Clever. She was pretty and smart. A great combo. But probably out of his league. Oh well, let's see what happens, he thought to himself.

"What house are you in?" Grant asked, referring to her sorority. Delta something was the answer. Grant didn't really pay attention to what she said. He was just looking at her.

The next hour was the most amazing conversation of Grant's life. It was about everything and nothing. Grant found out that Lisa Taylor was the daughter of an accountant and lived in Bellevue, which was the richest town in the Seattle area. She was pre-med. Yeah, right. A girl this beautiful would be pre-med for about two semesters and then get an easier major.

Lisa felt drawn to Grant. She didn't really know why. He was cute and tall—6' 2"—but there were cuter boys there that night.

This Grant guy was interesting, unlike all the Bellevue boys who were so predictable. Grant had a realness to him. The kind of realness you didn't see in her affluent suburban world where things were... predictable. He was absolutely different than anyone else she'd ever met. Opposites attract.

She didn't know why, but she felt safe around him. He had a flow, an ease. He seemed more mature than the other freshman boys. She felt like there was plenty to learn about him. Interesting things; interesting in a good way. He was simultaneously brilliant and goofy. Not "goofy" in a weird way. Irreverent. But polite at the same time. It was hard to explain.

The main thing that drew her toward him was his sense of humor. He was a blast to be around. During the long conversation, her sides literally got sore from laughing. She'd never been around anyone like him.

Grant was scared to death. This seemed like the most important conversation of his life; he was a loser talking to a pretty girl. That's scary. He was pulling it off, though, apparently making it look easy.

He had learned from real life scary things — actual threats to his life — to use the fear as a way to focus on the task at hand. To focus on getting away from a knife-wielding maniac, on rappelling off a cliff during a search and rescue, on making a great first impression on an amazing girl. Grant was good at conquering his fear.

"Do you have a major yet?" Lisa asked Grant.

"I think I'll do history," Grant said. "American History." He didn't go into the Revolutionary War stuff because she probably wouldn't care. And he didn't want to seem "weird."

"Where are you from, Mr. Pickle Lover?" she asked with another one of those beautiful smiles.

Grant was afraid of this question the whole time. He had been trying to steer the conversation away from this topic, but knew all along that there was no way to not mention this. Oh well. Let's see what happens.

"Forks," he said. "I have all my teeth and everything."

She laughed.

"I've kinda heard of it," she said. "Where's that?"

"Out on the Olympic Peninsula," Grant said. "Clallam County."

"What does your dad do there in Forks?" she asked. Grant could feel his perfect girlfriend slipping away.

Grant looked her right in the eye and said, "He's an unemployed, abusive, former logger."

Silence.

"Just kidding," Grant said. "My dad's a photographer."

She laughed. This guy was so entertaining.

Whew.

"You had me going there with that logger thing," she said.

The conversation went on. Grant felt a buzz like he was drunk, except that he'd had only one or two beers. He was in love.

Great. A loser had fallen in love with a rich sorority girl. This probably won't end well. Oh well. He realized that he couldn't possibly forget about her so he would be stuck with either a broken heart or the best thing to ever happen to him. He mentally shrugged. We'll see what happens, he thought to himself.

Lisa spotted someone and said, "Hey, I need to say 'hi' to my friend. I'll be right back."

Grant finished the beer he'd been nursing and thought about how lucky he was. Everything seemed to be going really well. This might turn out to be a disaster, but tonight was smooth sailing so far.

Lisa hadn't come back yet. It had been five minutes. Grant was getting nervous. Then it was ten minutes and still no Lisa. Grant was worried. Then it was fifteen minutes. Grant started looking for her. Panic. She wasn't anywhere.

Grant had been ditched. Damn it. It seemed to be going so well. Crap. He went back to his dorm and thought about how his whole life was over now. No matter what he tried, he would be a loser. Forever. Not even college was helping him.

The next day he went to class, but couldn't concentrate. Lisa was all he could think about. While he was walking, he bumped into things right in front of him because he was so focused on her, and feeling like his life was over at age eighteen.

Grant came up with a plan. A stupid plan, but a plan nonetheless. He couldn't remember her last name, so he would go to each of the twenty or so sororities and ask for "Lisa" and see what happened.

He went to the first sorority and asked for "Lisa." The girl at the door asked for a last name. Grant said, "That's the part I don't know." The girl said, "We have several girls here named Lisa, so I really need a last name before I call someone down." Grant left. This was going to suck.

He went to the second sorority on that street and knocked. Guess who answered the door? Lisa. What are the odds? Grant thought. This was meant to be.

Lisa seemed very thrilled that he was there. He acted like he meant to be there, instead of the fact that he was on a desperate mission to salvage his life from ruin.

"Oh, hey, hi," Grant said like he wasn't alarmed at all. "I was just following up from the party last night. You kinda disappeared."

Lisa smiled. She assumed he remembered what sorority she was in and had come to see her. "I'm so glad you came by," she said. "I went to say 'hi' to my girlfriend and she grabbed my arm and took me over to the Beta house. I thought I could get back to see you, but I couldn't." She seemed to be telling the truth.

"Well, let's go get something to eat," Grant said. "Some place with pickles." Lisa burst out laughing. That was how he asked her out on their first date. Pickles. It actually worked.

Grant and Lisa were pretty much inseparable for the next three and a half years.

Chapter 5

History

Grant joined a fraternity of good guys. The fraternity wasn't the bunch of dicks he assumed they would be. Several of them came from small towns like he did. Most of them seemed to be like him; they were at the UW to get good jobs and have some fun.

Grant was doing really well in class, especially history. He took an introductory class on the Revolutionary War and after about two weeks, his professor, Professor Estes, asked him to stay after class.

"Where did you learn so much about the Revolutionary War?" He asked Grant.

"The library." Grant wasn't trying to be a smart ass.

"What is the one question you would ask a Founder?" his professor asked. This was his standard question for seeing if a person was a serious thinker on this period of history or not.

"Oh, that's easy," Grant said. "I'd ask Thomas Jefferson why he thought the American Revolution turned out so differently than the French Revolution."

"What do you think President Jefferson would say?" Professor Estes asked.

They spent the next two hours talking about the differences between the American and French Revolutions. The basic answer was that the American colonies had a tradition of self-rule and diverse religious backgrounds, while France was run top-down and only had one religion. The American revolutionaries were also very conscious of how most revolutions end up—a bloodbath of terror by opportunistic politicians. Also, the American revolutionaries did not try to hunt down and kill all their Loyalist opponents. They hung some of them, of course, but they let most of them either go to Canada or reintegrate into America if they pledged not to cause trouble. Reconciliation was the difference.

Grant shrugged and summed up his point to Professor Estes. "The Founders were practical people," he said. "They understood that they needed the former Loyalists to be doctors, businessmen, farmers, laborers. The nation wouldn't last long if it was constantly re-fighting that war among its people. At some point, a country must put all the old vendettas aside and get on with building roads, establishing institutions, growing businesses… living life. The Founders prized the country actually working after the Revolution more than they wanted to hunt down people they hated. That's where the French went wrong."

Professor Estes was taking it all in. He just sat there for a while.

"Are you in the History Department?" he asked Grant.

"Yes, I'm an American history major," Grant said.

"Would you like to work for me as a researcher?" Professor Estes asked.

Grant blurted out, "A job working on this? Getting paid to learn about the Revolutionary War? Hell, yes." Then he corrected himself. "I mean, yes, Professor."

Grant ended up producing a senior thesis paper on the differences between the American and French Revolutions. It was even published in a scholarly journal, a very rare honor for an undergraduate. For a senior seminar project, he wrote about the differences between the guerilla warfare in the American and French Revolutions. He compared the theories of Mao and those of the American revolutionary guerilla leaders and found that tactically, they were largely the same.

The UW was so different than Forks. Grant thought that just about everyone he met, especially the rich kids, lived in such an artificial world. In their world, food was always in the grocery store, the power was always on, and the police always came when they called 911. They had no idea what being hungry was like, what a cold night was like, or what violence was.

Lisa fell into this category. Grant couldn't expect a beautiful, charming, future doctor girlfriend to be a hillbilly. In fact, her being a hillbilly would defeat the whole purpose of Grant starting a life in the suburbs with a respectable job and a respectable wife. Hillbilly was exactly what Grant was trying to get away from.

But every time Grant saw how the affluent Bellevue people lived, he kept wondering how this could be sustained. No one else seemed to be wondering about this. He couldn't get his mind off of this topic: American life was unsustainable. He thought about it all the time, in between thinking about Lisa and his future life in the suburbs.

American history was great and all but Grant found something that was even cooler, and that would pay better.

He had always worked at least one job since he was kid. He wanted to earn some more money — partying and having a girlfriend wasn't free — so he took a job at the federal prosecutor's office as a photocopy clerk. He got to meet all kinds of lawyers and FBI agents. It was very cool. He quickly realized that he could be a lawyer.

Grant was drawn to the law. His mind naturally worked like the law: elements, applying the facts, coming to a conclusion supported by a law, and making arguments. He could instantly pick up on legal theories and could remember every detail of legal cases and history. It was weird. He was made to do this.

Many people he respected were telling him that he should go to law school. He brought up the idea with Lisa.

"Law school would be great for you," she said with a huge smile. "We could do med school and law school at the same time." She had stayed a pre-med major and was getting straight As. She was actually going to be a doctor. She was also probably very glad that she could tell her family that her boyfriend from little old Forks was going to law school. It sounded a lot better than a "history major." And way better than "unemployed logger."

Grant remembered his conversation with his Grandpa: "Only rich people can be lawyers." Well, now, he was about to be one.

The one thing Grant didn't think about much during these years was Forks. He was completely wrapped up in Lisa, school, working, achieving, achieving, and achieving some more. He was getting papers published, planning on law school, and was in a very serious relationship with a gorgeous soon-to-be doctor. He was accomplishing everything he set out to. And more. Lots more. This was the path he thought about when he was nine. It was all coming true.

Chapter 6

Law School and Marriage

About a year into their dating, Lisa invited Grant to meet her parents. Grant was nervous. They would be on to him and his hillbilly past.

Past? Yes, it was his past now. He was a completely different person. He wasn't a loser anymore. He was a respected person. He figured he could pull off meeting the parents.

When they drove to her parents' house, Grant could not believe how big and beautiful it was. It was the nicest house he had ever seen. Later he would think about it; they had a nice house, but it wasn't a mansion. It was just so much better than the shack Grant had grown up in.

Lisa's dad, Andrew "Drew" Taylor, was a partner in a giant national accounting firm. Her mom gardened a lot. When he met Mr. Taylor, Grant shook his hand firmly and said, "Pleased to meet you, Sir."

Lisa's dad appreciated the "Sir" part but said, "Please, call me Drew." Grant nodded.

Lisa's mom, Eileen, seemed nice. He lightly shook Mrs. Taylor's hand and said, "Pleased to meet you too, ma'am."

"Call me Eileen, Grant," she said.

So far, so good.

They got to know each other. Surprisingly, Lisa's parents both grew up on farms in Eastern Washington. Eastern Washington was the rural part of the state. It was nothing like Seattle. Lisa's parents were down to earth people. They had worked hard, achieved a lot, and were respectable people. Lisa and her parents actually appeared to like each other; it seemed so different than how Grant grew up. He felt comfortable around them, but in their nice home he still felt like a hick masquerading as a college student.

They had dinner and Grant was not making any mistakes. He knew which fork was for salad and which was for dessert. He didn't try to be funny or to be... himself. He was playing it safe.

"So, Grant," Drew said, "Lisa tells me you're a history major. What do you plan to do with that?" He didn't say it like a put-down; he was genuinely curious.

"I plan on going to law school," Grant announced with pride. The Taylor's eyes perked up. Lisa hadn't told them that; she wanted to surprise them with the good news in person.

Going to law school was the right answer. "I am interested in being a judge, perhaps," Grant said. He never used the word "perhaps" except in fancy settings like this.

Law school? Maybe a judge? That was music to the Taylors' ears. The night went well. The Taylors were nice and they seemed to think Grant was OK. No one asked about Forks.

Grant took the law school entrance test and did very well. He got into the University of Washington and didn't even use the Indian thing.

Lisa got into the UW Medical School the same year. They were set.

Now it was time to get married. It wasn't even a "decision"; they both knew it was going to happen. Grant proposed to Lisa by getting on his knee. She said "Of course, Mr. Pickle Lover." They were ecstatic.

Next came the first year of law school and med school. This was the year of homework; crazy amounts of homework. Both were doing well in school. Lisa really liked medical school, and she was thinking about being an emergency room doctor. She was competitive and loved the challenge of making life and death decisions.

Grant loved the law, which wasn't a surprise, but he really disliked most of the people in law school. They were mostly arrogant. Grant wasn't sure why they were that way, because he was as smart as or smarter than they were. They were so impractical. These future lawyers couldn't do anything other than spout off theories. They were like an exotic flower grown in perfect greenhouse conditions; these impractical idiots couldn't survive a day out in the countryside. None of them had ever worked a day in their lives. Most were spoiled little brats. What happened in class one day illustrated it all.

Grant was in Trial Advocacy class, which is where students learn how to do a trial. It included examining witnesses, opening and closing arguments, that kind of thing. They used a made up case for their trial. Grant was assigned to defend an alleged gunman who held up a liquor store. The evidence showed that the defendant held a semi-automatic pistol in his left hand, clicked off the safety, and shot the victim. Grant knew something was wrong. He asked the witness (played by someone in his class) if she was absolutely sure that the gunman did this with his left hand. She was; it was definitely his left hand. She was left handed herself and recognized a fellow lefty.

"Handing you what's been marked Exhibit 23," Grant said in the mock trial to the witness, "can you identify this?"

"It's a drawing of the gun," the witness said. It was a low-budget mock trial so instead of a real gun for an exhibit, they just had a drawing of it.

"Can you look at the drawing of the right side of the gun?" he asked.

"Yes," the witness said.

"Now please look at the left side," Grant said to the witness. "Do you see anything that looks like a little lever?"

"Yes," the witness said.

"In the picture, do you see that little lever on the right side of the gun?" Grant asked.

"No," the witness said. "It's only on the left side."

"Thank you," Grant said with a grin. "No further questions."

Everyone looked surprised. Was that the end of the questions? He hadn't proven anything.

Grant then said to the "judge" (played by the professor), "Your honor, I move to dismiss the charges because I can prove the defendant is innocent."

"Please do," said the judge, with disbelief in her eyes.

Grant was enjoying this. "Your honor, the safety is a little lever," he explained since this professor had probably never touched a gun in her life.

"It is on the left side of the gun," Grant said. "It is impossible to click off the safety on the left side with your left hand. A person's left thumb can't get over the frame of the gun to click it off. It can only be done with your right hand." He demonstrated with his hand.

The gunman could not have used that gun with his left hand. Either the witness was lying or that gun wasn't the one used in the crime. Regardless, that was a reasonable doubt and it meant that his client would not be convicted.

Grant was so proud of himself. An innocent man was set free in this mock trial. Grant, the hillbilly from Forks, had outsmarted all the smart people from places like Bellevue. All because Grant had actually shot guns and knew that you could only use your right thumb to click off the safety on a Smith and Wesson semi-auto.

The professor thought about it and agreed that the defendant was innocent. Grant expected a discussion about how important it was to review the evidence and to think on your feet. However, what came next shocked Grant.

"What are some reasons why handguns should be banned?" the professor asked the class. What?

A discussion of gun control — a one-sided discussion of the entire class versus Grant — went on for the rest of class. No one said, "Hey, Grant, way to go on solving the mystery. Glad your life experience led to an innocent man not going to prison."

Grant could not believe it. What a bunch of impractical pricks. That about summed up his view of law students.

There was one exception — Bill Owens. Grant first noticed him because he heard something from him that no one else had at the UW Law School: a Southern accent. Grant got to know him and found out he was an Army officer attending law school part-time. Military and from Texas — two cool points in Grant's book. But, they were two definitely uncool points in the book of everyone else at the University of Washington Law School.

Bill Owens was the only friend Grant had in law school. They hung out a lot because, well, they were the only ones who would hang out with hillbillies like them.

Bill and Grant were different than most students in another way: they worked. Bill was in the Army full time. Grant worked at the state Attorney General's Office all during law school. Good résumé material. It was part of his plan to be a successful lawyer; to be the exact opposite of the Forks loser. Grant worked about twenty hours a week and had a full course load. He was used to it. In fact, not working would have seemed weird to him. He learned a lot of practical skills as a law clerk at the Attorney General's Office. He was learning how a government agency made decisions and what motivated them.

Grant's favorite class, in one sense, was Constitutional Law. He loved the Constitution. What a magnificent and brilliant document. He didn't know why, but he innately understood the Constitution. It made absolute sense to him.

But Constitutional Law was taught by a socialist; a female professor who really seemed to hate men, especially men who disagreed with her. God forbid someone challenge her; that would lead to viciousness as Bill found out one day.

"Mr. Owens," the professor said in a condescending tone, "please describe the holding in City of Richmond v. J. A. Croson Co."

This was a case that held that reverse discrimination — in that case, a mostly black city council passing an ordinance giving racial preferences to minorities based on past racial discrimination — was unconstitutional. It seemed that a group of black politicians was enriching some black-owned businesses. White politicians had been doing the same for white-owned businesses for years, but that didn't make it right. Racism was racism.

Bill explained in a matter-of-fact tone, "Croson held that racial preferences based on past discrimination can instead be unconstitutional race discrimination when there is evidence that past racial discrimination is no longer present. The court held that government must be color-blind, neither against racial minorities nor for them. Just neutral." That was exactly what the case held.

"Oh, color-blind," the professor said, dripping with sarcasm. "I notice you seem to have a Southern accent, Mr. Owens. It doesn't surprise me that you think 'color-blind' means taking away opportunities for racial minorities."

The message was received by the whole class. The professor was a hater and it was easier to just let her do her thing. She had the power, and one better not get in her way. It was pretty obvious that she picked out the one Southerner in the class for her demonstration of power.

Bill was unfazed. He went on to give a great defense of how the Constitution required color-blindness. But it didn't matter. His "class participation" grade, which was a third of his grade, was zero and he got a mediocre grade in the class, despite doing very well on the written test (which was graded anonymously).

This demonstrated to Grant that the left-wing people running everything were intolerant bullies who had some deep hatred of people like Bill and Grant.

Then it hit Grant. He wanted to be a lawyer to fight bullies. Lawyers could sue the government when they hurt people. Lawyers could sue big business, big labor, big anything on behalf of the little guy. In that moment, Grant knew exactly what he was going to do with his law degree.

This was reinforced when a federal judge gave a speech at an event Grant attended. The judge, who was appointed by Reagan, was not invited to speak by the law school. A private group, the conservative and libertarian Federalist Society, invited him to speak.

The judge's speech was on how lawyers can fight bullies. The judge said, "When you boil it down, the law is about protecting people from other people trying to take advantage of them. The law is about protecting people's liberties and rights." This made complete sense to Grant; it explained everything about the law.

This is what he was supposed to do. Grant had found his purpose. He wanted to be a judge; or at least a lawyer who fought bullies.

Chapter 7

Olympia

Grant and Lisa had opportunities to relocate just about anywhere in the U.S., but they wanted to stay in Washington State. They loved it there; the beauty of it, and the generally laid back people.

Lisa quickly found a job at a Tacoma hospital. Grant needed to find a lawyer job in Tacoma or nearby Olympia, which would be hard for him. Not because he had a bad résumé, but because he was "conservative." Washington was not a hospitable environment for conservatives.

The State of Washington had a very large government. Per capita, Washington's government was much larger than most states. For the most part, people in Washington State were liberals, at least in Western Washington around Seattle. In Eastern Washington, which looks a lot more like Idaho, people were largely conservative. The rural areas in Western Washington outside of the Seattle metropolitan area were largely conservative, too. Most people lived in the Seattle area. They had all the votes in the state that were needed to run the more conservative areas like their little parks and nature preserves. People in Washington State, just like the rest of the country, had been taught for generations that government was there to help the little guy and prevent evil corporations from exploiting them. Everything good came from government; everything bad came from a lack of government. Kids doing well on standardized tests? That came from government spending money on education. Kids not doing well on standardized tests? That came from a lack of government spending on education. Everything in life could be explained by the "fact" that government needed to do it, and needed to do more.

Of course, most people in Washington State didn't really think of it this way. They didn't think about it at all. They were happy to have a politician or bureaucrat or the media explain that every issue can be resolved through government action. They didn't think about what this really meant; they were just happy to have it taken care of. Running a business in Washington State was not easy. Taxes were very high and could be "interpreted" by the taxing authorities to mean that a person always owed more. Labor laws meant that firing an employee, even one who is stealing from the company, was very difficult. As for building on one's land, the environmental impact studies and permits made their land the government's land that they may get to use if Big Brother said so.

A group known as the Washington Association of Business was formed to represent businesses and to fight against government abuses. They were similar to a statewide chamber of commerce, except they had more balls than any chamber of commerce. WAB was an association of small business only; big businesses, which usually went along with government and received special breaks as a result, were not allowed into WAB.

WAB was run by a real character, Ted Foster. He was in his early forties and looked like a weathered Detroit factory worker, because that's where he came from.

He was a fighter, and was very effective. He was hated by bureaucrats and politicians. WAB and Ted Foster became a semi-household name in Washington State because they were regularly demonized in the newspapers and by the politicians.

WAB was located in Olympia, the state capitol of Washington, which was the town where Grant needed to find a job.

WAB was looking for an in-house lawyer to sue the government on behalf of members being terrorized by absurd regulations. Their current lawyer, Julie Ramirez, was moving to Texas to get married and, as she put it, "live in a state that is still free."

Julie's husband was in the Army at nearby Ft. Lewis and was friends with Bill Owens, who promptly told Grant about the opening at WAB in Olympia before the position was advertised.

Grant applied and nailed the interview. Ted loved the fact that Grant was from scrappy Forks and had experience from the Attorney General's Office. Grant's confidence from all the things he'd been through and conquered was appealing to Ted. The interview was supposed to be twenty minutes, but it ended up lasting two hours. Grant got the job.

Olympia was about an hour and a half south of Seattle. It was a beautiful town, right on the water; the southernmost end of the Puget Sound. It was an easy walk from the state capitol, which was breathtakingly beautiful with its grand rotunda, down to the waterfront of the Pacific Ocean. Mountains only a few miles away jutted out. Mountains and the ocean in one package — it can't be beat.

There was one downside to Olympia, however. Almost everyone worked for government in Olympia. They were mostly state employees; mid- to high-ranking bureaucrats who staffed the headquarters of the zillions of state agencies. They said that Olympia was a "company" town and the company was government.

But Grant was not complaining. He got his dream job that allowed him to carry out his purpose in life. Lisa had a great job, too. Life was good.

He had almost thoroughly transformed himself from hillbilly to lawyer. He was very proud of that. This had been the plan. The only residual vestiges of Forks were his love of fried foods and other unhealthy things, like drinking too much on occasion. However, having a bucket of fried chicken and a half rack of beer was getting less and less common for him. He was eating food that young professionals eat. He even started to eat sushi. He traded the Pabst Blue Ribbon for microbrews.

Grant and Lisa finally had a little money for the first time in their marriage. They did all the things that people in America do when they have a little money they bought things. And more things.

Grant started wearing Dockers and polo shirts. He even took up golf. He wanted to be the typical American white-collar professional. Lisa was happy to resume her former life of plenty, which had been put on hold by medical school, and she filled up her closet with clothes and shoes. They took vacations. Nothing extravagant, but they were living very, very comfortable lives of American professionals. Looking back at this time, Grant called it the "Dockers years."

The Matsons got to know the other WAB families. They spent time with Ted Foster and his wife, Joyce. There was also Brian and Karen Jenkins. Brian, who was in his forties and looked very distinguished, was WAB's chief lobbyist. Brian was a great guy who worked hard for the small businesses in WAB; he was not the typical lobbyist that lines the halls of the capitol building. He was a genius at legislative strategy. His wife, Karen, was great. She was beautiful and about a foot shorter than Brian. Karen and Lisa really got along well because Karen came from a wealthy family. Karen wasn't spoiled, but she was used to nice things.

Another of the three WAB senior staff families were Ben and Laura Trenton. Ben was the WAB political director. He got people elected to the extent it was possible to elect decent people in Washington State. He raised lots and lots of money for candidates. He knew all the rich Republicans in the state, and with a few phone calls, could raise buckets of money. Ben was dedicated to his "guys," the small businesses of WAB. He constantly chose conflict with squishy moderate Republicans over the comfort of being a "money guy" on the Hill, as the state legislative building was called.

Ben was destined to be a politician himself, if the voters in Washington State ever wanted a change from big government. He was a very handsome guy, who at age thirty already looked like a future elected official.

His wife, Laura, complemented the future elected official by being a very beautiful wife. At first, Grant (and probably most other people) found it hard to relate to her because she was so attractive. People assumed she would be bitchy and unintelligent. She was neither. She was genuinely nice to people and smart as a whip.

The Fosters, Jenkins, and Trentons were the only conservatives the Matsons knew. These four families were like pilgrims from a far off country who settled in a new and different land. They had a bond because they were so different than those around them. They would get together every year for a giant Super Bowl party and, a few months later, a Fourth of July party with all their kids playing together.

These parties were joyous during this high point of the easy times when everyone was making a ton of money and Grant and the WAB guys' careers were going great. They were climbing the ladder. They were the only thing close to a conservative "government in waiting" as they were often called. Everyone knew if a Republican somehow managed to get elected, that WAB would be staffing the new administration. It felt great, even though they knew that the odds of a Republican winning were so remote. They could dream.

At one Super Bowl party when Grant and Ben drank about a thousand beers, they went outside during half time to get some air. The kids were running around and it was getting loud.

Grant handed Ben a beer and said, "Here you go, Governor."

Ben laughed and then said, "You think that's possible? You know, someday?" Ben seemed serious. Or drunk. Or both.

Grant was feeling particularly honest, given the many beers. He said to Ben, "Hell, yes it's possible. If this state ever gets its head out of its ass… oh wait, that will never happen. So, no, man, I don't think it's possible."

Grant could tell that Ben was a little hurt, "No, I don't mean you'd suck as a governor," Grant explained. "You would be great. It's just that…"

"It would be insane to think I could ever be governor," Ben said, after snapping back into reality. "I was just playing with you."

Ben was in a part of the yard that the neighbors couldn't see, and he took a big piss. "Hey, look, the Governor is pissing in his yard!" Ben yelled. They laughed so hard it hurt.

Grant would remember "Governor Ben" pissing in his yard for years. There was something about it that he couldn't get out of his mind. It was like the path. It was like he was seeing the future, but he wasn't. It was hard to explain.

Grant's job at WAB was great. In addition to traditional legal work, he also lobbied. He saw how laws were passed. It was ugly.

He witnessed no outright bribery, but legislators were typically not very bright. They did what lobbyists said, especially lobbyists for government, unions, environmentalists, and big business. The Republicans usually listened to WAB, but listening was about all they could do.

The Republicans weren't exactly pure and wonderful. They had no power so everything they did was designed to try and achieve some power. There was no plan to do anything good once they got power; they just wanted it. Even in the past, when the Republicans controlled the state House and Senate, they still managed to pile up more government. A little less growth in government, but a net increase, nonetheless. Republicans were more interested in getting re-elected than in actually decreasing the size of government. Getting re-elected in Washington State meant promising "more funding for our schools," "protecting the environment" and all that. Just a little less than the Democrats.

Republicans spent much of their time on social issues, which meant they alienated most of the voters in liberal Washington State. It was pretty sad. Grant saw firsthand the reasons those in political circles said that the Democrats were the "evil" party and the Republicans were the "stupid" party.

Most of Grant's work was representing WAB members in lawsuits against the government. His first case was for Big Sam's Plumbing. Big Sam, who fit the name at six feet four inches, installed a water heater for a customer in some typical mildly corrupt medium-sized city in Washington State. It turned out that the customer was a city council member who was despised by the mayor. Big Sam didn't get a permit to install a water heater, because no one ever did, although the building code technically required one. So the Mayor announced his concern that the council member had broken such an important safety law. Big Sam, who was a very bright guy, wrote an extremely elegant letter to the editor of the newspaper about how stupid it was to require a permit to do something that people did all the time. The newspaper published it and the mayor looked like an idiot.

The mayor had the city attorney convene a special grand jury and charge Big Sam and the council member with the crime of installing a water heater without a permit. It was a gross misdemeanor, punishable by up to one year in jail. Conveniently enough, they announced the charges two days after the election. Big Sam was terrified about going to jail for installing a water heater. He was a WAB member so he called them.

Grant made a public records request to the city for all the water heater permits ever issued. It turned out that in a city of 90,000, exactly two water heater permits had been issued in the past ten years. A few thousand hot water heaters had been installed without permits, or criminal prosecution.

By the time Grant got the records from the reluctant city, Big Sam's trial was in a few days. He started the case on the day before Thanksgiving. This was exactly what he loved. Big Sam was being bullied and Grant had some special skills that could beat the bully. He took Thanksgiving Day off, but worked the next day and all weekend on the case. He found a very obscure legal doctrine called "procedural equal protection" that stated it was unconstitutional if a person exercises a constitutional right like free speech (such as writing a letter to the editor) and then is the only person prosecuted for a particular crime. Grant wrote a brief on this that was amazing. He put it on Tom's desk.

On Monday morning, Tom called Grant into his office. "You wrote this?" He asked Grant. "Over the weekend?"

"Yep," Grant answered. "Why, is it bad?"

"No, it's magnificent," Tom said. "I found the right lawyer for this job."

Grant filed the brief. The judge not only dismissed the charges, but also sternly lectured the city attorney and mayor on procedural equal protection. "What's wrong with you people?" the judge asked the city attorney to loud applause by the audience. The headline in the paper was "What's wrong with you people?"

Big Sam cried when the judge dismissed the case. He shook Grant's hand and said, "I thought I was going to jail and would lose my business. Thanks, man." They had a celebration lunch that included many beers. Grant was in his glory.

Big Sam's case illustrated how government seemed to act in Washington State during that time. There were isolated jackasses like the mayor and city attorney, but the courts generally could be trusted to right a wrong. It took some work from a motivated attorney, but it could be done. When Grant later looked back at Big Sam's case, being charged with a crime for installing a hot water heater seemed like the good old days. Back then, the corruption and government lawlessness were just isolated incidents instead of the norm. That would change.

Chapter 8

The Docker Years

Grant was headed out to a big New Year's party. He walked by the mirror in the hallway of his house. Who the hell was that? This guy had on Dockers, a polo shirt, a gut, and Acura keys in his hand. Seriously, who was that? The scrappy kid from Forks was nowhere to be seen. Instead, the mirror reflected some lame suburban guy.

Grant was in his thirties now, and a father of two children. Their girl, Amanda, was five and their boy, Cole, was two.

Grant loved being a dad. He constantly thought about all things he would do differently than his parents did. He realized how many bad things had been taught to him during his upbringing. When one of the kids cried, for example, Grant would start to get mad but then would catch himself. For a split second, he would think that he had a right to resent all the stuff he had to do for the kids. But then would realize that normal parents love their kids. And he definitely did love those kids. But he had to constantly fight against what he had learned from his childhood. It was hard because Grant and Lisa had such radically different childhoods.

Grant worked nearly all the time. He loved his job and he was continually trying to improve his résumé. He wasn't doing anything around the house like repairing simple little things. Instead, he spent his time writing articles, giving presentations, volunteering for bar association committees, working on campaigns. He thought his time was so valuable that someone else should do the work around the house.

That someone else was often Lisa, whose time was also valuable. Naturally, over time, she began to resent her role as the only one doing house repairs. She couldn't believe that her former logging town husband was so worthless around the house. It pissed her off. A lot.

When things broke, it led to an argument. Grant would respond by noting how many important things he had to do for work right then. Lisa would respond with something like, "Oh, I guess saving people's lives isn't as important as what you do." Things became very unpleasant in the house, which gave Grant yet another reason to be at work. It was a vicious cycle.

When Grant later looked back on the "Docker years," the one thing he was ashamed of was squandering all the skills he had in Forks and becoming a dependent, soft, fat, typical suburban American. He became what would later be known as a "sheeple" (a combination of a "sheep" ignorantly grazing without thought and "people").

Grant, who worked very hard, was a sheeple. As a sheeple, he fit in just perfectly in the Cedars subdivision where they lived. The Cedars was an upper end place. The houses weren't mansions, but they were upper end. Almost everyone who lived there was a state employee; many were assistant directors of state agencies. People were nice … well, Grant assumed they were. He never actually got to know most of them.

One exception was the Spencer family two houses away. They were not government employees. They were friendly and their kids played with the Matson kids. They were Mormon, but didn't meet all the stereotypes about a male-dominated household that tried to convert everyone. They were just regular people who, as Mormons, did slightly "weird" things like have a year's worth of food stored. And they didn't drink. The Spencers were the only other "conservatives" Grant knew of in the neighborhood.

The rest of the people in the neighborhood were unknowns. It was weird. Grant knew which agencies his neighbors worked for but didn't know much else about them. They would wave when they drove by, but Grant didn't know their names. In fact, Halloween was the only time he would see them when he took the kids out trick or treating. By the time Halloween rolled around the next year, he had already forgotten what his neighbors looked like and what their names were. Why even learn their names? He only talked to them at Halloween, which was fine with Grant. They were mostly liberals or, as Grant called them, "libs." They all put up Democrat yard signs during election season. Putting up those yard signs was like a display of loyalty to the great and wonderful God of government.

Grant hated all the Democrat yard signs in his neighborhood, so he put up his own yard signs for Republicans and even an occasional Libertarian. Once those signs went up the first time, some people in the neighborhood stopped being (fake) polite to him. They were a little cold toward him. Most still waved, but a couple of them were downright hostile.

Grant was actually proud that these people didn't like him. They were the ones using their government jobs to hassle the little people and take everyone's money to waste on their stupid utopian dreams. They were the kind of people who had plumbers charged with crimes for installing water heaters.

Chapter 9

The "A" Word

Grant's son, Cole, was two years old now. He wasn't talking much. Grant was a little worried, but he didn't want to bring it up.

Manda, as they called Amanda, was the perkiest and most outgoing child on the planet. She had red hair and was the center of attention in any setting.

Lisa was her competitive self. A person has to be competitive to make it through medical school but she was a little too competitive sometimes. She had to master everything she set her mind to. She knew what was best because she had looked into it and her worthless husband just worked and then collapsed on the couch to watch football. "If you want something done right, you have to do it yourself," was, unfortunately, becoming her motto. Even more unfortunately, it was true, given her workaholic and overweight husband.

But, all the comforts of the suburbs made things fine. Nice house, nice cars, nice furniture, all that. They weren't in debt but they had lots of stuff.

Lisa was also concerned about Cole not talking. She took him, without telling Grant, to a pediatric specialist.

"Autism."

That's what was wrong with Cole.

"Autism." What a terrifying word. It meant never talking, having to live in an institution. Lisa cried all the way home from the doctor's office.

Grant cried when Lisa told him of the diagnosis after the appointment. Their "perfect" life wasn't so perfect now. One of their kids wasn't going to be a doctor or a lawyer. He would probably have to live in an institution. It was devastating.

But the diagnosis explained a lot. As they would later find out, Cole had a normal IQ, but had extreme difficulty communicating. He could not understand many words and he couldn't speak them. Later, at age seven, he could speak and understand words at a two year-old level.

Amazingly, Cole could read years ahead of his age. He didn't always understand what was written, but he did pretty well. He had a photographic memory. He could recall a license plate he had seen two years earlier. He could tell extremely slight differences in detail between things. He could understand mechanics and figure out devices instantly. He was an absolute whiz on the computer. Basically, his extreme lack of verbal communication was made up for by his extreme understanding of visual things.

It was very frustrating for the little guy. Cole would be tired and want to sleep but he couldn't say it. He knew what to say but the words wouldn't form. None of the grownups could understand what he wanted. He would try to talk and they would ask, "Are you hungry? Do you need to go potty?" No, I'm tired, he would try to say. I want to go to bed now. Then he would cry. He cried a lot.

Lisa, the competitive one and the doctor, went to work learning everything about autism. She bought dozens of books on the topic. She crafted a very detailed plan to teach Cole to talk. It centered on visual things. She made index cards with words on them, like "eat." She would show a card to Cole and he would know it was time to eat. He understood that because it was written down, it wasn't words someone was saying to him. Cole soon progressed to showing Lisa or Grant the "eat" card, which meant he wanted to eat. It was like sign language, but with index cards.

Cole began using the cards less and less and began using simple words. The words were still fewer and more basic than kids his age, but he was learning. It was like he was stuck in France and everyone spoke French except him. He had to figure out how to get things done with simple words and hand motions like one would if they were surrounded by people speaking only French.

Kindergarten was the first big test. Lisa worried that the teachers wouldn't accept Cole; Grant was ready to sue them. But, the teachers in Olympia were great. They made educating Cole a top priority. The kids were also great to him; they took him under their wings. For all the bad things Grant thought about government, he had to admit that the Olympia schools were excellent. They were taking care of his little Cole and that was all that mattered.

Cole got better and better. By his later years of elementary school, he could string sentences together. It was still very hard for him to understand people he wasn't used to. People like his family had gotten used to how to talk to him, but others didn't know.

Manda took amazingly good care of her little brother. She spent a lot of her free time helping him talk and asking him questions to get him to talk. It was heartwarming. Cole came to depend on his big sister. When she was gone, Cole would ask, "Where is Sissy?" He could handle her being gone, but he was much more comfortable with her around.

Grant had a nontraditional father/son relationship with Cole. They were very close and Grant spent all the time he could with Cole. But not being able to communicate well put a crimp in the formation of the relationship. Grant learned that hanging out with Cole meant just being in the same room with him; it didn't mean talking. Cole got more and more comfortable with Grant just being there and not trying to talk to him all the time. Once the comfort was there, then Cole would let Grant talk to him.

Even when Cole was in middle school, Grant felt like he had a young boy instead of a middle school student. Grant would notice other dads talking to their sons like Grant talked to Cole, and then realize that the other boys were three or four years old. It was very hard on Grant. He loved Cole, and Cole was doing so much better than a kid with a full case of autism, but Grant still struggled.

Cole was on a little league team. They gave him a few breaks like pitching him soft balls. At first he didn't get the part about running to first base but once someone showed him, he did fine. He even hit a homerun one time and ran the bases. He would be OK. Different, but OK.

Cole's autism had a big effect on Grant. He realized that the "perfect" suburban life — a nice house, lots of stuff, vacations — wasn't so perfect. Family was what mattered. Grant felt this urge to disregard the expectations of being a "normal" suburban family and became fixated on ensuring that his family could make it through whatever bad things came their way. Grant was the man in the family, and this was what men did. He started working more reasonable hours and stopped letting his mind be occupied with how to climb the résumé ladder.

Grant became a Christian. One night he just said, "God, I can't do this on my own. I need You." Right as he said that, he had the overpowering sensation that everything would ultimately be alright, but after lots of misery and sacrifice. It was more than just optimism; it was a certainty that amazing things were ahead of him. It was the path again: He couldn't see into the future, but he knew — with absolute certainty — the general direction things would go. He started to see that people put into his life would be part of the coming amazing things and that he and they had been placed in this place at this time for a reason. He didn't want people to think he was crazy so he didn't talk about it. He essentially became a secret Christian.

During this time, Grant kept thinking about how he was the man and it was his job to get his family through whatever came in the future. He thought about how dependent they were on society. They relied on many other people for things like food, fixing things, personal protection. These were all the things that he used to know how to do in Forks but had lost. It was just a little thought at this point. He didn't actually do anything to act on the little thought. But he thought it. Over and over again. It was like someone was trying to tell him something.

Chapter 10

Other People's Money

Grant's work at WAB was going great, but it was coming at price. The part he loved the most was working for WAB to help its members who were getting screwed by government. It was extremely satisfying to have people like Big Sam break down in tears of gratitude. Grant thrived on that.

There was a price to it, though. Grant fought people all day, every day. Suing the government is not easy. They fight dirty. They would constantly pull tricks and underhanded stunts. They would lie and Grant would lose cases where his client was right but unwilling to lie to counter their lies. The bureaucrats on the other side would try to set Grant up. They filed a complaint against him with the Bar Association, which had the power to take away his law license. He was completely innocent, so he won, but it was incredibly stressful. This stress began taking its toll. His blood pressure was starting to go up. He would come home from work — the "fist fight" as he called it — and would snap at his wife and kids. He would apologize but he couldn't just go from a fight to the calm of his home in an instant.

One time, Grant was driving home after a junior government attorney he was winning against had falsely accused him of trying to physically threaten her. Even as he was nearing his house, he was still frothing mad that this lawyer would accuse him of that and that she might call the police and then he'd have to prove his innocence. Grant pulled in the driveway and hit the garage door button. He knew that when he hit that button he had to put all the anger and fighting away. He owed that to Lisa; it wasn't fair for him to come home and be furious for hours. But, Grant couldn't stand it. Someone had falsely accused him of a crime. Yet he had to just be calm and tell his wife he had a good day at the office. Grant stopped in the driveway. He just stopped.

Then it hit him. He was a fighter. Grant fought people all day long. Not with guns or fists, but with law and politics. But it was fighting just the same. He was learning how to fight; how to not fear his opponent, and how to channel the anger into an advantage while controlling his outward emotions. Grant didn't want to fight, but he was always found himself in a position where he had to do so to help innocent people. He realized that ever since he punched his dad in the face that he had been placed on a path of fighting and winning. He felt like these obstacles were being placed in front of him to teach him how to fight.

You are being taught to fight. You will need this fighting spirit even more for what's next.

What was that? It was like an outside thought, as if someone was talking to him, but not with words he could hear. It was... an outside thought. But it was loud and clear.

Grant was stunned. He just sat in the driveway for a while. Did that just happen? Was an outside thought talking to him? That was crazy. But there was no mistaking it. An outside thought had spoken to him.

The kids came out of the house because they heard the garage door go up but hadn't seen their dad come in. As they were coming up to him, Grant was in a trance realizing that all these fights he was forced to take on had a bigger purpose. The outside thought had said so. It was crystal clear.

Grant rebelled. He didn't want to listen to the outside thought. He screamed at the steering wheel, "I don't want to fight! I want to be normal. Why do I have to do this?"

The windows were up so the kids didn't hear him. He snapped out of the trance and saw his two fabulous kids. They were so happy to see him; smiling and waving. How could he be in a bad mood when they were so happy to see him?

A few days later, back at the office, Grant got a call from a WAB member named Ed Oleo. His case was unusually egregious but it illustrated what was going on in the larger sense of things.

Ed was a real estate agent who owned a small real estate agency. He was a nice guy. He caught the head of the Board of Real Estate Licensing, a corrupt man named Bart Sellarman, under-disciplining an agent for a large real estate agency. The under-disciplined realtor had stolen almost a million dollars from clients but, because he had connections, got a $1,000 fine. Ed was outraged and started talking to other real estate agents about how Sellarman was giving sweetheart deals to some realtors. Word got back to Sellarman that Ed was accusing him of corruption.

Ed had to have a real estate license to be in business, and

having a real estate license meant that the Board had the power to inspect every aspect of Ed's business. Lo and behold, Ed was selected for a "random" audit by Sellarman. Ed wasn't concerned; he had always been honest so they could look at whatever they wanted.

Sellarman found that Ed had improperly allowed "unlicensed" realtors to work at this company. Ed was puzzled because all of his agents were fully licensed. It turned out that a law mandating that an agent from another state had to take the Washington real estate exam before selling real estate had been repealed about two years ago. The new law said there was a grace period, and that the out-of-state realtor could take up to one year to get his or her Washington license. Sellarman found that one of Ed's agents had only had an Oregon license for eight months but then got a Washington one. But, Ed explained, this was legal now.

"That's not my interpretation," Sellarman told Ed. Sellarman told Ed that the new law, passed by the Legislature, did not apply until the Board wrote regulations enacting it. Yes, but the law says what it says, Ed argued, and it was passed by the Legislature. No "interpretation" in Board regulations is necessary. Besides, Ed thought, no state agency could write mere regulations overturning a statute passed by the Legislature.

Grant backed Ed and explained to Sellarman that the statute is the law; it doesn't take Board regulations to make a law of the State of Washington effective. This was not good enough for Sellarman. He revoked Ed's license for violating a repealed law. Then Sellarman revoked the real estate licenses of all of Ed's employees for working at an "unlicensed" real estate company. Sellarman didn't care about all these innocent people; he was vicious, vindictive, and, thanks to how much power the good people of Washington State had handed to their "public servants," had the unlimited power to do this.

Of course, the law didn't allow taking away the licenses of people based on repealed laws. But it would take a "hearing" in front of the Board of Real Estate Licensing which was presided over by Sellarman. Ed and his employees could appeal to the county court in Olympia that heard all the appeals of state agency decisions. The judges on the court were very pro-agency. Olympia was a company town and making sure government worked smoothly — that is, got its way — was the job of most people there, including the "impartial" judges. Ed and the employees could appeal to the court of appeals, and then the state Supreme Court.

Each one of these three or four steps would cost Ed about

$50,000 and take nearly a year, while he had no license to be in business and couldn't make any money. So he had "due process" appeal rights, but they cost more money than anyone had, and took longer than anyone could take. This was big government's approach to Constitutional rights: they still exist, but we've created a system where no one can actually use them. You have appeal rights; good luck exercising them. Now do what we say.

Ed got physically ill over this. Besides nausea and vomiting, he had a host of other ailments. The ordeal was devastating. Long-standing clients were leaving in droves. Ed's wife was furious at him for "making a big deal" out of Sellarman's corruption and thereby costing them money. She threatened divorce and made him move out for a while. He was a wreck. He had spent hundreds of thousands on his attorney, who was getting beaten repeatedly in court. The judges kept deciding that the Board had "discretion" to carry out its important regulations. After all, the Board had to have "discretion" to protect the public from all those evil companies.

Out of money and totally desperate, Ed called WAB. Grant took the case.

About this time, a new junior lawyer came to WAB to help Grant with all the cases he was getting. Eric Benson was a smart guy who was fresh out of law school. He was really devoted to the cause; even more conservative than Grant. He was a libertarian, actually. Eric shared Grant's hatred of government and actually hated it more. Eric would stay up at night thinking of ways to defeat bureaucrats. Eric was Grant on steroids.

Eric started working with Grant on Ed Oleo's case night and day. Eric had dug up some interesting information out about Sellarman and his finances. (Grant was afraid to ask how Eric got the information.) It seems that Sellarman, who earned a relatively modest state salary, had all kinds of assets like boats, a race horse, and a condo in Mexico. It was obvious Sellarman was taking bribes to let people off if they paid him. By the time Grant and Eric were done with Sellarman, the Board of Real Estate Licensing agreed to drop all the charges against Ed and his partners and settled the retaliation claims for $200,000. Sellarman was not fired, of course.

On the day he had to hand over the check for the $200,000 of tax payer money, Sellarman confidently told Grant and Eric, "So what? It's just other people's money. We've got more. Much more. See you in round two."

WAB's attempts to get the Governor's Office to fire Sellarman were laughed at. Sellarman, it was explained, was "protecting consumers." Government was not protecting people — it was terrorizing them.

No one outside of WAB seemed to care. Grant wanted to scream to them to forget all that crap they learned in school and on the news about fair government employees protecting the public by using reasonable regulations. That might have been true forty years ago, but now government had so much more power. Ed's business was in the hands of a guy like Sellarman who could shut him down just to get some quick bribes or to get even. The courts were letting it happen. It took something unusual like finding out about Sellarman's corruption to stop it.

Ed's view of how government worked was forever shattered. "I'm a Democrat," Ed told Grant and Eric at their celebratory dinner after winning. "Hell, I even donated money to the Governor's last campaign and she's the one who just told us that Sellarman is a faithful public servant doing his job." He was stunned by all of this.

"I thought," Ed continued, "that all these agencies were here to help people and be the one fair referee in the system." Ed looked like he was now embarrassed to be saying it. "Everyone I know thinks like I used to. My friends think I'm making all this up until they see the check Sellarman had to write me. They all think like I used to. How can everyone be so wrong?"

"I know, man," Grant said. "I deal with this all the time." That's all Grant could say.

"They're evil bastards," Eric said. "Evil. That's the answer."

The majority of regulators were not like Sellarman but it only took a few like him to make the system corrupt. Grant started to feel like there were two universes. One universe was where normal people just went about their business not caring about what was happening, and another world where Sellarmans were out destroying people. The universes existed simultaneously. Why didn't people care? Why?

Ed, Grant, and Eric were silent for a while, trying to figure out the answer. It was beginning to ruin the celebratory mood of the dinner. Then Ed looked Grant and Eric in the eye and said something that was obviously hard for him to say.

"When are people going to stand up and fight back?" he asked. "When are we going to put a stop to this?"

"Soon," Eric said with a smile. He looked like he would enjoy that day.

Grant thought and answered. "The problem, Ed, is that only a small percentage of the population ever gets screwed like you did. Most people just live off the system and don't care. But the number of Ed Oleos out there is growing and growing. The government is getting more bold and brazen each year. They're drunk with power. No one can really stop them. They're creating more Ed Oleos. That's how it will stop."

Grant paused. "I hope."

Chapter 11

A Country Boy Can Survive

The phone rang in the middle of the night. Grant knew that was never a good sign.

"Hello?" He mumbled.

"Grant, it's mom." He hadn't heard her voice in several years. Grant had not had any desire to go back to Forks for a visit, and his mom and dad never invited him. Things were always so tense on the few occasions when they were together. Larry was jealous of Grant's success and interpreted all the good things in Grant's life as a slam on Larry. And Larry hated Lisa. She was the "stuck up" one who made Grant leave the wonderful life he could have had in Forks. Grant and his parents were living totally separate lives.

"Your father died," Grant's mom said. She started crying uncontrollably. She had devoted her whole life to that piece of shit. Now he was dead and she didn't know what to do with herself.

Grant didn't feel any emotion at all. What kind of person doesn't break down in tears when they find out their father is dead? Me, Grant thought. That's who.

Sometimes, Grant amazed himself at how unemotional he could be, especially when bad things were happening to bad people. Instead of sympathy for them, Grant would mentally shrug.

Grant was nice to his mom and told her he would be out to Forks in a few hours. Lisa had awakened. She really hated Larry for all the mean things he had done to Grant (although Grant never told her all the things). Grant didn't even think to ask her to come to Forks for the funeral. He just left.

The drive to Forks was a time of reflection. Grant realized during the drive how much he had changed since he lived there. College, marriage, law school, law jobs, kids, successes in his profession— he was a totally different person. It was hard to put into words.

As Grant got closer and closer to Forks, he came upon landmarks that reminded him of growing up. Memories came flooding back.

The place hadn't changed much. Now that he had been living in suburbia, the place seemed like more of a dump than he had remembered it. Was he getting too good for Forks? That thought scared Grant.

The sun was coming up and he could see all the signs that people lived differently in Forks. They had gardens, fishing boats, and wood piles; signs of self-sufficiency. The pickups had gun racks. It was apparent that they could get by much better in hard times than in beautiful neighborhoods like the Cedars.

Grant started ruminating again about how dependent he and his family were on society functioning flawlessly. A man needs to take care of his family; you can't do it when you're dependent on all the comforts you're living in now. He'd thought this a thousand times recently.

All the things Grant saw in Forks that early morning reminded him of a skill he'd lost. He didn't garden; Lisa would laugh at him for suggesting they put some potatoes in their immaculately landscaped yard. He hadn't fished in years. He hadn't split wood either, and probably couldn't fall a tree like he could back then. Guns. He hadn't shot in years.

Grant went to his old house. It was more of a rundown shack than he had remembered. There was a strange newer pickup in the driveway.

Grant parked his Acura, which looked absurdly out of place at the shack.

He knocked on the door and his mom answered. She was in terrible shape. Steve was there. It was great to see him, all grown up. Grant assumed the pickup was his.

The occasion didn't lend itself to idle chitchat. Grant comforted his mom; he owed her that. He got down to business, planning the funeral and making arrangements. Larry had died of a heart attack.

Grant's sister, Carol, arrived a few hours later. He had kept in touch with her, on and off over the years. She was a professor at the University of Washington teaching literature or something. She seemed to be doing well.

The funeral was a blur. Grant was just there because he was supposed to be. He kept feeling guilty that he wasn't sad. But he wasn't. He didn't really know his mom and dad. His childhood seemed like a lifetime ago. It was; he had a new life.

After the funeral and consoling his mom until she fell asleep, it was late and Grant went out onto the front porch. Steve drove up. It was so good to see him and be able to catch up. Steve had married a nice local girl and they had three kids. Steve was not logging, of course, since the state and feds had virtually prohibited logging for the sake of the supposedly endangered spotted owl, although there seemed to be a lot of them flying around. Steve managed the local auto parts store.

"I need to get out of here," Grant said. "Let's go have a beer."

"Roger that," Steve said. That's what Steve and Grant always said back in the day when they worked the radios on CAP searches.

Grant looked at his Acura and said, "Why don't you drive?" Steve smiled. They left for one of the two taverns in town. No one recognized him in Forks, which was just fine with Grant. Besides, who has a beer after their dad dies? He didn't want people to recognize him.

In his conversation with Steve, Grant focused on how Steve was living. He made a little bit from the auto parts store, but he hunted, fished, gardened, and did some small custom logging jobs on the small pieces of land still available for logging. Grant was drawn to how Steve lived. He realized that Steve and his family could live just fine if the auto parts job went away. They could feed themselves. And they were perfectly happy. They didn't need big screen TVs or a closet full of clothes they never wore.

Another thing Grant focused on was the community in Forks and how it banded together. Steve talked about friends giving him deer meat and how he repaired a guy's boat for free. Everyone knew carpentry, electrical, and even welding skills. Steve had a pretty well-equipped home shop and could just about fix or build everything there. This was how everyone lived in Forks.

Then a song came on the jukebox. It was one of Grant and Steve's favorite songs from high school, "Country Boy Can Survive" by Hank Williams, Jr. Steve and Grant were singing along to the lyrics:

> I live back in the woods, you see
> A woman and the kids, and the dogs and me
> I got a shotgun rifle and a 4-wheel drive
> And a country boy can survive
> Country folks can survive
>
> I can plow a field all day long
> I can catch catfish from dusk till dawn
> We make our own whiskey and our own smoke too
> Ain't too many things these ole boys can't do

We grow good ole tomatoes and homemade wine
And a country boy can survive
Country folks can survive

Because you can't starve us out
And you can't makes us run
Cause one-of- 'em old boys raisin' ole shotgun
And we say grace and we say Ma'am
And if you ain't into that we don't give a damn

Wow. That was it. A country boy can survive. Grant can't.
Steve can plow a field all day long and catch catfish from dusk till
dawn. Ain't too many things that ole boy couldn't do. You can't starve
'em out and you can't make 'em run. These old boys would, sure as
shit, raise that ole shotgun.

That song explained everything missing in Grant's life. It
explained the thoughts he was having about being dependent. He was
having them because, unlike most people in the suburbs, Grant
actually knew how rural people could survive. Grant could see how
dependent he was because he knew how people lived without being as
dependent. Grant could see it; regular suburban people couldn't.

"Hey, Steve," Grant asked, "you still got that old Hank Jr. tape
we used to listen to?"

"Nope," Steve said. "But I got the CD." Oh, that's right, Grant
thought. It had been many, many years since anyone had tapes.

"Does it have this song it?" Grant asked.

"Yep," Steve answered.

"Can I borrow it for the trip home?" Grant asked. "I'll mail it
back to you."

"Got it in my truck," Steve said with a smile.

All the way back to Olympia, Grant listened to that song. Each
line had a profound meaning to him. So did the landmarks as he drove.
Especially the sign that said, "Leaving Forks."

Chapter 12

You are the man. Do something.

By the time Grant pulled into his neighborhood in Olympia, everything had changed. He was noticing things he had never noticed before.

When he was on the outskirts of Forks, Grant noticed all the signs of independent living he'd seen earlier like the wood piles and fishing boats. They got fewer and fewer the closer he got to Olympia. The denser the population became, the fewer signs of independent living he saw. On the outskirts of Olympia, there were no more signs of independent living; quite the opposite.

On the highway as he came back from Forks, Grant started to notice all the semi-trucks. They were everywhere. They were full of everything people needed to live. Trucks full of food, gasoline, medicines, and parts to run all the machines and gadgets everyone relied on. What if the trucks stopped rolling?

When he was back in Olympia, Grant stopped at the grocery to get his favorite lunch: stir fry at the deli in the store. He and Lisa rarely cooked anymore; they ate take out pretty much exclusively. As soon as Grant walked into the store, he noticed things he hadn't noticed before. He noticed that there was a stunning variety of products, but not too much of any given product. For example, in the chilled drinks aisle near the deli, there must have been fifty kinds of cold drinks — but only six or so of each one. Where was the inventory they would use to restock?

For the first time in his life, Grant walked around the parking lot to the back of the store. He was on a quest to answer this nagging feeling about being dependent.

Grant walked around the outside of the whole store. There was no giant warehouse with the inventory. There was only a loading dock with semi-trucks constantly coming in and out.

Semi-trucks. That's how they did it. It was "just-in-time inventory." It meant that stores kept just a little bit of product on hand and ordered more when that little bit was sold. This saved the store money by not having to pay interest on inventory while it was sitting before being sold, and it saved on the cost of shelf space. Just-in-time inventory explained why the store would be out of milk and bread within two hours of the announcement that some snow was coming. When that happened, Grant had seen otherwise nice people become angry when there wasn't any of a particular kind of food that they liked. The idea of going through two days without that one kind of Belgium goat cheese was too much for some people to bear.

What was wrong with me? Grant wondered. Was he really walking around a grocery store thinking about how much food they had? What a weirdo. He went back and got his stir fry. He ate it and headed home. The nagging feeling wasn't going away.

When he got home, Grant saw that Lisa and the kids were out somewhere. He started looking at things in the house. The food pantry. It had maybe a week's worth of food? The particular cold cereal Manda always ate: two days' worth. The pancake mix Cole loved: maybe enough for three days. This explained why they were going to the grocery store about every other day. The Matson household had a just-in-time inventory system, too.

Grant looked at his computer. They couldn't do much without it. Businesses would be done for in a crisis; no internet, no business. America would grind to a halt in about twenty minutes without the internet. How would all those stores order more inventory without the internet?

Electricity was even more critical. Without electricity there would be no internet, plus no refrigerators, lights, or anything. Grant scanned around the living room. Everything ran on electricity. Everything.

He went out to his car to get his phone. In the garage, he noticed that he had no tools. In Forks, everyone had tools. Not just hand tools, but chain saws, shovels, everything. He noticed the furnace in the garage. It ran on natural gas. That seemed like a pretty stable thing to supply, but it took electricity to turn the fan that delivered the heat. Grant remembered the two-day power outage a couple of winters ago and how cold it got in the house.

Well, we have a fireplace, right? He thought. Except that he had never actually had a fire in it. Lisa said it would make a mess and she didn't want to use it. The fireplace was a decoration. Besides, they didn't have any firewood. That would look "junky" at their immaculate house.

The Matson house relied on water coming out of the tap. The

water had never gone out. But there was a giant water treatment plant serving about 100,000 people in Olympia. What if a key part broke and it took a semi-truck or FedEx to get a replacement to the plant?

What about security? There was no crime in their comfy neighborhood. In fact, Grant could only recall once ever hearing a siren and that was a fire truck going to a barbeque that got a little out of hand. That was it. He had wanted to keep his old .22 at their house, but Lisa said no. She didn't want a gun in the house. Grant offered to get a trigger lock, which was reasonable given the kids. Still no. "Guns are dangerous," she said. So Grant's .22 — the one that he had slept with that night he waited to be stabbed by his dad — stayed in Forks. Calling 911 would have to be their only way to stop crime.

At this point, that nagging feeling about dependence was screaming to him. A criminal, or a group of them, could drive right into the Cedars, get out of their car, walk into any house or knock the door in, and do whatever they liked. That last thought was horrific. He knew what criminals did when they found defenseless pretty women.

You are the man. Do something.

There it was again. The outside thought. Talking to him clearly, without speaking. Just a thought from somewhere in his mind.

Grant was listening this time to the outside thought. He knew what he needed to. Grant was going to do something.

Chapter 13

Capitol City Guns

Grant got in his car and went to the local gun store, Capitol City Guns, that he'd driven by a hundred times. It felt weird — dirty, actually — going into a gun store. He didn't want people to see him going in there, like it was a porn store. He sat in the parking lot, gaining the courage to go in. He started to chicken out. Lisa would get so mad if she saw him at a gun store.

What is wrong with you? Take care of your family.

The outside thought was getting louder. Grant thought again about what criminals would do to Lisa if they had a chance. Maybe the kids, too. It was the most horrible and terrifying thought.

In he went. He knew from Forks that a shotgun was the perfect home defense weapon, so that's what he was going to get.

The second he walked in the store, he knew he'd done the right thing. There was nothing scary or "dirty" about a gun store. It was like any other store.

The sales people in the store were very helpful. They could spot a yuppie getting a first gun a mile away, and they wanted to help. Grant got an inexpensive pump 12 gauge, a Winchester 1300 Home Defender. It would do. He got one box of twenty-five shells and a trigger lock, too. He paid cash; no credit card for Lisa to find out about. He had just cashed an expense check from work reimbursing him for a few months' of miles he had driven on WAB business. He had been planning to turn the cash over to Lisa, as usual. Not anymore.

Right then and there he decided he would start to put the cash from expense checks in an envelope in the car. This is how he would spend money without Lisa knowing.

Grant noticed that, unlike the grocery store, Capitol City had plenty of inventory in the back. It made sense that a gun store wouldn't have just-in-time inventory. If the grocery stores are empty, then people will be flocking to gun stores.

Did I just have that thought? Grant wondered. What is wrong with me? That trip back to Forks had really changed him. Now he saw signs of American society's dependence everywhere he looked.

The whole experience of walking into a gun store was over in about twenty minutes. He filled out the paperwork and got his shotgun.

"Isn't there some kind of waiting period for getting a gun?" he asked the sales clerk.

"Nope," the guy said. "Not in Washington. No waiting period on long guns, only handguns."

After calling a phone number where the police checked out that Grant wasn't a felon, the clerk rang up the sale and handed Grant a large rectangular box labeled "Winchester." That was it. Grant was now a gun owner.

Grant thanked the clerk and picked up the rectangular box and put in his car. When he got out to his car and put the box in his trunk, Grant chuckled. That was easier than I thought, he said to himself. Then it hit him: he had changed. A half hour ago he was a helpless and frightened sheeple. Now he was a gun owner. He immediately felt more at ease. The world isn't so scary when you can protect yourself.

As he left the gun store parking lot, Grant started to wonder how he would get the gun into the house. What if Lisa was home? He felt like he was smuggling contraband. He laughed again because many husbands were going to the porn store and then smuggling it into the house. He was just trying to have a gun to defend them. What a horrible husband he was.

On the short trip from Capitol City Guns to the Cedars, Grant practiced his line. He hated lying to Lisa but, as the Jack Nicholson's character in the movie "A Few Good Men" said, "You can't handle the truth!" That was it. She couldn't handle the truth and he needed to do this.

Lisa was unloading some groceries — of course, it had been since yesterday that they went to the grocery store — when Grant came home. He walked in with the shotgun box.

"Hey," Grant said, "look what my dad gave me. Mom said he wanted me to have it. Don't worry, it came with a trigger lock." Grant was afraid for her to see the shotgun. It was one thing to see a box, but another thing to see a scary gun.

Lisa glared. But she was thinking. She had secretly been wondering why Grant didn't have a gun in the house. She had heard about a friend of a friend who had a prowler on the front porch and it took several minutes for the police to come. And the trigger lock would take care of the concern about the kids. She saw lots of things in the ER from unlocked guns and kids.

"Let me see the trigger lock," she said. Grant opened the box and the trigger lock was on. She thought about it. This gun actually made sense. She was actually a little proud that her couch potato husband was finally taking responsibility for something around the house like their security. Maybe he wasn't so worthless, after all.

"As long as the trigger lock is always on," Lisa said. "I mean always except if there's a robber. And the bullets are kept separately. And the gun and the bullets are kept up high where the kids can't get them."

Grant couldn't believe how well this was going. "Of course," he said. "That's perfectly reasonable." It was.

Grant was a gun owner, and his wife was OK with it. That felt pretty good.

A few days later, the nagging feelings about dependence came back. The power went out for a few hours and Grant's mind went into a whirlwind thinking about all the things that needed electricity. He realized that when the power was off, the police were hamstrung. Defending his family was up to him. You can't outsource your family's security. You have to man up and get it done.

A few days later, Grant decided to try out the new shotgun. He swung by a sporting goods store to get a second box of shells; it would be less "embarrassing" going into a sporting goods store than a gun store. He would leave the first box of twenty-five shells at home for home defense. He had asked the clerk at the sporting goods store where to shoot. They told him about a gravel pit outside town where people shot. Grant headed there with his box of shells and his new shiny shotgun.

Grant knew how to shoot a shotgun from growing up in Forks, but he ran into something he hadn't experienced before. The new shotgun was jamming. Oh great. It must be broken. He would go return it and get a new one.

A guy shooting at the gravel pit, who looked like a country boy, came up to him.

"That thing jammin'?" the guy asked.

"Yep," Grant said. "I think it's broken."

"Let me see if I can fix it," the guy said. He quickly took the gun apart for cleaning and asked if Grant had ever lubricated the bolt. No, he hadn't.

"You know how to do that?" Grant asked, pointing the bolt in the guy's hand.

69

The guy looked at Grant like he was an idiot. "Yeah. It's not hard." After a squirt of oil, the gun ran fine.

Grant realized that he was such a sissified and dependent suburbanite that he didn't even know to perform simple maintenance on a shotgun. His immediate thought when something didn't work was to get a new one. Like a sheeple consumer. The idea of fixing it never crossed his mind. That's what highly trained specialists did. Lawyers didn't fix things.

Oh, God, did he just think that? How stupid was that?

What if he had tried to use that shotgun when someone was trying to kill his family? What if it had jammed because he'd never test fired it?

A few days later, Steve called and said he would be in Olympia for some auto parts business. They got together and started talking about how suburbanites like Grant lived. Steve said something that stuck with Grant for the rest of his life.

"We're living under a false economy," Steve said.

Exactly. That's what had been bugging Grant. This was all fake and couldn't go on. Steve, the auto parts store manager in Forks, knew more about reality than Grant's economics professors at the University of Washington. Those idiots told everyone that America could just have a service economy and not build anything, and that whenever there was a downturn the government could just print and spend more money. What could possibly go wrong?

Grant kept asking Steve about how he lived back in Forks. He was fascinated about how much Steve could do: build things, hunt, and fish, can food they grew in their garden, all of that. The nagging feeling about dependence was there again, but Grant knew that he couldn't just start living like Steve did in Forks. It was really bugging him.

Chapter 14

Survivalist

Grant was feeling his oats. He was not afraid to look at guns. Hell, he'd just bought one and successfully smuggled it into the house. He was invincible.

It was much easier going into a gun store the second time as opposed to the first. Grant went back to Capitol City and looked at all of the cool guns. Wow. He had forgotten how much he loved them.

The expense-check envelope in the car was full, so he bought a .38 revolver; a gently used Smith & Wesson with a three-inch barrel so it wouldn't kick as much as a snub nose. It is hard to go wrong with one of those; simple to operate, and ammo is relatively cheap and plentiful. He went out to the gravel pit. It shot beautifully. He loved it.

He had fallen back in love with guns. They felt so good in his hands. When he handled one, he didn't feel like a dependent suburbanite. Grant remembered how safe he felt with a gun. The ogre couldn't hurt him when he had one. He was safe.

He went back to Capitol City and got a Crimson Trace laser grip for the .38. It put a red dot exactly where the bullet would go. It made aiming almost effortless. It was so easy that Lisa, or any new shooter who didn't practice using guns, could do it in a stressful situation. And a revolver was very simple to operate; no cocking, no safeties, no magazine or slide that could jam.

At the gun store, Grant saw that guys buying handguns could avoid waiting five days to pick up a handgun if they had a concealed weapons permit. As whacked out as Washington State was, at least they had good gun laws. A permit was only $35, so he got one. He now had a concealable revolver and a permit to carry it.

But he didn't carry it; that would be weird. He kept the permit secret from Lisa. She would think he was a gun-crazed nut. He put a trigger lock on the .38 and hid it where Lisa would never find it. He hid the box of .38 ammo; the one box of fifty shells. That should be enough.

As he was taking baby steps toward being prepared, the nagging thoughts about dependency were getting more intense and frequent. Grant kept thinking he should learn about things. He needed to learn — actually, relearn — how to survive. Not just how to build a fire in the woods. He needed to learn the survival mindset. He had to get in the habit of figuring out a solution on his own instead of depending on someone to supply him food or fix something.

Grant went to the bookstore to find books on "survival." He was looking at the books secretly; he didn't want anyone to know what he was looking at. It felt like the first trip to the gun store. It was like he was looking for a book like "Bestiality Illustrated."

Grant meandered over to the "Outdoors" section of the bookstore and waited until no one was looking. Then he pulled a book, the *Special Forces Survival Manual*, off the shelf and looked at it, shielding it so no one could see the title.

That book had things in there about building a fire and making traps to get small game. That wasn't the kind of survival knowledge he needed. Oh, sure, it was good stuff to know and he planned on learning that at some point. But right now, at this early stage of his journey into prepping, he needed to find a book that would tell him how to be an independent man. There were none.

Grant left the bookstore empty handed and disappointed that there wasn't some book he could read that would teach him everything he needed to know. This survival thing might be more difficult than he thought.

When he got home and saw that Lisa wasn't there, Grant got on his computer. He did a Google search for "survival." He erased his browsing history so Lisa wouldn't find out his secret, shameful interest in something so sick and wrong. He started to laugh at himself; it's not porn, it's learning how to save your family and live through bad situations. Since when is that a shameful thing?

Grant had an iPod and liked podcasts. So he searched the iTunes Store for "survival," and many bizarre podcasts came up. Some of them were the crazy tinfoil hat kind of "survivalists": the government is going to round you up and put you in camps, the Jews are taking over the world, etc. That image of a survivalist was exactly what Grant was afraid of. "Survivalist" seemed to mean "white supremacist" and "conspiracy theorist."

Great, Grant sarcastically said to himself. He was going insane. He was worried about society breaking down and only a bunch of weirdoes shared his concern. If the only people who were survivalists were weirdoes, then he wasn't a survivalist.

Grant clicked on one last search result: "The Survival Podcast."

The stats showed that exactly 173 people were subscribing to this podcast. It probably sucked.

He listened for a few minutes. Whoa. The guy doing the podcast wasn't crazy. He was really smart. He was practical. He talked about how to store food, how to learn skills, how to grow a garden, alternate sources of electricity and water. Jack Spirko was his name. He did this podcast while he was driving in his car. Grant was hooked.

Besides the non-nuttiness of the guy and the practical information, the other thing that Grant liked about the Survival Podcast was that Spirko seemed to be just like him. He had grown up in the country and lived a lot like they did in Forks. Spirko got a big job and turned into a suburban guy, but felt like the whole thing was a fake. Just like Grant. Spirko returned to his country boy roots and was telling everyone else who would listen— all 173 of them— about how they, too, could get more independent and survive whatever might be coming. Spirko made it clear that he wasn't a racist or an anti-Semite. He was a libertarian.

Grant hit the button on iTunes to become a subscriber to the Survival Podcast. He could feel that something bad was coming to America. It was the strongest nagging feeling he'd had up to that point. The economy seemed to be a giant fraud. The analysts on CNBC kept saying that things were fine but Grant didn't believe them. Jack Spirko was telling people to get out of the stock market. That was preposterous; the Dow was at 14,000. Spirko was adamant.

Then it happened. All kinds of banks were failing. There was full-on panic in the U.S. It looked like the financial system would melt down.

Grant kicked his survival preparations— "preps" as Spirko called them— into high gear. He felt bad for reacting so strongly and perhaps panicking, but he felt the need to get food and guns ASAP. When Grant thought about the preps he needed to do, the nagging feeling would stop nagging and start encouraging him.

Chapter 15

Prepping

Grant was really worried about Lisa finding out that he had lost his mind and was a "survivalist." He needed to persuade her why having a little food and security would be a good thing in these troubled times. She was smart and surely would understand that when the Dow drops 40% and the government is taking over banks and whole industries, that something unusual was happening and it required some thinking outside the box.

He was wrong. Grant had allowed Lisa to manage the money long ago. She was smart and did a good job at it. Grant remembered back to a previous summer, when he could feel what was coming, when he sent Lisa a link to a news story about the CEO of a huge European bank. He was not some kook. The banker was predicting a financial meltdown and credit crisis in the U.S. in the upcoming fall. Grant emailed the story to Lisa with the message, "maybe we should diversify at least some out of the stock market." She got a little mad. She told him that she was a very capable money manager and that getting out of the stock market when it was up to 14,000 was crazy because at this pace, it would be at 16,000 by Christmas.

Grant knew Lisa. If she had said they're staying in the stock market, selling now would mean she was wrong. If anything, this meant that if the stock market dropped, she would want to buy more stock because the prices were low. Sometimes when she had a choice of admitting being wrong or doubling down, she would double down. She wasn't mean; she just thought she was right. And Grant had always sat on his ass while she managed the money, so she was probably justified in not appreciating his last-minute "expertise" on the matter.

Grant would have rather bought some gold, which was at $900 per ounce, and some silver, which was at $17, but he had no choice. More stocks it was. He knew that Lisa would never back down and admit that a "survivalist" got it right. He was now even more worried about her finding out about his secret life. The more prepping he did, the more he was defying her. That's how she would look at it.

Grant felt a wedge coming between him and Lisa. But he couldn't go back to being a dependent suburban sheeple. He had actually thought about what happens when 911 doesn't answer the call and when there is no food at the grocery store. Once you think those thoughts, you can't just go back to not caring. You have to do something.

Be a man, Grant kept hearing the outside thought say.

Be a man.

Well, if Lisa was going to double down, so would he. Grant realized right then and there that he had to prepare for what was coming. There was no choice. He kept thinking how he would feel when his kids were hungry and his family was terrified to leave the house, and he would know that he could have done things to prevent it but he didn't want to make his wife mad. There was no choice. No one was going to do this for him. It was up to him.

Realizing that it was up to him and that he had to do it was a relief. He had been trying to figure out a way to get Lisa on board. It wasn't going to happen. He was going to play the hand he was dealt. Grant had a job to do. He was the man, and protecting his family was his job.

No one said this would be easy, Grant kept repeating to himself. If prepping were easy, all the sheeple idiots would be doing it. Instead, they were going to Applebee's and gorging themselves on food trucked in 1,500 miles and putting it on their credit cards.

He listened to a Survival Podcast episode about storing food and learned that some foods stored better than others and were cheap. Grant focused on oatmeal, pancake mix (Cole's favorite food), beans, rice, and pasta. He specifically wanted food that could be cooked using only water and heat. He didn't want things that had to be baked or required milk or other ingredients. The foods he focused on also had to be easy to store for long periods, and be items that his family would eat. They wouldn't love it at first, but they'd eat it. Especially when there was no food in the stores.

Grant went to the local Cash n' Carry, a discount grocery store that sold in large lots. It wasn't a Costco or Sam's Club. It was different. It was a combination of discount grocery store and restaurant supply store. It sold things in gigantic lots; and very inexpensively.

Grant was afraid to go into Cash n' Carry. It was like the gun store or looking at a "survival" book; only crazy people did that. He expected to see militia people or survival whackos in there. He was

76

doing lots of things lately that he'd never done. Might as well add walking into a Cash n' Carry onto the list.

Grant sat in the parking lot for a few minutes getting his courage up. It was getting easier and easier to do these things now that he'd started doing them.

He watched the people going into the store. They seemed pretty normal. No obvious weirdoes. Grant got out of his car and strolled in like it was no big deal. As he got to the door, he realized it was, indeed, no big deal. He was just going to a Cash n' Carry. It wasn't like he was going to buy heroin.

Grant walked in. He was relieved just being in Cash n' Carry. Look at all that food. A prepper's dream. It was amazing. The prices were unbelievable. Fifty pounds of pancake mix was $35. That would make 200 breakfasts (using one cup of mix per breakfast). That's less than $0.18 a breakfast! And that's $0.18 now, but that same one cup of pancake mix would be worth $10 if there wasn't any more on the store shelves. But how to store it?

Spirko talked about using a food vacuum sealer. Bacteria needed oxygen so if food wasn't exposed to it, the food would last for years. The vacuum sealer sucked all the air out of the food. Adding some oxygen absorber packets would add even more years to the food. Oxygen absorbers were optional; vacuum sealing alone would do the trick. Grant got a good vacuum sealer, a bunch of sealer bags, and some oxygen absorbers. He was ready to put up several months' of food.

But where? He couldn't store the food at his house; Lisa would find out. Grant had seen a rental storage unit place on the way in to the Cash n' Carry. That's where he would store the food. Then he remembered a storage unit in downtown Olympia, down in "bum town," which was near his office. Grant would use the money from the expense checks to pay for a small storage unit.

Grant looked at all the food in the Cash n' Carry and left without buying anything. He wanted to get the storage unit first and make sure he had a place to keep the food before buying. He went to bum town and got a small storage unit. He felt like a criminal renting a storage unit; they probably wondered if he was going to stash the bodies of his murder victims in there.

It was unusual to pay for a storage unit with cash, but they still took his money. Grant had to use his credit card — which Lisa would know about if a charge ever went through — to guarantee payment so he had to make sure he came in once a month and paid with cash. Oh well. This was better than not having a place to store the food and therefore not getting any.

With the storage space taken care of and the vacuum sealer, Grant went back to Cash n' Carry. He bought fifty pounds of beans. He got a variety of red beans, black beans, navy beans, kidney beans, and pinto beans in five-pound packages. He bought fifty pounds of rice. He got ten one-pound packets of gravy. Rice and gravy: that's good eatin'. Lots of carbs, some fat, and some salt.

Grant began thinking about nutrition. He realized there was "normal times" nutrition and "crisis" nutrition. In normal times, when healthy food is everywhere, it made sense to stay away from lots of carbs, fat, and salt. That's how the calories pile up when people are not physically active; no one needs all that salt when they're not sweating.

But in a crisis, when food is scarce, carbs are critical. Same for fat, which is a necessary part of a human diet. It's just that with fast food drive-thrus, people got way too much of it. During a crisis, everyone would be physically working harder, doing lots of things they didn't do before the crisis, like walking places when there's no gasoline available. There probably wouldn't be air conditioning, so people would sweat a lot more and need the salt. Besides, foods with carbs, fat, and salt were cheap and easy to store. Nutrition was one of the many topics where the "normal" rules were backwards in "crisis" times.

Grant also got fifty pounds of pancake mix. Cole would love the reassuring sameness of a morning with pancakes. Pancakes need syrup. The Cash n' Carry was out of gallon jugs of syrup. On a hunch, Grant went to the dollar store. He'd never been to one before; he'd never had to because he could afford the regular grocery store.

Grant found the dollar store to be a prepper's paradise. Everything was truly one dollar; they didn't even have price tags. Most things were off brand, but who really cared. The food aisles were amazing. He quickly realized that the grocery stores were charging double or sometimes triple what the dollar store was. And the neat thing about the dollar store selling something for a dollar was the unit size. It was smaller than normal. It made for handy small packages that could be stored and used one by one. For example, Grant got sixteen-ounce glass bottles of syrup for a dollar. He got twenty of them. The smaller bottles would be better than a gallon jug of syrup; easier to pour, less mess, less waste. Smaller bottles could also be given away to needy neighbors. That's harder to do with a gallon jug. Grant looked closely at the sixteen-ounce syrup bottles. They were glass and had a decent screw-on cap made of metal. They could be washed out and used to store lots of things when the syrup was gone.

Grant got almost $100 of food at the dollar store. That was two shopping carts brimming to the top. He got boxes of tea bags, big cans of spaghetti sauce, flavored mashed potatoes, and cases of canned vegetables.

He got lots of cheap housewares there, too. He got ten can openers. What good is canned food without a can opener?

Grant started thinking about can openers. A can opener would be worth its weight in gold in a crisis, when fresh food would be hard to get. There would be warehouses of canned food. A can opener was another thing that could be handed out to a needy neighbor. The dollar store had cheap toilet paper, toiletries, over the counter medicines, work gloves, bungee cords, and just about everything else. For a dollar.

After learning what the dollar store had, Grant went back to the Cash n' Carry to finish off some meal ideas. Now that he had two cases of big cans of spaghetti sauce, he got some twenty-pound boxes of spaghetti noodles. They would go great into vacuum seal bags and stay fresh for years. A twenty-pound box of spaghetti noodles was $19. That meant twenty good-sized dinners of a pound of spaghetti and a big can of sauce were about $2 each. And it would store for years.

It cost a lot less to prep than to buy normal groceries. But Lisa and the kids would never eat this stuff in normal times. In a crisis, however, it would be the best tasting spaghetti they had ever had and they'd be thankful they had it when others didn't.

Grant's car was filled up with food. He took the vacuum sealer and an extension cord and went to the storage unit. Since it was in "bum town," Grant knew he needed to be careful. For the first time in his life, he packed a gun. He put his .38 in a little pocket holster and slipped it into the front pocket of his jeans. It fit perfectly. He had the permit; might as well use it. He realized that he needed to pack the gun quite a bit for practice to test out the holster and just the mindset of carrying a gun.

The mindset was a big deal. A person carrying a gun thought differently. They were more aware, and avoided trouble so they wouldn't have to use it.

The front door at the storage unit had a sign that food wasn't allowed in the units. That was a dilemma. He would be careful not to leave even a crumb in case there were mice or rats (he'd never seen any signs of them there). Luckily, it was late evening on a Sunday so the manager wasn't around. There was a surveillance camera at the entrance to the units so Grant used a plastic bag to cover the labels on the boxes of food.

It took several hours to seal up all the food. Grant carried all the food up the stairs, sealed it, and put it in organized piles. He realized that he needed big plastic storage tubs like the kind they put the Christmas decorations in. He'd get those later; he didn't have any room in the car for them with all the food. It was extremely reassuring to be sealing and organizing so much food. He kept thinking about a financial crisis and what an empty grocery store would look like. Then he'd look at the month or two of food he had for his family. He was proud — he was a man doing his job. The nagging thoughts were gone.

This is just the beginning of your work.

There was that outside thought again. Grant listened carefully to it this time.

Chapter 16

Getting in Shape

One of the things Grant realized from hauling all that food up the stairs to the storage unit was how tired he got. Winded, in fact, just carrying a case of canned vegetables up the stairs. Not a little winded; full-on stop and rest with a pounding heart kind of winded. He could never do all the things he needed to do in a crisis if he was this out of shape. He looked at himself. He was fat. For the first time in his life. He had noticed the gut a few years ago, but now he was genuinely fat. And weak. He never exercised. He worked in an office and sat on the couch on the weekend. He knew something was up when he started wearing XXL shirts but he never thought it was a big deal.

You will need to be physically strong for what's coming. Get strong.

The outside thought had been right about everything else. Grant decided to do what it said.

Lisa had always been in good shape. She stepped it up and got in great shape a few years ago when the kids were in middle school and late elementary school and were much lower maintenance. She did it by joining the gym in town where everyone worked out. A few years ago, she had asked Grant if he wanted a membership and, predictably, he said no. It hadn't surprised her. Why would Mr. Workaholic and couch potato want to exercise?

Now Grant saw everything differently. The world wasn't just about working and eating and sitting on the couch. There were actual dangers out there. Being out of shape could get him killed. Or being weak could get his family killed. His pathetic physical condition was more than just another prep to work on. It was a symbol of what he'd become: a fat, useless sheeple. This had to end.

When he got home from the storage unit, Grant said to Lisa, "I've been thinking that I'd like to join the gym." She was stunned. She assumed he'd be there a week or maybe two and then drop it.

Going to the gym for the first time in his life was horrible. He didn't know how to dress. He just wore some shorts and a t-shirt; he wanted to fit in there. He did. That was a relief.

The first machine he got on was an elliptical trainer. He looked around and other people were setting it on twenty minutes. No problem. He could handle twenty minutes of walking, so this would be a breeze.

Or not. After three minutes he was winded. It was the same full-on winded he got from walking up the stairs at the storage unit. Three minutes? It was even on the lowest resistance setting. This would be impossible.

Like everything else you've accomplished?

The outside thought had a good point. How hard could this be compared to transforming himself from a Forks loser to a respected attorney? Focus on the task at hand. Create manageable goals. Track progress. Work hard. Getting in shape would be just like anything else. Besides, he had to do this. His life and the lives of his family literally depended on it.

He went to the gym the next week and did five minutes. Then six and soon ten. He got up to twenty minutes and then went a second time each week. Lisa was amazed.

Grant started eating better. More precisely, he started to notice what he was eating. Everything he had been eating was unhealthy. And the portions were huge. He started eating medium-healthy foods but not going insane with health food. He realized that he often ate a lot at a meal because that's how they did it in Forks. He would go outside and work splitting wood or something for several hours so he had to load up on food at mealtime. There were no breaks every few hours for a little snack of healthy food. But in Olympia there was no wood splitting and there were always some decent snacks around. Just put some carrots in the refrigerator at your office; how hard is that?

Grant started to lose some weight. Slowly, but it was noticeable. Lisa was noticing. She didn't ask why he was doing this; she was just happy he was. Grant realized the first benefit of being in better shape: more interest from his wife. This was great. That alone was worth it; saving his life and his family's was up there too, but don't discount the motivation of a little more sex.

Pretty soon, the twenty minutes twice a week became thirty minutes three times a week. He added mild weight training to his elliptical work out. Since he didn't have pectoral muscles in his left side, he couldn't use all the weights. He had one of the trainers help him. He was using some weight machines on fifty pounds. In a couple of months, he was up to 100 pounds and had quadrupled the number of repetitions.

"Hey, you have some actual muscles," Lisa said one night. Yep, he did. The night went very well from there on out. Motivation.

Now that he was in decent shape, doing things around the house wasn't so hard. He was doing projects in the yard and could do lots of errands on the weekends that Lisa used to do. He was doing about ten times more around the house than before. It was like a rebirth. Lisa was starting to change her mind about her formerly worthless couch potato husband.

This meant everything to Grant. He felt like he had some making up to do for the years of being a slug. He was earning back her respect after years of frittering it away. He knew he needed her respect for what was coming. Lisa would never abandon her home and way of life to follow a fat couch potato into a dangerous unknown. But she would follow a strong man who had earned her respect.

Chapter 17

More Capitol City Guns

Being in shape meant that he could do things outdoors much better; like shooting. Lots and lots of shooting.

Shooting was fun, but it also had a very useful purpose. Grant knew that when the grocery store shelves were empty the people would panic. They would fight with each other to get food. When the gas stations were running out of gas, they'd fight over a place in line to get some. At first people would be rude and cut in line, then they would have fistfights, then they'd shoot each other if it got really bad. The cops would be too busy to deal with any of this. And, if it stayed bad for long, some dirtbags would band together and try to steal food and other supplies. That meant guns were critical; first to defend yourself and then your band of people.

Armed groups of Americans fighting for food and gasoline? Oh, come on. That's crazy. This is America.

That was the problem. It was America. People expected those things to just be there. They had no backup way to feed themselves. And, worst of all, they had the expectation that things would just be there.

If everything Americans expected weren't immediately available, they would get mad and afraid. Very mad at whomever they blamed for the shortage and very afraid because they would instantly realize that they were completely screwed if the semi-trucks stopped driving up to the grocery store every few hours. The anger and panic would combine and have a multiplier effect. It would be a chemical "freak out cocktail" of adrenaline, fear, egging on by others, and rage. It would be almost psychotic. People would do things they never even imagined.

Whenever Grant was thinking about something like this, the history major in him would ask how people in the past had dealt with it. Human beings acted in rather predictable ways.

The answer was frightening. All over the world and in every time period there were shortages like the ones Grant knew were coming. They never went well. The freak out cocktail would kick in and some people would kill and steal. Not all of them, of course, but a small portion of them killing and stealing caused real problems for everyone. Lifelong friendships would be ripped apart over a piece of food. Trustworthy people would turn on one another. Governments— dictatorial and brutal— would rush in to "restore order." It was always to "restore order," but the order was theirs. The population must be disarmed and dependent on them for their "order" to work. Then the government leaders could do whatever they wanted. Getting to do whatever they wanted was the prize; and sometimes was worth causing the crisis in the first place. World history had too many examples to even start to list off.

History also showed that gangs would form to protect their members and to get the things they needed, like food. Bad gangs took various forms in history: pirates, many police forces throughout the world, and mafias. They took various forms but did basically the same thing.

In reaction to bad gangs, people would form good gangs. They would be self-protection groups that shared work and food. Examples of good gangs in history included isolated towns, religious and ethnic groups, and people who banded together for protection. Bad gangs would attack good gangs. Some good gangs would get out of control and turn into bad gangs. But a gang— mutual protection and sharing of labor and resources— would be the primary unit of society when fancy civilization broke down.

There was no reason to think that today's America would be any different. In fact, there was every reason to think it would be worse. No other society in the history of mankind ever had so much prosperity and food and luxuries so easily available. Never. No society had ever been more dependent on these things just being there. No society in history ever had so far to fall. Americans were spectacularly expectant that things would always be perfect. It would get ugly when this changed.

You can't even imagine.

There was only one sensible thing to do. Get some guns and self-defense training. Not some militia whacko thing. Not playing army. Not going out raiding and stealing like the gangs. Grant had no desire to end up being the very thing he was trying to protect himself and his family against. He just wanted to get the right mindset and training, and meet like-minded people so they could be a good gang.

It was absolutely obvious that Grant needed to know how to

use guns himself and he needed enough to equip a small group like his family and probably other families. As important as this task was, Grant had two limiting criteria. The first was that he would not break the law by buying machine guns or anything crazy like that. The goal was to survive; being in federal prison was not a smart survival move. His second guideline was that he would not spend so much money that it prevented him from doing all the other necessary preps. It would be stupid to have $10,000 worth of guns and ammunition, but no food. Guns, as much he enjoyed them, would not be some expensive hobby justified by the need to prepare for the roving hordes. Guns were a tool and one part of the preparations he needed.

The shotgun and his .38 were just the start. Grant began dropping by Capitol City Guns periodically to see what they had. He was also saving up his cash. He was taking his time and re-educating himself about guns. He knew the basics, of course, from Forks, but his information was a little dated. He knew about shotguns and hunting rifles. But his gun knowledge stopped over two decades ago. Since then, semiautomatic pistols— even ones made partially out *plastic*— and "assault rifles" began to dominate the market.

The first thing Grant figured out was what he needed. Needed, not wanted. The Survival Podcast and the guys at Capitol City talked about a "four gun" battery: a shotgun, centerfire rifle, a handgun, and a .22 rifle. The shotgun was for home defense and hunting. The centerfire rifle was for hunting bigger game and stopping people out at longer ranges. The handgun was to stop bad people at close urban distances and was easy to carry and conceal. The .22 rifle was for small game and keeping shooting skills sharp with inexpensive ammunition.

Grant had the shotgun and handgun already. He needed a centerfire rifle and a .22. He wished he could get the .22 rifle he had back in Forks, a 1930s Winchester model 63 pump action, but he wasn't going back there and asking his mom for a favor. He figured he'd get the .22 first, practice with it, and then move up to the centerfire rifle.

He was getting to know the owner of Capitol City Guns, a guy named Chip. He was a thin silver-haired gentleman in his late fifties or early sixties and always had a smile.

One day, Grant came in and asked Chip for a suggestion on a good .22 rifle.

"Oh, that's easy," Chip said. "A 10/22. They've made about five million of them. Maybe six. Seriously. Everyone has one. You can get parts and accessories everywhere."

Grant remembered the 10/22 from Forks. Chip was right;

everyone had one. Grant asked to see one. It was a great little .22. He got one, along with some extra twenty-five-round magazines, the steel-lip ones recommended by Chip. Grant got some targets and went out to the gravel pit.

The 10/22 was great. It was very accurate and very easy to shoot. He spent as many afternoons as possible at the gravel pit plinking; it was great fun. He got a scope for it and learned how to mount it, courtesy of Chip.

Once he had his rifle shooting skills back after hours of 10/22 plinking, he decided it was time for a centerfire rifle.

Grant went to Capitol City Guns looking for a centerfire rifle. He assumed he would get a normal centerfire rifle like a bolt-action deer rifle. That's what everyone had in Forks. When he walked in, though, he saw a wall of M-16s. Well, they were actually AR-15s, the civilian version of the military rifle. They were beautiful. They just looked bad ass. And totally solid. Grant was drawn to them. He had done his homework on ARs and knew that they were very reliable, easy to use, light, and were just about the perfect gun for a variety of uses.

"Chip, could I see one of those?" Grant said pointing to a plain vanilla AR-15. It had a carry handle and a twenty-inch barrel. A standard issue A2.

"I don't know if I should do that, Grant," Chip said very sternly. "Once you hold this, you'll buy it, and then another. Are you ready to join the brotherhood of AR owners?" Chip asked with a devious grin.

"Let's see," Grant said with a devious grin of his own.

The AR-15 felt fantastic in Grant's hands. Wow. It was an amazing tool. He couldn't believe that a civilian like him could hold it, let alone buy it. He *had* to have it.

"Wrap it up, I'll take it," Grant said to Chip with a huge smile. It was liberating. Grant would own an "assault rifle" of his very own.

Owning an AR-15 was the definition of liberty. As flawed as America was, at least a citizen could own something like that. He looked at the gun, which looked exactly like a military rifle (because it was), and thought, "This is freedom." Grant also thought that it would be much harder for the government to impose a dictatorship on the country when regular people like him had these.

Grant never wanted to use it like that; he hoped that the only thing he ever pointed it at would be a paper target. Grant fervently hoped that. He recalled the figures of the Revolutionary War who constantly talked about not wanting to fight a war. They weren't cowards; they ended up being the bravest heroes. They were decent human beings who just wanted liberty and a good life for themselves and their families. They worked hard to achieve that without guns. But they all had guns and knew how to use them. None of them were murderers who enjoyed it, but many of them ended up killing. They deeply regretted it the rest of their lives, although they'd had no choice.

Grant couldn't wait to field-strip that beautiful thing and put it back together again. He watched YouTube videos on how to do it. One day when Lisa was gone, he field-stripped the gun and put it back together. It took a long time the first time. The brand new gun was really tight; he thought he couldn't get some parts out at first, but eventually he did. It felt awesome to be working on an AR-15. He was no longer a helpless sheeple.

Shooting it was amazing. It was just plain fun to shoot. Little to no recoil. Accurate as can be. He was in love.

He shot it almost every weekend. He had a membership at the local rifle range, which had a covered area that was a must in rainy Washington State. Grant was getting very good with the AR. He was operating it smoothly, like a pro. He surprised himself at how good he was getting.

What a contrast. Grant was getting excellent on an AR out on the shooting range, but when he came home he had to hide it. He kept his AR in a gun case in the garage. It was high up on a shelf. Lisa never saw it or knew that he had an AR. He didn't show it to the kids. In fact, he didn't show it to anyone. Grant didn't want people knowing that he had such a "machine gun," although it was a perfectly legal rifle. In a crisis, they might try to steal it or insist that Grant protect them. Other people who had them, and who could be trusted, could know.

Grant bought a few books on ARs and learned a lot about them on the Survival Podcast forum. He went to Capitol City Guns and hung out; he learned even more about them there.

Grant was becoming a regular at Capitol City. It was like a barbershop where guys went even when they didn't need haircuts. He was forming strong friendships there. There were many people from different backgrounds there. He was the only lawyer, but among the "regulars" there were a manager of large retail store, an airline pilot, a general contractor, and a computer guy. Grant would bring donuts. Others brought chicken and pizza. It was a great place. An oasis of "normal" people in liberal, government-loving Olympia.

The guys at Capitol City were Chip's family. He had been

married earlier in life and divorced. His daughter came to the store once in a while. She was a beautiful young lady. Chip lived alone and his parents had recently died.

One day, Chip, who was having a rough day, said, "You know, Grant, you guys are my family. Thanks for being my family." He seemed like he was going to cry.

Grant didn't know what to say. He just shook Chip's hand and said, "My pleasure, man. I feel the same."

One of the most interesting people who hung out at Capitol City was "Special Forces Ted." He was a Green Beret at Ft. Lewis. He was in his mid-forties, had black hair, and was always tanned from all the deployments in sunny parts of the world. It was hard to miss him when he walked into the store in uniform. He literally had a green beret on his head. His name was Ted Malloy, or, as Chip called him, "Special Forces Ted." He got that name because there were two Teds: him and Ted the UPS delivery guy who came in every morning with packages. To distinguish the two, Chip started calling one "UPS Ted" and the other one "Special Forces Ted."

Special Forces Ted came into the store because Chip took care of him. Chip would get customized rifles and accessories for Ted, usually at cost or sometimes below cost. Ted started to get customized rifles and gear for his team and other Special Forces soldiers. The teams were in Afghanistan then. Chip would hook them up with the good gear that they couldn't get from the Army. Ted was very appreciative.

Special Forces Ted became a regular at Capitol City. He would be retiring soon. He just went through a nasty divorce. Now that he was leaving the unit, his Army buddies wouldn't be around like they were in the past. Ted's "family" of his wife and his soldiers had instantly vanished. His whole world had changed in a matter of a week.

Capitol City Guns became Special Forces Ted's extended family. He and Chip were particularly close because they were similar; they didn't have a family anymore so the guys at the gun store became the family.

Special Forces Ted got a kick out of Grant. He thought most lawyers were worms. (Grant agreed.) Ted liked Grant's attitude. It was so refreshing to see a lawyer in a suit taking apart an AR. Ted especially liked that Grant knew his own limitations; Grant wasn't a mall ninja. A "mall ninja" was a military wannabe. It's a person who buys cool tactical gear and walks around a mall to show off to people but has no clue how to actually do anything tactical. Ted liked that

Grant was trying to learn tactical things and knew that he started off not knowing crap about it.

Grant had enormous respect for Ted, which was easy to have once he learned about the things that Special Forces do. Most people think Special Forces are commandos who parachute behind enemy lines and blow up bridges like in the movies. They can do that, and sometimes do. However, Special Forces mainly send in a small team of usually twelve soldiers into an enemy-held area and link up with indigenous fighters who are on the same side as the Americans. The twelve-man Special Forces team trains, supplies, motivates, and leads the indigenous fighters to attack the enemy and gather intelligence for regular American forces.

Special Forces soldiers need to be more than just excellent gun fighters. They must be part salesmen and part diplomat to get indigenous fighters to join the American side and stay loyal. They must know how to effectively govern the areas they're in. They need to know how to keep the indigenous fighters happy by, for example, making sure their villages have food, water, and security. This is actually much harder than blowing up a bridge.

Besides the lack of a family, the other connection Chip and Special Forces Ted shared was that Chip was a former solider. Not a Green Beret, but a supply guy who had combat experience in Vietnam. People who think the Green Berets do all the important stuff, while the supply guys don't, obviously have no idea how it works. It's pretty hard to win a firefight with no ammunition. Where does that come from? The supply guys. Ask George Washington and Mao how important supplies and logistics are. Supply guys had saved more than one Green Beret's ass. Ted respected Chip. They were becoming like long lost brothers.

One day at Capitol City, Ted and Chip were looking at a gun when Grant walked in. The gun was beautiful. It was the most recognizable gun in the world and the international symbol of terror and rebellion. It was an AK-47.

"Uh oh, hide it," Chip said to Ted when Grant walked in.

"Roger that," Ted said and clumsily tried to hide it.

Grant wondered if he had stumbled into the sale of an illegal fully automatic machine gun. That didn't seem like the kind of thing Chip would do.

"Sorry you had to see that, Grant," Chip said very seriously. "Because now you'll want one and then another, then another." Chip was grinning.

Ted picked up the AK and demonstrated how to hold and shoot it. He took it apart in a few seconds and put it back together. It was so simple to do. It was designed to be used by uneducated peasants throughout the world.

Ted explained to Grant, "This thing is so rugged that you can leave it in mud for a while, shake off the excess mud, clear out the barrel of course, and it'll fire. That happened to me once in the Philippines." Ted explained that the AK shot a different cartridge than the AR, which Grant already knew, but he also knew not to interrupt a Green Beret and say, "Yeah, I know."

Ted continued, "The AK uses the 7.62 x 39 cartridge, which has more knock-down power than the AR's 5.56 x 45, but drops a lot past a hundred yards. So, for short to medium range work, that is, shots inside a hundred yards, the 7.62 x 39 is a really great cartridge. I love an AK for that range. Besides, these things look terrifying. That's a plus. People will surrender because of that. It's nice to not have to shoot people."

Chip added, "There are probably several million AKs, and their cousins the SKS, in circulation, so there is lots of AK ammo out there. We sell almost as much 7.62 x 39 as 5.56. We always have cases of 7.62 x 39 here." Grant thought that in a crisis it would be good, when he couldn't just go to the store to get more ammo, to have a gun in both of the common calibers, 7.62 x 39 and 5.56. If one were hard to get, he could use the other rifle.

Grant had done his homework on the Survival Podcast forum and knew that quality varied enormously with makers of AKs. Chip's was a good brand.

"Can I see that?" Grant said with a smile because he knew he would be buying it, and then another, someday.

"Oh, you'd like to see this?" Chip said with the devious grin he often flashed.

This particular AK was even more badass than a normal one. It was an "under folder," which meant it had a stock that folds under the gun so it's much shorter, but the stock can still unfold and be used like a regular rifle. With the stock folded up, it just had a pistol grip. It looked like a terrorist gun. Grant thought it would be good to have a short rifle that could easily fit into a car or even under a jacket.

"Wrap it up, I'll take it," Grant said, just like when he had bought the AR. Grant had enough cash in the expense-check envelope, so he went out to the car and got it. He had enough left over for some magazines and a case of ammo. He was set.

The AK was a fantastic gun. Grant shot it frequently and got as good on the AK as he was on the AR. He operated the AK so smoothly he could have passed for a trained professional. He could consistently hit a target at fifty yards, switch over to one at a hundred yards (and hit most of the time), come back to one at twenty-five yards, and then get a few more at fifty yards. It felt great. He felt absolutely safe with an AK in his hands. Nothing could harm him. Nothing.

Chapter 18

We won. Now what do we do?

Things were also going great at work. WAB was getting famous for fighting the power. It felt fabulous.

It was an election year. That meant that the pathetic Republicans would come to WAB groveling for money and promising to fight for small businesses. Yawn. Grant and the other WAB guys had heard this before.

A new face appeared. He was Rick Menlow; a young and slightly nerdy guy in his late thirties. He was a Republican county commissioner from Snohomish County, which was part of the Seattle suburbs. His district was gerrymandered to include the rural areas of that county so the Republicans could have at least one seat. That was "fairness" in the one-party state of Washington. The Ds would throw the Rs a bone now and again.

Menlow was running for State Auditor. Washington had a very strong auditor's office. The auditor could basically investigate anything that involved state or local government spending of public funds. That was a huge part of the Washington state economy, unfortunately.

The current auditor was a Democrat hack. She used her office to cover things up. "The State Auditor did not find any wrongdoing," is what the government would say when someone found something out like when Sellarman, the Real Estate Board guy, was doing something corrupt. That was exactly what happened in the Ed Oleo case; the State Auditor found no wrongdoing. Move along, nothing to see. Only crazy people thought there was anything wrong with government.

WAB interviewed candidates to decide whether to endorse them. A WAB endorsement was sought after by Republicans. It meant lots of votes from small businesses and quite a bit of money. WAB's PAC was brimming with money thanks to all the court victories they were having. It seemed like WAB was the only counterweight to the government in the state. That would end up being dangerous for the WAB staff and their families.

The WAB interview was conducted by Tom Foster, Ben Trenton, Brian Jenkins, and Grant. Candidate interviews were one of Grant's least favorite things. The politicians coming before them were such lying shitbags. And pathetic. Why would any Republican run in Washington State? There must be something wrong with them to go through that.

When it was Grant's turn to ask the candidate a question he asked Menlow, "What would you do differently than the incumbent if you were to be the State Auditor?"

"My job," Menlow said flatly.

Good answer.

"How so?" Ben asked.

Menlow smiled like he'd been waiting to tell someone his plan. "I would fire most of the people there and use the resulting money to hire outside auditors to actually audit state and local governments. You guys know all the stuff I'd find. I would tell the Legislature that if they try to defund my investigations, then they're trying to prevent me from uncovering what they're doing."

OK, this Menlow guy was saying all the right things. But he was a Republican running statewide. There hadn't been a statewide Republican officeholder in almost three decades.

WAB decided to endorse Menlow, put the endorsement in their magazine, which went out to about 20,000 small businesses in the state, and donate the maximum contribution of $2,000. Menlow would lose, but WAB would do what they could. They never really thought about it much more.

A few weeks later, Eric came running into Grant's office very excited.

"Did you hear the news about the State Auditor?"

"No. Is it good?" Grant asked.

"Oh yeah. Wait till you see this." Eric was practically running to Tom's office where there was a TV.

A small crowd had gathered around the TV. The local news was playing a grainy video of a police dash camera. It showed a drunken woman in a business suit doing a sobriety test. Then she shoves the cop, jumps in her car, and takes off — only to hit a little kid in a cross walk! Then the camera catches her screaming, "Do you know who I am! Don't fuck with me, pig!" Finally, the police tackled her and then tried to give first aid to the kid, who was a little girl.

The room of WAB staff was silent. Stunned. No one could believe it.

"She's done," Tom finally said. "Call Menlow. We've got a campaign to run." There was blood in the water. The WAB staff was charged up and running on adrenaline.

The Democrat State Auditor tried to resign the next day. This would give the Governor time to appoint another friendly person to make sure things kept getting covered up at the State Auditor's Office. But it was right before the election so the Auditor's name was already on the ballot. There was only one other name on the ballot: Rick Menlow.

In the next few days, WAB raised a ton of money for Menlow. It wasn't too hard. WAB was the 900 pound gorilla of the "right wing" in Washington State. The media constantly replaying the drunken State Auditor screaming "Do you know who I am!" didn't exactly hurt Menlow's campaign. WAB polling showed Menlow would win so there wasn't much drama for election night. It would be a rare celebration instead.

The WAB staff, including Grant, went to the Republican election night "victory party." Grant had gone to one a few years earlier but quit going. They were like funerals. There never were any "victories" on election night.

The first returns came in a little after 8:00 p.m. Menlow was winning but it was surprisingly close, though, 52% to 48%. A drunken lunatic running over a child still got almost enough votes to win with a "D" after her name. Grant hoped that those voters simply didn't know what had happened. But, with the constant repeating of the video of her on TV, most of the people in the state must have seen her running over that little girl. That meant a sizable portion were still voting for the State Auditor because she had that all-important "D" after her name on the ballot.

WAB staff were invited to Menlow's hotel room at the party. At this joyous moment, they were all silent. They still couldn't believe that a Republican—and one who promised reforms, no less— might actually win an election in ultra-leftist Washington State.

Then Menlow's cell phone rang. Everyone knew what that meant. The concession call from the other side.

Menlow was very polite and respectful. When he hung up he wasn't smiling. He looked scared.

"Well, that was the concession call." Menlow said, still very disturbed. "Oh crap. We won. Now what do we do?"

Menlow's campaign manager, an attractive and savvy-looking young woman named Jeanie Thompson, blurted out, "Dunno. Maybe a transition team?" Everyone in the room laughed. No one had any plan whatsoever for actually winning. This was the first time it had actually crossed their minds.

Menlow pointed at Tom and said, "We need to talk." It was pretty obvious that the people in the hotel room would be the transition team. It was an electric feeling. Finally! The good guys had won. We can do some good things, Grant thought. Finally. It was their turn to fix things.

Not surprisingly, WAB essentially ran the transition. There was no one in the Washington State Republican Party who remembered how to do one since they hadn't won any statewide elections in over thirty years.

So WAB just made it up as they went along. Grant, Ben, and Brian were the main WAB people working the transition team. They were Olympia insiders and knew all the things necessary to come into a state agency and transform it.

The ring leader of the old State Auditor's bureaucrats was Nancy Ringman. She was the Chief of Staff. She was a hateful little troll.

Like most of the other people running Washington State (and the rest of the country at that point), she was a baby boomer. Similar to so many others of her generation, she grew up in the 1950s and early 1960s, was raised by "squares," rebelled against all that was official American squaredom in the late 1960s and early 1970s, went to college and learned about how great socialism was, got various jobs, and excelled in her career. She had to prove "woman power" to everyone and do it all: career and kids, although the career was more important. She had to be tougher than any man because the "old boys" would try to trip her up.

The problem with that mantra was that there were fewer and fewer "old boys." Most of the work force at the management level, especially in government, were either female baby boomers like Nancy Ringman or feminized male baby boomers who felt guilty about being male and didn't want to look "macho."

Nancy Ringman revered government. It could solve all problems. In her mind, the only bad thing in the world was people who got in the government's way. Why did those people oppose all the great things government could do? They were greedy, that's why. Greedy people wanted to keep their ill-gotten gains.

Nancy was the typical Olympia bureaucrat, and she lived in the Cedars, along with Grant. She knew that Grant worked at WAB, which meant that he was one of those evil people.

Grant didn't really recognize Nancy at first. He didn't recognize most of the people who lived in his neighborhood. One day, when Grant was over at the State Auditor's Office meeting with the new Auditor-elect, Nancy saw him. To say that she hated Grant was an understatement. But her job was on the line so she thought she'd try the pleasantries that had gotten her this far.

"Oh, hi, Grant," she said. "I'm Nancy Ringman. Your adorable children come over to trick or treat. I'm on Whitman Street. I understand you're helping Auditor-elect Menlow on, " she couldn't bear to say "transition." "Helping him on some matters," she finally said. Nancy was trying to smile, but it was coming off as gritting her teeth.

Grant didn't hate Nancy, although he would be entitled to. He just thought of her as typical of everything that's wrong. She and the rest of the government-worshipping baby boomers needed to make room for a new generation of people. The new generation who had borne the brunt of all this wonderful government and knew what was wrong with the utopia the baby boomers had created— and who weren't so corrupted by the system that they could actually fix things. All Grant could think when he was talking to her was, "Get out of the way." But he didn't say it out loud.

Obviously the old Chief of Staff would need to go. That was a top-level change that Menlow himself needed to do. Grant, Ben, and Brian would do all the rest of the firings. At first, Grant felt bad about firing people, although most were crappy at their jobs and many of them were lazy. They all, to one degree or another, had covered up bad things. But it was still hard to fire someone.

They all had jobs waiting for them in some other state agency. The government knew how to take care of its own. The State Auditor's Office hacks would come out of this unscathed. They didn't see it that way, though. Even though they had guaranteed jobs— most were actually making more at their new agencies run by fellow Democrats —they still felt entitled to do the job they wanted to do. They actually felt it was entirely their choice which job they had. And, in the past, they had always got what they wanted. The old Auditor's staff viewed the voters as idiots who were meddling in their careers.

The question was how deep the firings would go. Of course, WAB thought they should go very deep. Clean house.

Menlow, however, was a nice guy. He didn't want to fire everyone. He was a politician; why make enemies he didn't need to?

"If we fire everyone, who will run the agency?" Menlow asked them in one of their meetings. "Now that I'm the Auditor, if this place screws up it's my fault." In hindsight, this should have been a clue to Grant that Menlow wasn't a reformer but rather just a new bureaucrat.

Ben could see what was happening. He dealt with politicians all the time. "Yeah, but you ran for this office to change things. To start doing good things. Remember when we asked what you'd do different and you said, 'my job.' Well, your job is to fire these corrupt shitbags."

Menlow frowned at the "s" word; he didn't like swearing. He regained his composure and said, "Yeah, I guess you guys are right. But let's leave the rank and file workers. They didn't do anything wrong."

"Yes, they did," Grant said. He retold the story of rank and file State Auditor's employees not doing anything about Sellarman at the Real Estate Board. Grant gave other examples of State Auditor's employees who hadn't lifted a finger even when irrefutable evidence of corruption was presented to them.

"Besides," Grant said to Menlow, "even if the rank and file didn't personally do bad things, they have loyalties to the people who made the decisions."

"And," Brian added, "Because so many illegal things have happened in the State Auditor's Office, the rank and file have a motive to help cover it up since they were involved, too." Good point. All the rank and file employees were accessories to the misconduct and would act like accessories by trying to thwart the investigations.

Menlow was silent, thinking about what he should do. The silence continued. Tom could see that Menlow was reluctant to fire people and that WAB couldn't force Menlow to grow a pair of balls.

Finally, to let Menlow save face, Tom said, "The people elected you, Mr. Auditor, not us. It's your office. It's your choice on the rank and file."

After some more discussion, Menlow said he wouldn't fire the rank and file. "Or some of the mid-level managers," Menlow added. So Menlow had gone from wondering if he should fire the rank and file to now thinking he should keep some of the mid-level managers, who were definitely guilty in all the corruption of the State Auditor's Office.

Menlow said, "One more thing, guys. I need someone to go after agencies on behalf of citizens. Grant, you want a job here?"

What? Working for the government?

"Yes," Grant blurted out. It surprised even Grant that he said that. "What, exactly, would I do?"

"Take in citizen complaints about state and local government and then use the full power of the State Auditor's Office to investigate the complaints." Menlow was smiling, knowing that Grant wanted to do this. Menlow was also smiling because he knew he could leverage WAB's credibility with the right wing and never have to worry about being thought of as too soft on state and local agencies when he had hired a WAB pit bull like Grant.

"Special Assistant to the State Auditor?" Menlow said. "How does that sound?" Menlow knew what Grant would say.

"The full power of the State Auditor's Office?" Grant asked. After Menlow had just gone soft and decide to keep most of the old employees, Grant was wondering if Menlow would really do any reforming.

"I get free reign to go after people who broke the law?" Grant asked. He needed this authority to do his job.

"Yes. Full authority," Menlow said. This was the political compromise Menlow was making; keep the old employees, but hire a pit bull to go after corruption. It seemed like it would work, at least everyone in that room hoped it would.

"Done," Grant said and extended his hand for a handshake. "So, boss, when do I start?"

That was it. Government-fighter Grant Matson had just become a government employee. For a good cause, of course.

Chapter 19

A Hillbilly with a Law License

Why in the world would Grant want to be a government employee? Grant loved WAB, but he realized that he could do more of what he was meant to do— fight government corruption — at the Auditor's Office. Work the problem from the inside. Tom, Ben, and Brian understood. They were happy for him. They knew that they would still see him all the time.

Work at the State Auditor's Office was great. Grant actually got paid to help people who were getting screwed by the government. And he didn't have to send them a bill. And Grant had the authority of the State Auditor's Office behind him so he could do great things for people from the inside. Grant was now a white-collar sheepdog fighting back against bullies. It was pure heaven.

The first few months of work at the Auditor's Office were the "honeymoon period" when everything was wonderful. One of the people Grant got to help was Joe Tantori.

Joe ran a firearms training facility for military and law enforcement. It was a compound; secure as hell. It looked like a mini Blackwater facility. The military didn't want onlookers seeing how they trained.

Joe's facility was about two hours north of Olympia on the Puget Sound. There were numerous Navy bases in the Puget Sound and they did not have training facilities for firearms, which seemed weird. One of those bases was the Naval Magazine Indian Island where they stored munitions for the various naval installations in the Puget Sound. The second base was the Bangor nuclear submarine. Both bases needed a place to train. So did all the various local law enforcement agencies and even the federal law enforcement agencies on the Sound like the Border Patrol and Coast Guard at Port Angeles. Joe's range was it.

Joe constructed an extremely safe complex of shooting ranges and located it far from any neighbors so they wouldn't be bothered. He had a few hundred acres of buffer.

But that wasn't good enough. One of the distant neighbors was one of the three elected county commissioners. A few days a year, when the air temperature was just right and the winds were perfect, the commissioner could hear the faintest sound of gunfire. This was unacceptable. The commissioner started his quest to shut down Joe's facility.

The county, without a warrant, "inspected" Joe's facility. The Sheriff, who knew that the search was illegal, would not go along with it. So the county's land use enforcement officer, who was part of the county environmentalist clique that had elected the complaining county commissioner, conducted the search. The county land use department then ordered Joe to close it based on a repealed version of the land use ordinances. That's right; a repealed ordinance. Just like the Board of Real Estate tried with Ed Oleo. When the law won't allow what the government wanted, why not just use a repealed version of the law?

Joe brought it to their attention that the ordinance had been repealed and that the county had given him a building permit to build a shooting range exactly where he did and to the exact standards they specified. That wasn't good enough. Joe's lawfully permitted facility did not fit the land use department's "vision" for the area; a "vision" which did not include "violent" things like a shooting range and men in military uniforms. The hippies who dominated the county didn't like the "militarization" of Joe's land even if it was completely legal. Law and property rights needed to yield to the community's "vision."

This started five years of litigation, which cost Joe almost a million dollars. The land use department enforcement officer would periodically appear at Joe's range and inspect it, despite the fact that he had no warrant. This was completely unconstitutional. But Joe's remedy was to go to court — expensive and time-consuming court. An elected judge, who knew the "community's vision," did not include Joe's lawful and harmless use of his own property, sided with the county over and over.

In all this litigation, Joe had sent the county a subpoena for all the communications between the county commissioner, land use department, and the hearing examiner deciding the administrative appeal of the building permit. The county said no such documents existed. One morning a package appeared on at the main gate to Joe's facility. It contained several years of emails between the commissioner and the judge that said things like, "Do whatever it takes to shut down Tantori" and "I don't give a fuck about the law. Shut that asshole down." One reply from the hearing examiner said, "Anything you say, boss." The smoking guns.

Except Joe was out of money. He had the smoking guns but no money to get them in front of a judge. If the county judge ignored them, he could probably get the court of appeals to care.

Joe called WAB, where Eric was able to help. He got Grant, who was now the "Special Assistant to the State Auditor," involved, too. Grant demanded to see how much money the county was spending on that the lawsuit, which freaked out the county.

The real help for Joe came from Eric at WAB. He ended up getting Joe a new trial because of the obvious bias of the judge, and the trial was a success.

After the new trial, Joe could use his range again, and he was elated. Grant got to know Joe and Joe invited him and Eric out to the range one winter day. Eric couldn't make it.

Joe didn't know if an Olympia lawyer like Grant had ever shot a gun. He wondered if the fragile lawyer could handle the cold weather. They went out to the range with some steel targets in the shape of a human silhouette that fell down when they were hit. Joe handed Grant an AR-15 and said, "I bet you've never seen one of these." Grant thought he'd have some fun with Joe.

"Hey, I'm a lawyer," Grant said, "I don't know anything about guns. Is that a machine gun? Can I see it?" Joe gave him a safety briefing on how to run an AR. Grant listened patiently, pretending it was the first time he'd heard these things.

"You ready to shoot it?" Joe asked. "Don't be scared. It hardly kicks at all."

"OK. I'll give it a try," Grant said, like he was afraid. He took the AR, kept the muzzle pointed in a safe direction like a pro, looked down range, racked a round with an effortless pull of the charging handle, shouldered the rifle, smoothly clicked off the safety, got in a perfect shooting stance, and fired.

"Ping!" on the steel target. "Ping, ping, ping," on the other targets. Grant kept moving from the left to the right in between shots to make it harder for anyone shooting at him to hit him. He hit every steel silhouette. He clicked the safety back on and handed it to Joe. Joe was shocked. He didn't know what to say.

"I'm not your average lawyer," Grant said with a smile.

"What branch were you in? Marines?" Joe asked.

Grant laughed. "Nope. I'm UCG."

"UCG?" Joe asked. "What's that?"

"Untrained Civilian Goofball," Grant said. They laughed.

Grant winked and said, "Well, untrained when it comes to formal training. I bought one of these and shoot a little on the weekends." They shot together all day. Joe taught Grant some tips and tricks.

Ammunition was not a concern. Joe had cases of 5.56 ammunition. The Marines would bring ammo by the pallet and not shoot all of it, so he got the leftovers for personal use. Joe could not believe that a lawyer could run an AR like that. Grant could not believe that a guy he knew had cases of ammunition.

"So, you're a lawyer and you can shoot like this?" Joe asked at the end of the day. He still couldn't believe it.

"Yep," Grant said. "I'm their worst nightmare: a hillbilly with a law license."

They both knew who "they" were. People like the bastards who had tried to bankrupt Joe.

Joe felt like he could trust Grant. So he told Grant something very sensitive that he had been thinking for a long time but didn't want to tell anyone. Joe had a security clearance and had to stay in the good graces of his military and law enforcement clients. He couldn't be a "revolutionary."

"Have you heard of an organization called 'Oath Keepers'?" Joe asked.

"Is that some religious thing?" Grant asked.

Joe laughed. "No, that's 'Promise Keepers.'"

Joe explained that Oath Keepers was a large national organization of currently serving and veteran military and law enforcement. The "oath" in Oath Keepers was the oath every military and law enforcement person takes to "uphold and defend the Constitution, against all enemies foreign and domestic."

And domestic. Those words rang in Grant's ears.

Joe, who was former State Patrol SWAT guy, said, "We take a pledge to not enforce ten unconstitutional orders we might receive. Like to round up guns." Joe told Grant about the other nine unconstitutional orders Oath Keepers pledged to not enforce. Things like conducting warrantless searches or detaining Americans as "unlawful enemy combatants."

Wow. This stuff was getting serious. A large national organization of military and law enforcement people pledging to not round up guns. This was not BSing over beers. This was serious.

"What I like about Oath Keepers," Joe said, "is that they're not militia whackos. They don't want to overthrow the government. They want people to honor their oaths. That shouldn't be too controversial."

Joe couldn't figure out how people were putting up with what was happening so he had to ask Grant, who was an Olympia insider.

"When are people going to rise up?" Joe asked. "I mean, I'm no radical or anything, but this system isn't working. If they can do this to me," he said referring to the illegal searches and attempts to take away his property, "then they're doing it to millions of other people. What's up? What's going to give?"

Joe stared off at the water surrounding his compound. "I mean, I don't want anything violent to happen. But people will not put up with this much longer."

"It's a numbers game, Joe," Grant said. "Now there are only a few Joe Tantoris or Ed Oleos." Grant told Joe the story about Ed's fight and Ed asking the same question Joe was.

"But every year," Grant continued, "they get more reckless and think they can get away with anything. There are more Joes and Eds each year. It's growing exponentially as they get greedier and more power hungry. They can't stop themselves. So next year there'll be double the numbers of people like you, quadruple the next year, and," Grant did some quick math, "sixteen times the number the year after that. Pretty soon enough people get it."

Grant paused and looked Joe right in the eye. "It's coming, Joe. I don't want it, but I can't see how it's avoidable. The Joes of the world will eventually fight back."

Grant had been thinking a lot lately about how such a collapse would unfold, so he decided to tell Joe what he thought would happen. He hadn't been able to tell anyone else this, but Joe had shared his involvement in Oath Keepers, so Grant would return the trust by telling him what he really thought would happen.

"It will build slowly," Grant said. "It'll take a period of years. First it will be by people like us moving to better states like Texas. Look at how many businesses are fleeing California. Then it will be by cheating on their out-of-control taxes. A Patriot voting block will develop and get stronger each year. Elections will become nasty. They'll try to destroy Patriot candidates. They'll cheat on the vote counting, which is shockingly easy when their people control the machinery of the voter counting. They'll start to charge Patriot candidates and any of them who actually get elected with crimes. 'Tax evasion,' probably."

Grant went on, "A tax protest movement will start up where

people openly refuse to pay taxes. They won't be able to afford them and the government can't put everyone in jail. Oh, and the government will scare the population with horror stories about 'militias.' They'll pass all kinds of 'emergency' laws. The sheeple will be terrified about the 'crisis' and rally around the good government who is just trying to protect them."

This was the scariest part for Grant. "Then there will be an event. I have no idea what it might be. It could be real or concocted by them. 'Right-wing terror' of some kind. It won't matter if it's real or made up. It will shock everyone. By this time, with all the new 'emergency' powers they give themselves, the Patriots will realize that they need to do something now or it will be lost forever. We will. Protests, some turning violent. There will be assassinations. I don't condone that, but it will happen. The government will crack down even harder, losing more and more support each time they do. At each of the stages, the economy will get worse and worse until it basically stops functioning."

Grant paused. He didn't want to say what he really thought. "Then things get ugly."

Joe took it all in. He knew all this was true but he'd never heard another person say it, especially someone who had a front row seat to what was really going on like Grant.

"Yep." That's all Joe needed to say.

Joe felt he could fully trust Grant. Joe knew he had to do something about what was happening. Hopefully he wouldn't have to do anything drastic, but he had to do something. He couldn't let this happen to more people.

"You, my friend," Joe said to Grant, "are welcome back at my range any day. Bring friends."

Joe looked at Grant in the eye again and said, "I'll bring some of mine."

Chapter 20

A Busy Ant

It was spring after another Grant's trip to Joe's facility. Plants were blooming, but not many people felt a joyous springtime rebirth. Most were gloomy. The economy was horrible. Most were very worried about losing their jobs, some had lost them, and everyone knew someone who had. People were scared.

The country had just elected another big-government President. People were figuring out that he wasn't the "moderate" he said he would be. Plenty of people were afraid of what this new President would do. He seemed to be making the bad economy worse.

While some people were panicking about the economy, Grant was not. In fact, he felt much better than he had just a few months earlier. He had about three months of food in the storage unit and an AR-15 and an AK-47 with plenty of ammo, magazines, and even spare parts. He was starting to develop a network of friends who could help in a crisis. Most importantly, he had the survival mindset.

Grant knew that bad times were coming; he had a plan and some supplies, but most of all he knew that "normal" things would be coming to an end. He was mentally prepared for the massive changes — civil unrest, food shortages, personal tragedies — that were likely coming. He did not suffer from normalcy bias, which is when people are confronted with massive change, like the grocery stores not having food. They can't accept the new reality. They assume everything is like it's always been; that things will be "normal." Instead of adjusting to the new situation, they try to shoehorn the old "normal" into the current reality. They might, for example, refuse to believe that the stores don't have food. They might believe outlandish things like one particular store is out of things now but the other stores have plenty. They are so biased by what "normal" used to be that they can't operate in the current situation. It's a combination of denial, wishful thinking, and not knowing how to function in the new situation. Normalcy bias gets people killed. They make terrible decisions when they refuse to believe how bad things are.

Instead of the normalcy bias most people were suffering from, Grant channeled the anxiety of the economy and political climate into action. He added to his food storage. He went to Cash n' Carry and got more beans, rice, spaghetti, and pancake mix. He got lots of sugared drink mix because he knew people would need the calories of sugared mix and because he knew that water might need to be treated with iodine or bleach to purify it and having some flavoring could make it much more drinkable. He started getting a few items during each trip he made to Costco for the regular things his family ate. He got cases of tuna, canned turkey, cans of refried beans, and packets of instant oatmeal.

He got a lot of oatmeal. Oatmeal met all of his criteria for prepping food; it only required hot water, stored forever, was cheap, and his family would eat it. He got eight boxes with fifty-five packets of flavored oatmeal. That was 440 servings. Each box was $9, so that was about $0.16 a serving. He vacuum sealed the oatmeal envelopes. They would last for years and years now that they were sealed.

Another thing Grant stocked up on was spices and flavorings. Beans and rice get pretty bland after a while. Eating deer and other game meat required some spices. Hot sauce would make all the difference in the world.

The dollar store came to the rescue again. He got big canisters of flavorings and sauces for $1. Soy sauce, barbeque sauce, hot sauce — all $1. He got about a dozen one-pound canisters of table salt. Salt had a million uses and would be an invaluable seasoning, especially for someone sweating a lot. He also got a lot of coffee and tea. He didn't drink much of either, but he knew others would. It was cheap, and nothing is more soothing than a cup of coffee or tea.

It took water to make coffee or tea. More importantly, without water, a person was dead in three days. Grant marveled that some preppers would spend thousands on guns and ammo and neglect water. If the grid goes down, water treatment is something that will fail. Waterborne illness is a real danger.

Grant got a Berkey water filter. It used microscopic pore filters to screen out everything that could hurt a person. Raw sewage could be converted into drinkable water. It cost about as much as a case of cheap ammo. What a bargain.

Grant was also stockpiling medicines. He learned on the Survival Podcast forum how to make some great first aid kits. Not the Band Aid kind of kits. These were medium-duty trauma kits. Grant also bought many over-the-counter medicines. He had hay fever so he purchased several thousand non-drowsy allergy pills from Costco for next to nothing. They would last years as they didn't have an expiration date. Grant also got hundreds of caffeine pills. He and his colleagues might need to be awake a lot.

Grant got tons of vitamins, too. He went to Costco and got a few 500-pill multi-vitamin bottles and vacuum sealed their contents. A multi vitamin a day could keep the doctor away.

Since little cuts could easily kill people when there were no hospitals or pharmacies, Grant realized that he really needed some antibiotics. But he couldn't get them over the counter, and forging one of Lisa's prescription pads seemed like an extremely bad idea. What to do?

Grant learned on the Survival Podcast about fish antibiotics. They were the same as human ones, except they said "Not for human use" on them for legal reasons. The antibiotics were used to treat diseased aquarium fish. They were available without a prescription, at a tiny fraction of the price, and could be stored for years in a cool place. Even when they expired, they were still safe, though they might lose some of their potency.

Grant looked this up on the Survival Podcast forum and found out dosing instructions for humans. He discovered several great internet sites for ordering them. For about $60, Grant had enough perfectly good antibiotics to treat a dozen differing infections. He printed out the dosing instructions and vacuum sealed them with the antibiotics. What a life saver.

Now Grant had enough food and medicine for about six months in his storage unit. There was only one hitch; he had to get from his house to the storage unit to get them.

He figured a crisis probably wouldn't unfold instantly; he would have at least a few hours to get there and load all the stuff. However, loading the stuff might be a problem. There was only one of him and no one else knew about the stash. Lisa, who was a foot shorter than him and very petite, could not lift the big tubs. Oh well, no plan is perfect. Having all those supplies about two miles from his house was much better than not having anything.

Grant started wishing he had a place to put the food, a place far from the city where things would be safer. A "bug out location" or "BOL" as they were called in the prepper community. A BOL would be great, but he didn't have a fortune lying around.

Chapter 21

The Cabin Miracle

Grant's mom was calling. That was weird. She never called.

"Hi, Mom," Grant said. He had decided long ago to be civil and respectful with his parents. He didn't have to like them and he didn't have to visit them, but he did have an obligation to treat them as normally as possible. He wasn't a hater.

"Grant, the city is taking the homestead parcel," she said. The homestead parcel was his Grandpa's land in Oklahoma. It was not the ranch Grant would visit as a boy, but was a forty-acre parcel of land granted to Grant's great grandfather in 1904 as an Indian allotment. It was next to the ranch and was where Grandpa's brothers and sisters grew up in the 1920s. The homestead parcel was now owned by Grant's mom and her siblings. The homestead had enormous meaning to Grandpa and Mom and others in the family. It was sitting in what was now suburban Tulsa. It was worth a fortune, but the family did not want to sell it.

Grant asked his mom about the details. The city was using good old eminent domain to get the land for a song and then would probably sell it to developers and make lots of money to fund city government. It was an outrage, but as Grant explained the law to his mom, there was nothing they could do about it except to get as much money as possible for the land.

That's what happened. When all the legal stuff was over, Grant's mom would receive her portion of the proceeds, about $250,000.

She said to Grant, "The accountant told me that we have to spend the money on real estate within the next two years or we get taxed on it."

Great. The government takes your land and will then tax you on the "capital gain" of your "windfall" which is actually the forced sale of your land to them. But, on the bright side, it meant that Grant's mom had to buy some real estate soon or have a good chunk of it taxed away.

That's when it just came to him. A cabin. It was brilliant. That's what he could do. Get a cabin. It would be about the same amount as the inheritance. In that moment, Grant wasn't thinking about how the cabin would fit into his preps. He was just thinking about how he had always wanted a cabin.

In college, Grant spent a lot of time at his friend, Jeff Kozan's, cabin near Seattle. He absolutely loved it there. It was on the saltwater on an inlet to Puget Sound. He could not describe why he loved it so much there. It was away from the city. It was quiet. Every single time he went there he had a great time.

One time, Grant, still the poor kid from Forks struggling through college, told Jeff, "Someday I'll have a cabin like this. Not sure how, but I will." Even back then in college, when it seemed impossible to actually have a cabin later, Grant knew — *knew* — he would have one. It was now that time. Grant could have a cabin.

"What should I do?"Mom asked.

"Buy some real estate," Grant said. "I want to get a cabin nearby, on the water. Something simple but something that the kids can grow up in and have great memories of." Grant then started to realize how a cabin would be the perfect bug out location. A place to go when a crisis hits. A place to store food and other supplies. A place to hunt and garden when food was scarce. A place to be safe.

He went on to describe to his mom the things he sought in a bug out location. He wasn't telling his mom about the survival uses for the place; she didn't need to know what he was doing. She was too old to travel there from Forks, anyway.

A bug out location needed to be away from the city, but not totally out in the boonies. This would allow Grant and his family to get out of a city in a crisis, but there would be enough people around the bug out location to help him protect it and to trade with. He wanted a place on the water; saltwater, preferably. Olympia was right on the Puget Sound so there were hundreds of inlets and coves on the saltwater. Saltwater had clams and oysters and plenty of fish and a person could connect by boat to anywhere else in the area. A lake didn't allow that. And mosquitoes didn't live in saltwater.

The past few years, on occasion, Grant would drive around some of the saltwater cabin areas near Olympia and dream about owning one just like Jeff Kozan's cabin in college. Grant had some nearby areas in mind. He described them to his mom. He wanted a place that was an hour or less from his house so he'd actually go there often — like every weekend.

This is really happening, he thought. He knew — *absolutely knew* — that this "cabin" was going to be more than a place to have family barbeques in the summer. He was simultaneously amazed that this was happening, while at the same time he was calmly planning it out. It was the future and the present all at once. There was that feeling again; the future and present at the same time. Intertwined. Happening at the same time.

Grant's mom said she could take a portion of the proceeds of the eminent domain proceeds and give it to Grant.

When the conversation was over, Grant said goodbye to his mom. He felt a little guilty taking the money because the homestead meant so much to her. But, Grant didn't decide to sell it and she'd be taxed on the money, so the guilt quickly dissipated.

Grant told Lisa the great news. She didn't seem so happy. It was pretty obvious that she didn't like the idea of Grant's idiotic family that had been so cruel to him, suddenly giving him something so substantial. Besides, Lisa and Grant had worked extremely hard for so long and had built amazing careers and they couldn't afford a cabin. Now Grant's family was just handing one to him.

In addition, a "cabin" was not Lisa's cup of tea. It meant a second set of bills, a second set of maintenance, and a second set of all the crap that comes with owning a house. And Grant wasn't exactly good at doing anything around their real house, although he was getting much better.

"I'm not doing crap out there," she said. "No laundry, not paying the bills, nothing," she said. Her response wasn't exactly the joy of getting a free cabin he had expected.

"OK," Grant said. It was very clear to him that his years of being a suburban slug were now catching up with him. She had a good point. He quickly said, "I'll do everything out there." He knew that sounded like a kid saying they'll feed the stray dog, while the parent knows they won't.

Grant knew how to get Lisa to warm up to the idea. He told Manda about it. She was instantly excited. Jump-up-and-down excited. She thought of the endless possibilities of sleepovers with her friends. Having a cabin was a big boost in the popularity standings. Cole was not too interested. It was hard to describe to him with words what a "cabin" was.

Grant and Manda spent that summer searching for cabins. During the evenings, they would get on the internet and look at listings. They would prioritize them and then make a list of places to go see that weekend.

Grant had never seen Manda, who had turned fourteen, so organized about anything. He was used to having to tell her over and over again to put her dishes in the dishwasher and do her homework. But, now she was presenting him with stacks of color-coded and prioritized real estate listings with the prices highlighted. When she cared about something, she could be very organized.

That summer, they drove all over the area, even out a few hours from Olympia. Cabin shopping was magnificent. Grant and Manda were having a great time, and they were bonding.

They came across some incredible properties. The real estate market was in the tank. Prices had fallen enormously. It was the perfect time to have money to spend on real estate.

The first place they looked at in person was a cabin on Harstine Island. It was an hour and half drive from Olympia, which was longer than they wanted. But it was on Harstine Island, which was just a twenty-minute boat ride from Olympia. They drove out there and the first thing Grant noticed was that Harstine Island had a bridge providing the sole land access to the island. That could be a big plus since it would be easy to defend. But, if it were taken or destroyed, residents of the island would be in bad shape.

Harstine Island had a mix of full-time residents and part-time cabin owners. It was beautiful there. There were lots of water views and the big evergreen trees Washington State was famous for. It was very secluded.

The Harstine cabin was nice. Located on a small hill overlooking the beach, the cabin was modest, but very cozy. It was on two acres with a sturdy out building that would house a boat, truck, and tons of other equipment. It had a huge clearing that would be perfect for gardening. There were a few apple trees; perfect for having food year after year without having to plant anything. The layout was easily defendable because the driveway was rather steep and would require anyone coming up it to expose themselves to the many hiding places along the driveway. It was a perfect bug out location; a comfortable place to live, with plenty of gardening space, an out building for equipment, and defensible.

There was no access to the beach, though. They would need to rely on friendly neighbors. Grant assumed he could find them. Grant and Manda asked Lisa and Cole to come and see if they liked it. Grant assumed Lisa would love it.

She didn't. "How do we get to the beach?" she asked.

116

"Friendly neighbors," Grant answered.

"I don't want a beach house with no guaranteed beach," she said.

Grant was furious, although he knew she had a point. Oh well, they would need to find another place. Harstine Island was off the list.

He and Manda went back to the drawing board. Manda found another very promising cabin on the internet. Grant saw the picture of it and knew that this was the one. So did Manda. They drove out to it one gloriously sunny Saturday. There was nothing more beautiful than the Puget Sound on a sunny day. The mountains in the background. The inlets and the sound. Huge evergreen trees everywhere. Beautiful.

This cabin seemed to be perfect on paper. It was about forty minutes from Olympia. It was out in the country, but not so far out that it felt like a park. It didn't have a ritzy "resort" feel.

The development it was in was Pierce Point, which consisted of a group of about 500 lots. Not all of the lots had anything on them. "Development" wasn't the best word to describe it because that usually meant a new subdivision.

Pierce Point wasn't new. It was a combination of middle class homes and cabins that were nice, but not too extravagant. The middle class homes were on the way in to the place. The cabins started popping up closer to the water. Some were very nice; most were small houses on the water. There were some lots with RVs on them. There were a few junky homes, but this was a rural area and not everyone had tons of money. Most of the homes were well kept. They looked like working families lived there. Most driveways had pickups. Quite a few yards had playground equipment for kids. It looked like Forks, but nicer. There was quite a healthy mix of middle income working family homes and nice cabins.

The cabin they were looking at was on the very northern tip of the development. They went down the road towards the water. Big evergreen trees were all over but there were fewer down by the water. It was a rural, forested area down by the sea. It was perfect.

RVs on lots started to be replaced by cabins. Many were more aptly called "beach houses." The paved road ended with a sign that said "County road ends." Perfect. That was exactly what Grant wanted. A good paved road leading most of the way there and then a little county gravel road leading to seclusion. Perfect.

The gravel road was only a few hundred feet. The water on the left was beautiful. Grant saw the cabin they were looking for.

It was perfect.

It didn't look like a regular house. It was more like an A-frame cabin, but not tiny like a cabin. It looked like a typical Washington State beach house. The trees on both sides of the cabin provided a "mountain cabin" feel and then the water view offered a "water cabin" feel.

When they drove up, Grant looked at Manda and said, "This is it. This is the one." She nodded with a huge smile. Even at age fourteen she knew this was perfect.

They knocked and the owner was there. She was in her forties and looked like the mom of teenagers. Almost instantly, the owner liked the Matsons. She could see that her beloved cabin would be put to good use by a family of people who would have similar good memories made out there. Then she said something unusual to Grant.

"I need to sell this," she said. "I just got divorced, my job is looking like it's in trouble, and my ex-husband lost his job last year. We need the money. We'll sell this for a very fair price."

Grant couldn't believe it. The place was perfect and available for a song. He felt bad for the owner, but knew she needed to sell.

She gave him the tour. The outside of the cabin had a huge deck that looked out over the water. The view was amazing. The body of water was Simpson inlet, a finger of salt water about half a mile wide. The land on the other side was forested.

Standing on the deck looking at the water was so peaceful. It was amazing. It was exactly what he had been dreaming about.

They went down to the water. A short trail of about thirty feet led to a bulkhead. The bulkhead had a ten foot or so wide strip with a fire pit. The bulkhead had stairs that led down to the water, and the tide would come in on the lower part of the stairs. They were made of saltwater-resistant wood and looked very solid.

The beach was magnificent; not a sand beach, but a pebble beach. The tide was out about half way. The owner described how she could walk the beach all the way in both directions, north and south. To the south were other cabins.

To the north was nothing but trees and beach. Since the cabin was at the northern end of the development, the beach was uninhabited to the north. It looked and felt like a park or wildlife preserve along the beach. An eagle flew by. It almost seemed like the owner had ordered a show for Grant to convince him to buy the place.

They walked the beach a little way. How many times in one day could Grant use the word "perfect?" This was the place. He felt like he belonged there. There was that weird feeling of the present and future all at once.

Two other parts of the cabin were briefly shown, but not paid much attention. The first was the unfinished basement. It wasn't really a basement; it was a lower level to the cabin. It had a cement floor (the foundation of the cabin) and insulation on the walls; no drywall. The door going into it was on the ground level, but was lower than the cabin since the cabin was on a slope. The owner said, "You can store things here. Maybe a kayak." Grant knew what he'd be storing there — a year of supplies for his family. There was a bench in there that would be just right for working on guns.

The next little thing that the owner mentioned was a separate outside storage shed. It had the same siding as the cabin; thick wood with a thick coat of paint in perfect condition. The shed was about twenty yards from the cabin and surrounded by trees. "You could keep whatever in here," the owner said. It was empty and had a light. It was clean and seemed waterproof. Grant instantly thought about the food he had in the storage unit. It would fit perfectly in there.

There was one drawback to this place: no space to garden. Unlike the Harstine Island cabin, they could not grow any food here. Grant looked around to the surrounding lots. There was plenty of space on them. In fact, the lot next to this one was vacant. During a collapse, Grant could ask to use the neighboring lot for gardening and would give the owner a portion of the harvest. It wasn't ideal, but the cabin and area had so many other extremely compelling advantages that it was still the best location, by far.

The owner said, "Come and see the inside." It, too, was perfect. It wasn't fancy; it was somewhat outdated, and felt like a cabin, not a second home. It was exactly what Grant wanted. Who needs granite counter tops in a cabin? That seemed kind of wasteful, and Grant couldn't afford it, anyway.

The place was solidly built and in great shape. The furniture was decent. Although it wasn't in style, it wasn't cheap stuff that would fall apart. There was a main living area with huge window doors that looked out over the deck and onto the water. There was a nice wood stove, and an eating area. The kitchen was small, but solid and decent. A stove, sink, refrigerator, cabinets; everything someone would need. Next to it was the master bedroom and a full bathroom, which included a shower. That would be very welcomed after a day of playing on the beach. Or for living out there full time if his family ever had to flee their permanent home.

The owner smiled at Manda and said, "Come see the loft." They went up the stairs to a huge loft. It was one big room with two

119

beds, a couch, and tons of floor space. It was the perfect sleepover place. It could easily fit ten people. It, too, had huge windows that looked out at the water. The trees on the sides of the lot gave it a secluded feel.

Grant didn't want to let the owner know how perfect the place was. That would increase the price. "Thank you for showing us your cabin," he said. "We have quite a few more to look at."

"The furniture comes with the place," the owner said. She obviously wanted to sell the place.

"Aren't we getting ahead of ourselves?" Grant said, trying his best poker face. He didn't want to insult the owner and really wanted to tell her how fabulous her cabin was, but this was not the time.

Grant and Manda went home and talked the whole way home about how to get Lisa on board. Manda was his little co-conspirator.

About a week later, Grant took Lisa out to the cabin. He picked an especially perfect day with bright sun and warm temperatures, which were cooled by a slight breeze from the water.

When they drove up, Lisa looked the place up and down. She was silent. She walked up onto the deck, looked out over the water and said, "My deck chair will go here." She was smiling.

Thank God. She liked this place. The tour took two hours. Lisa didn't do anything she didn't want to do for two hours, so this was a good sign.

Manda was Lisa's tour guide and was the most convincing little salesperson ever. Grant heard her up in the loft say to Lisa, "This is where all my friends can stay. I can't wait! Don't you love it, Mommy?" Lisa couldn't resist Manda, especially when she called her "Mommy."

Cole liked the place. He thought they were going to someone else's house. He thought it was a neat place.

"Do you want to go down to the water and throw rocks?" Manda asked Cole.

"Oh, yes," he said. Lisa smiled. They closed on the cabin a few weeks later.

Now you have the place. Fill it up with supplies.

Grant understood that. But he didn't understand the next outside thought.

Then work on the relationship to get her out here.

Why would that be necessary? Lisa loved this place. Didn't she?

Chapter 22

I Will Wear the Pants I Want to Wear

Getting the cabin touched off a flurry of prepping. Grant saw a million things that needed to be done, and he was happy to do them. He needed to install a motion detector light, for example. The cool thing about the cabin was that it was his place; he didn't need to consult Lisa on whether to do something like install a motion detector. At their house, he did. Well, more specifically, Lisa wanted to decide what needed to be done and when, but at the same time wanted Grant to just take care of things. She would get mad when she had to tell him to do things around the house. But, when Grant just did things on his own, she would get mad because he wasn't doing what she wanted him to do. Grant quickly learned that it was just as easy to have her mad at him for things he wasn't doing as for the things he tried to do. It was very frustrating.

In one rather heated discussion they had, Lisa said, "Why do I have to think of doing everything around here, like staining the deck?" Grant had been guilty of be being a fat slug and sitting on the couch for a few years, but now that he was prepping he was doing all kinds of things like staining decks.

"Oh, you mean the deck that I tried to stain in the spring?" Grant asked. "I asked you to show me the can of deck stain so I could get some more. I said I would get a pressure washer to clean it off, but you said we shouldn't pressure wash it and that you'd get me the right can of stain. Then you got busy. I asked a second time and you got mad at me for 'not just doing it.' You have your choice. I can do things on my own or you can control everything. But you can't have both."

That went over well.

"Why is it that you don't mind fixing things at the cabin?" She asked.

"Because I can do things on my own there," Grant said. "I don't need any permission."

She couldn't believe that she just set herself up that way. The cabin was becoming an issue. She didn't like that he had "his" cabin and would go there. He needed to be home staining the deck. He needed to do things at the house first, and then go to the cabin second. She was starting to hate that cabin.

When it came to doing things around the house, Grant had tried and tried to do things to her liking. He didn't know how to do some things around the house, but he tried. He did everything she asked and even suggested things that needed to be done. He had never, ever, once blown something off.

Grant had had it. He couldn't please her on this topic. So be it. He would just do his thing the best he could, prepare a place for them when the inevitable arrived, and… be the man, even when it's unpopular.

Grant realized that he loved Lisa too much. He was still — after over twenty years — so thankful she married him that it went a little overboard.

This led him to trying too hard, which led him to frustration. For the longest time, Grant actually thought that if he tried to stain the deck, that even though she basically wouldn't let him get it done, it was his fault. That was stupid, and over with. He decided to treat her more like any other person he had a close relationship with; try to please them but understand that you can't always. Then shrug and do your best. You still love them; you just don't expect to please them all the time.

Grant was finally free of the urge to please Lisa at any cost. Strange things started to happen. Like his pants.

Grant hated jeans. They were a little too tight and didn't have enough pockets. When he went shooting, jeans were not ideal. He needed shooting pants with cargo pockets. The kind all the other guys on the range had.

Grant went to a military supply store outside of nearby Ft. Lewis. This base had lots of units deploying overseas. In addition to the thousands of infantry troops, Ft. Lewis was also home to the First Special Forces Group and the Second Ranger Battalion. The military stores near Ft. Lewis sold custom gear to troops and military contractors going to a combat zone. Soldiers, especially the special operations guys, often bought their own stuff instead of relying on general issue gear when their lives depended on it. Contractors had no general issue gear, so they always bought their own stuff.

One of those stores near Ft. Lewis sold 5.11 brand "tactical" pants. They were designed for SWAT teams but weren't over the top "mall ninja" clothes. They looked like regular tan pants with cargo pockets, but each of those pockets were sized perfectly to fit two AR mags. The knees had padding on the inside for comfortable kneeling for long periods of time, such as when pointing a rifle at something. They weren't any more money than a pair of jeans.

Grant, who no longer viewed gun or military stores like porno stores, walked right in. He tried on a pair of 5.11s. They fit great. They were really rugged and well made. He wore them home. He felt more honest with himself wearing them.

When he walked in, Lisa looked at him and frowned. "What's with the pants?" she asked. That was kind of shitty of her.

"They're shooting pants. Is there a problem?" Grant couldn't just stop there; this kind of thing had been building for some time. "I'm a grown man. I will wear the pants I want to wear." That was the end of that discussion.

That felt so good that he went out and bought some slip-on work boots. They were rugged and comfortable; perfect for shooting. Some people called them "Romeos" while others called them "Georgia boots." Grant called them "hillbilly slippers." He came home with those and practically dared Lisa to say something. She didn't.

The next weekend, clad in 5.11 pants and hillbilly slippers and feeling like a real man for the first time in quite some time, Grant went to the storage unit. He loaded all the tubs into Lisa's Tahoe SUV and took them to the cabin. It took four trips. He started at 6:00 a.m. and got done at 9:00 p.m. He was glad he was in such good shape because it was hard work. He noticed that when he worked this hard all day that he needed about four meals and a snack. He craved salt because he was sweating a lot. He took mental note of this. He reminded himself to store more food than would be needed in normal times and to include "bad" things like salted food. At this point, he had a few months of food out at the cabin's storage shed. It was a rough estimate; it was hard to tell how much food they would eat or if they would have "guests" to feed.

Grant also had several thousand rounds of ammo, all clearly marked and in .50 Army ammo cans, the green rectangular ones with the handle; the kind people run with in war movies. Ammo cans are airtight and can keep ammo fresh for years and years. He got them at the local surplus stores.

Grant was astounded by how much ammo he had collected. He had been buying up ammo — a case here, a few boxes there — before each of the ammo scares that accompanied every election. Before the ammo scares, Capitol City Guns had plenty of cases (1,000 rounds) of

5.56 or .223 for an AR. Grant got a few cases of 7.62 x 39 for his AK and a few hundred rounds of .38 for the revolver.

He had also picked up a little .380 auto pistol, a Ruger LCP. It was tiny and easily fit in the front pocket of his pants. It was just a little larger than his iPhone. The LCP was so easy to carry. He carried it concealed whenever he could, which wasn't often given that he couldn't get "caught" with it by Lisa.

Grant had a few hundred rounds of .380 auto for it that he got before it disappeared. As crime went up and ammo scares raged on, many people bought concealable 380s and bought all the ammo they could. It became impossible to find .380 rounds anywhere.

Right as Grant started prepping, a huge sporting goods superstore, Cabela's, opened in the Olympia area. They had cases (250 rounds) of 12 gauge shells for about $55. Knowing that everyone had a 12 gauge, Grant realized that 12 gauge shells would be in extremely high demand after a crisis. They were cheap then, so Grant eventually got four cases. He purchased lots and lots of buckshot, too; almost a case of it. He'd get five or ten boxes (of five rounds each) every couple of weeks. He would also get bricks (500 rounds) of .22 ammo. Before the ammo scares, a brick of .22 was about $20 — four pennies a round. Much like 12 gauge, everyone had a .22. Grant thought that .22 ammo would become used as currency after a crisis.

Seeing empty — totally empty — gun store shelves during the ammo scares reinforced Grant's thoughts on how people panic and clean out the stores in the blink of an eye. There was something very unsettling about seeing empty shelves in a gun store. It was more than just that the prices were going way up and he couldn't shoot on the weekends because he couldn't get replacement ammunition. More disturbing, by far, was the knowledge that people were buying guns and ammunition in droves.

They must have a reason for doing that. They must be afraid of something. When about ten or twenty million people had the same idea, the inventories that were designed for normal demand for, say, a hunting season dried up almost overnight. People were hoarding ammunition. More than guns, ammunition was even more susceptible to hoarding because it cost less than a gun.

Grant found himself wanting to buy more cases of ammo even at ridiculous prices. Most of the time, he resisted. When a federal official announced one morning that the Administration had the goal of outlawing "assault rifles," Grant ran out and bought a half case of overpriced .223. Later, he was a little embarrassed by how much he paid, but he thought it was necessary at the time. Grant was investing in "precious metals" that just so happened to be capable of stopping people trying to kill you. Gold coins were great, but they couldn't do that.

Grant noticed one kind of ammunition was still plentiful during the ammo scares: .40 pistol. This was the caliber almost all police used and it was popular with civilians. They must have mass produced .40 ammo for the cops, because it was usually the only caliber available during the hoarding. Grant decided that .40 would be his semi-auto pistol caliber when it was time to get one.

There were many more guns in 9mm than .40. (They had roughly the same power to stop someone, with the difference between the two only mattering to internet forum debaters.) Since there was such a huge market for it, 9mm ammo was cheaper than .40, but so many people had 9mms, so the ammo flew off the shelves during the ammo scares. This meant that the large market for 9mm made that ammunition harder to find.

Grant figured there was much more .40 available because it was the "cop caliber" and manufacturers knew that cops would be practicing with their guns all year long and using a lot throughout the per year. Therefore, the ammo factories were geared up to constantly churn it out. Besides, law enforcement would order in giant lots; there might be some overruns and those cases would go into the civilian market.

Another lesson from the ammo shortage was that oddball calibers were the hardest to find. That 16 gauge was probably a great gun, but the stores only carried a few boxes of it; however, they had cases of 12 gauge. Grant realized that he should pick a few very popular calibers and stick with them. A gun without ammo is worthless.

Stocking up on ammo was a key prep. Grant remembered the first time he lifted a full case, 1,000 rounds, of ammo onto the counter at Capitol City Guns. He felt weird getting a whole case. Chip made him feel more comfortable by saying, "Just one?" Chip was serious.

There were sound reasons to stock up on ammo, other than the impending collapse Grant foresaw. First of all, there was almost no ammunition available during the ammo scares so Grant couldn't enjoy his hobby of shooting unless he stocked up. Second, the price of ammo, when it was available, was skyrocketing. It made financial sense to invest now in something that was rising in price, would last for decades, and would undoubtedly be used.

As much as Grant hated to admit it, there was an emotional reason to stock up on ammo. Having cases of it curbed his concerns about the future. There were real dangers out there to prepare for. It was amazingly comforting to be doing something about all the problems that were bubbling out there. He was taking action instead of sitting around worrying.

Any thinking person realized that there were plenty of things to be worrying about. It was obvious things were falling apart in the United States. The Federal Reserve was creating trillions of dollars out of thin air.

Many people did not know what the Federal Reserve did. Grant found out and was surprised.

A big stumbling block for Grant even wanting to learn about the Federal Reserve was all the weirdoes who constantly harped about how the Federal Reserve was a "Jewish conspiracy" to take over the world. Grant wasn't crazy, so he was reluctant to look into something that only seemed to be of concern to crazy people.

However, he took a few minutes and learned about the Federal Reserve. It wasn't a "Jewish conspiracy," and it wasn't complicated. It was a bunch of bankers of varying ethnic backgrounds and it was all out in the open.

The Federal Reserve was a central bank, basically the big bank that lent all the money to all the banks in the U.S. It was not a federal agency; it was just the biggest bank that had a license from the federal government to create money. Yep, that's right. They got to *create* money. Out of thin air.

Grant had always assumed the U.S. Treasury created money on printing presses and with the consent of Congress. He was wrong. The Federal Reserve, a collection of big banks, would decide, on its own, to create money by loaning electronic dollars to other banks. For example, one day the Federal Reserve might decide to loan a hundred billion dollars to a major bank in the U.S. or in a foreign country. The Federal Reserve did this by creating credits on their computers. They would just credit the electronic accounts of the other bank with one hundred billion. That meant— *poof* — the other bank now had account balances that said they had an extra hundred billion dollars. It was all electronic. There was no cash or gold or anything backing up the hundred billion dollars that the computer screen said existed. It just appeared in the other banks' accounts. Then the bank loaned out the hundred billion dollars in their account to other banks, and those banks loaned it to people. The other banks had to pay each other back, including the bank that had borrowed the money directly from the Federal Reserve. So, the Federal Reserve got its hundred billion dollars (that it just created on a computer) with interest. The Federal Reserve kept this massive sum of interest for itself and loaned some of it back. God only knows what else it did with this massive slush fund.

All of this was secret because it was not a government agency, so it wasn't subject to the Freedom of Information Act that allows the public to see most government documents. No one could find out about what the Federal Reserve was doing. Not even Congress.

Yeah, but what about that dollar bill in everyone's wallets? That was money, right? It said on it that is was a "Federal Reserve note." What's that?

Debt. It's a certificate of debt that says the Federal Reserve owes the person with the dollar bill one dollar (that they can just create with a few clicks of a computer). That's right: a dollar is just "debt"; it's not an asset like a small chunk of gold. Americans didn't trade money around; they traded debt.

Grant was driving up to a McDonald's drive-thru getting the kids Happy Meals when he realized that a dollar was just debt. He took out a $20 bill he had earned by working hard and gave that $20 bill to McDonald's in exchange for some Happy Meals. After giving Grant some change, McDonald's took that $20 bill and used it to pay their French fry supplier. The French fry supplier took the $20 in a bank account and bought potatoes. The potato farmer took the $20 now in his bank account and bought some fuel for his tractor. And so on. That $20 bill piece of paper was traded for Grant's labor, Happy Meals, French fries, potatoes, and fuel — things that are real and have value.

But that $20 piece of paper isn't "money" in the sense that it's worth anything. Labor, Happy Meals, potatoes, and fuel are things that are worth something. That dollar — a piece of paper representing debt the Federal Reserve owes the holder of the bill — is only worth something because things can be purchased in exchange for it. A person can get Happy Meals for that piece of paper because McDonald's believes it can trade that piece of paper for uncooked French fries. It's the belief that someone will accept the piece of paper in exchange for stuff that makes that piece of paper worth anything. If McDonald's and everyone one else started to say they wouldn't accept dollars, but would only accept some new currency like gold or silver, that $20 bill would quickly become just a piece of paper. A person couldn't feed that piece of paper to their kids. The whole system worked on a belief that that piece of paper was worth stuff because it could be exchanged for stuff. It was that simple. The whole system worked on a belief.

It hadn't always been this way. A hundred years ago, a twenty dollar bill was backed by an ounce of gold. Someone could take that twenty dollar piece of paper into a bank and say they'd like a one-ounce $20 gold coin for it. "Here you are," would be the answer as the bank teller handed them a one-ounce gold coin that said, "$20" on it. The $20 bill and a one-ounce gold piece were interchangeable.

That meant that $20 was worth a set amount: one ounce of gold. The value of the dollar couldn't fluctuate much; it was worth a set amount of gold. And could easily be traded for something of real value: gold.

Not anymore; not even close. When money can be created out of thin air, people will want to create lots of it, just as the Federal Reserve did. When there was a downturn in the economy, the politicians would call the Federal Reserve and beg them to create more money to loan to people to get them to spend it. "No problem," the Federal Reserve would say; it made interest on all that money it was creating. A few clicks of the Federal Reserve computer and the economy had a few billion, or even trillion, more dollars in it. People were a few billion or trillion more in debt (because all these dollars are really debt). More spending, more debt. The economy improves and the politicians get re-elected. What's not to love?

More spending and debt, that's what's not to love. Common sense dictates that such a cycle can't continue without a consequence. Inflation is that consequence.

If there are ten trillion dollars out there and then the amount is increased to twenty trillion, each dollar is worth half as much. There is only a certain amount of stuff to buy with those dollars; when there are more dollars chasing the same amount of stuff, it will take more dollars to get the same amount of stuff. As Jack Spirko on the Survival Podcast explained it, it is like playing a game of Monopoly. One player has a color copy machine and just makes twice as much Monopoly money. There are twice as many Monopoly dollars in circulation. Pretty soon, that Boardwalk property that was $500 goes up to $1000 because everyone has twice as many pieces of paper money.

Seeing an inevitable future, Grant would try to think about a Happy Meal costing $100. It was hard to imagine at first. Then he realized that the problem was thinking about a Happy Meal. Store some pancake mix or, better yet, grow your own food. Trade something with a farmer for some fresh beef. Get out of the system of debt and Happy Meals. People would be happier (and healthier).

After forty plus years of thinking that a person needs Happy Meals and had to pay for them with dollars, it was hard for people to adjust their thinking. Quite honestly, most people would have no reason to think about it if they didn't know how fragile the whole system is. But once they realized how fictitious all this, people would have a reason to think about these things. It was frightening.

Chapter 23

The Team

Grant was going to Capitol City Guns at lunch a few days a week. He loved hanging out with "normal" people instead of the bureaucrats who hated him at his State Auditor Office job. Capitol City was an oasis.

For some reason that Grant never fully understood, the guys at Capitol City really liked having him around. He was a lawyer and, now, a kind of high-ranking government official. Grant wasn't the average gun store guy, although the regulars at Capitol City included other white-collar guys. He viewed Capitol City not as a gun store, but where some of his best friends were. He brought food in and remembered guys' birthdays.

Grant shared stories with the gun store guys about all the government corruption. The guys couldn't believe it was that bad. When he started mentioning things that would then appear in the newspaper a few days later, they realized he wasn't making the stuff up.

Another reason they probably liked Grant at Capitol City was that he bought a fair amount of guns and ammo there. He traded in his Winchester 1300 shotgun that he never really liked for a tactical Remington 870. The 870 had a recoil-reducing Knoxx pistol grip and stock. One of the reasons Grant didn't like the Winchester was the recoil. This tactical 870, though, was easy to shoot. He got pretty good at reloading it quickly and using it aggressively at short ranges.

One of the coolest things about Capitol City was that they assembled AR-15s there. They had a shop in the store and, with nothing but a bunch of spare parts, assumed a few ARs at a time. Grant started to learn how an AR fits together from the guys. He learned that AR-15s were like Legos, and that the pieces fit together and were customizable. Pretty soon, Capitol City gave Grant and a handful of other regular customers "shop privileges." They could just walk into the store and go back to the shop and make ARs. Capitol City got free labor out of the deal and the guys got to learn how to make guns. It was very cool.

Grant's AR was fine. It was a standard A2 like the kind issued in the Gulf War (but not fully automatic, of course). Grant wanted a really customized one. He started collecting pieces — a bolt here, hand guards, a trigger assembly — and began putting them together with help from Chip. He got exactly what he wanted; the Magpul UBR stock that he loved, the stainless steel bolt carrier group that cleaned so easily, the Yankee Hill hand guards. He got a special barrel that Chip was working on. Everything was just the way he wanted. He had never had a gun built for him, by him.

When he was done, Grant had a totally fabulous AR. Chip was getting him parts at wholesale. It cost much less than Grant thought it would. He was very proud of it because he helped build it.

He got very, very good with that AR, going to the range every other weekend and practicing. He would alternate between his cabin and range time on the weekends. He was getting very good at shooting, and his cabin was looking great. He could truly relax on the range or at the cabin. That's where things were "normal" and he didn't feel like a weirdo for thinking about how America was on the brink of a collapse.

One day, Grant was on a lunch break from work and had a suit and tie on. He was working on an AR in the shop. He had the gun in a vice and was using a metal punch and a hammer. Chip came up to him and said, "A lawyer and a gunsmith. Wow. You don't see that every day."

Then Chip came up to Grant and whispered, "What are you doing this Sunday?" Grant thought Chip was inviting him to some weird church or something.

"Not sure," Grant said cautiously. "Why?"

Chip looked around. "Some of us do a little tactical shooting at a law enforcement range. Steel targets that pop down when you hit them. It's very realistic training, and a total blast. I don't want the others to get jealous by hearing me inviting you. We only let cool guys know about this."

This sounded like fun. It would be like Joe's range.

"Sure, I'm in," Grant said. "When and where?" Chip gave him the details.

Grant got up early on Sunday morning and got his gear together. He put on his 5.11 pants and his hillbilly slippers. He would look like a dork in jeans and tennis shoes and would lose his footing and not have any cargo pockets for magazines. Thank goodness he had his 5.11s and hillbilly slippers. At least he wouldn't look like a lawyer out there.

Grant felt like he was trying out for a sports team. He hoped his gear was cool enough, although he never tried to buy the latest and greatest tactical gear. Besides, he was in his forties and was a lawyer. He wasn't going to try to be a twenty-something tactical bad ass. He was an old white-collar guy who happened to shoot pretty well. He didn't want to turn into a mall ninja. Or, worse yet, a middle-aged mall ninja.

Grant got a dozen doughnuts — it *was* a law enforcement range — and headed into the sticks outside Olympia to one of the two rifle ranges in the county. His usual range was the other one so he was unfamiliar with the one he was going to.

When he got there, he saw a sign that said "Restricted. Law Enforcement Only." There was a white civilian Hummer parked there and an Asian guy standing next to it. He was tall, probably six feet, and looked to be in his mid-twenties. He was a tough looking guy, like from a martial arts movie, but one of the good guys; not a thug. He looked familiar. Grant thought he'd seen him at Capitol City but, for whatever reason, never met him.

The Asian guy saw the doughnuts and smiled. "You Grant?"

"Yep," Grant said.

"Chip couldn't make it but said you'd be coming to join our little group today," the Asian guy said.

Grant thought this guy was a cop, maybe a Fed. Oh well, Grant didn't have any illegal guns, so he wasn't concerned.

"I'm Bill Kung," the Asian guy said. "My friends call me 'Pow.'"

"Pow?" Grant asked.

"Yep," he said. "As in 'Kung Pow' — you know, Kung Pow chicken, the Chinese food. Some stupid attempt to mock my Korean heritage," he said with an even bigger smile. This guy was cool.

"Well, Pow, pleased to meet you," Grant said shaking his hand.

"Time to gas up," Pow said and started to load up magazines. He had about two dozen of them, AR and Glock mags. Pow had a Glock in a cool Kydex holster and a high-end AR with an Aimpoint red-dot sight. He loaded the magazines smoothly and quickly. He did a press check of his pistol and rifle, which is a check to see if there is a round in the chamber. He did it efficiently and without thinking, like he'd done it a thousand times. He probably had.

Some pickup trucks started to come down the road. There were three of them; a Ford, Chevy, and a Dodge. "The rest of the Team," Pow said.

Team?

What had Grant got himself into? He didn't know, but he liked it. Then he wondered if he was good enough for these guys. He was pretty good, but these guys were probably at a whole different level.

Each one of them got out of their truck. Grant had seen these guys before. They came to Capitol City pretty regularly, but he never really talked to them for some reason. Pow greeted them as warmly as he'd greeted Grant. Introductions were in order.

"Hey, guys, this is Grant," Pow said. "Chip said he's cool. Chip can't come today." The guys all nodded as if it say, "If Chip's cool with this guy, we're cool with him."

Pow introduced each guy.

"Grant, this is Scott Dogget," Pow said. "We call him 'Scotty.'" Grant shook his hand. Scotty was also in his mid-20s clean cut, and in great shape. Grant assumed he was probably military stationed out at Ft. Lewis.

"Over here is Wes Marlin," Pow said. "We call him 'Wes'," Pow said with a laugh. Wes was about the same age as Scotty and Pow, but looked even more military. He had a crew cut and was also in great shape. He looked Southern, for some reason.

"Pleased to meet you, Grant," Wes said with a Southern accent. Grant smiled to himself.

"Last, but not least, is Bobby," Pow said, "otherwise known as Bobby Nicholson," Pow said, as the third guy walked up to Grant to shake his hand. Bobby was a little thicker and shorter than the others, but was full of muscle. He looked like he would do just fine in a fight. He had a confident walk, but not a cocky strut. He seemed very at ease with himself and the world. He was dark, maybe half Hispanic.

Wes pointed at Pow, a Korean, and Bobby, part Hispanic, and said in his Southern accent, "We believe in diversity."

Grant nodded. "Diversity" was an odd thing to say. Who cared what race people were? And who counted people by quota?

"Yes, sir," Wes said in that rich Southern accent, "A Ford, Chevy, and Dodge. That's diversity."

They laughed.

They were looking at Grant's very yuppie Acura. Why didn't he have a pickup like them?

"That's my Tacura," Grant said.

"That's an Acura, right?" Bobby asked.

"Not when a gunfighter like me drives it," Grant said with a wink. "Then it's a Tacura. A tactical Acura." That got a good laugh. From then on out, Grant's car was known as the "Tacura."

"The new guy brought doughnuts," Pow said, the introductions being over.

They had some doughnuts and then unloaded their gear from their trucks. These guys were serious gun fighters. Holy crap. Gear and guns galore. Mostly ARs and Glocks, but some AKs and 1911s. Several Benelli semi-automatic shotguns. They must be military. Infantry definitely, but maybe Rangers. Maybe even Special Forces. Probably friends of Special Forces Ted's since these guys were often at Capitol City Guns, like Ted was.

Scotty effortlessly slid a full case of 5.56, which probably weighed thirty pounds, across the bed of the truck, jumped down onto the ground, and then picked it up like a bag of potato chips.

These guys were good. What the hell was Grant doing with them?

Grant's gear was not as cool as theirs. That was OK. It wasn't a contest for the most expensive gear. Their gear was genuinely good; not flashy. They all had 5.11 pants and bland t- shirts in desert tan or black. There was nothing flashy about these guys; they looked like professionals.

Pow told them, "Grant here is a lawyer."

They booed Grant and then smiled. Grant was used to it. Lawyers are rarely popular among normal people.

Grant asked, "What unit are you guys in?"

They laughed.

Bobby said, "I work for a defense contractor. White collar shit."

"I work at Hoffman Equipment Rental" said Wes.

Scotty said, "I'm a lab tech."

It was Pow's turn. "I sell insurance."

What? A white-collar "tactical" team? Grant didn't feel so out of place.

Grant realized that these guys were, like him, civilians who liked to shoot and had gotten pretty good at it. But unlike Grant, these guys weren't married and didn't have kids, which explained how they had the time and money to do fun things like unlimited guns, gear, and shooting. Grant realized he could learn a lot from them. And, finally, he had guys to hang out with who were gun guys.

The law enforcement range was great. It was a lot like Joe's. It had a 100-yard range with human-shaped steel targets. They made a "ping" sound when they were hit so the shooter knew he was hitting them. They were about one-half the size of a person, about three feet high. They had a spring in them so when they were shot, they fell down. There were numerous fifty-yard bays off to the side, all with steel targets. Shooting reactive targets, ones that let you know you've hit them, is a thousand times better than shooting at paper targets. There was something psychological about shooting a target shaped like a human being. Grant thought it would be easier to shoot a person after practicing on a human-shaped target.

They warmed up with a few magazines. These guys were smooth and reinserted fresh magazines lightning fast. They were very accurate, too. They looked exactly like SWAT guys or military contractors.

Grant was very good with the AR, but he didn't have a pistol. He had a .38 revolver, but it was not a tactical gun, so he didn't bring it. He had been meaning to get a good pistol but hadn't done it. Besides, he was building up his AR and AK ammo supplies.

"What? No pistol?"Pow asked. "Oh, man, I'm gonna hook you up with one." He went back to his car and got a spare Glock and holster. "It's a .40 and we normally shoot 9mm. Wanna try it?"

Grant was reluctant because he didn't know how to shoot a Glock and he didn't want to show his lack of skill to these guys. "OK, I'll give it a try," he tried to say confidently.

Pow proceeded to teach Grant how to operate a Glock. It took about ten seconds because, with no safety to forget to click off, the Glock was the easiest pistol on the planet to learn. Grant instantly loved the Glock. And, Grant noted, all these guys carried Glocks. That must mean something.

Pow loved teaching people how to shoot. It was obvious. Halfway into the training session, he said, "I consider myself a shooting instructor who doesn't get paid." He was really good at it.

Soon Grant was shooting the Glock well and hitting accurately on the paper targets. Pow taught him quick magazine changes and drawing from the holster.

Grant liked the .40; it didn't kick too much, although some people had said it would. The other guys were 9mm fans because it had less recoil and held more rounds in a magazine than the bigger .40, but Grant could handle the .40 recoil just fine and liked the fact that its round was slightly harder hitting than the 9mm. Grant also knew that .40 ammo was always available for purchase. That sealed it for him; he would be a .40 guy. He based that primarily on ammo availability.

It was time to use the Glock on the steel targets at twenty-five yards. Grant was nervous because the other guys were watching, and his lifetime experience with a Glock consisted of the last fifteen minutes. Oh well. He'd let the guys know earlier in the morning that he didn't think he was an expert. He was here to learn and have fun.

He got ready. Pow handed him a magazine. There were five steel targets. Pow yelled out "Threat!" which was the signal to start shooting. Grant put two rounds into four of the steel targets, missing only once. Then "Click!" He was out of ammo. Pow had purposefully loaded nine rounds in the magazine so Grant would have to show if he'd learned how to change the magazine.

Grant quickly grabbed a spare magazine, ejected the old mag, jammed the new one into the gun, racked the slide, and then dove onto one knee and put two quick shots in the last steel target. He had just reacted.

The guys were cheering. Why?

"Dude," Bobby said, "did you see that mag reload and dropping to the knee? That was awesome."

Grant didn't know that he'd done that.

Pow was very happy with his new student. "I gave you a mag with only nine rounds in it so you'd have to do a reload. Why did you go to the knee to do it?" he asked Grant.

Grant thought, "Well, if I'm reloading there's a better chance the other guys will get off a shot. I figured I needed to be a smaller target so I got down. It was just a reaction."

Then Grant realized that this instinct of his was exactly what it would take to be good at this. He was very proud of himself.

The Team was glad to have a good new recruit. And the recruit was a lawyer who instinctively drops to his knee for a mag reload. They spent the rest of the day shooting and taking turns teaching Grant things like how to transition from his rifle to his pistol quickly.

Grant was glad he was in the best shape of his life. This runnin' and gunnin' stuff worked up a sweat. The weight training allowed him to have the arm strength to point a rifle all day long. He was twenty or so years older than these guys, so he didn't want to be the tired old guy. He was fine, though, and kept pace with them. Grant realized that if he had to do this all day, every day, that being in shape would be an absolute must.

Grant had a blast. It was so much more fun than standing in place and shooting at paper targets. He realized that if people were shooting back, knowing how to stand in one place and shoot at paper targets would not be much help. In fact, just standing there out of habit could get a person killed.

That day, Grant found a new love: tactical shooting. He was good at it. He was thrilled to be on the Team, and could tell this was what he was supposed to be doing.

Chapter 24

Normalcy Bias

That day, when he came back from the range with the Team, Grant was elated. He was good at something really cool. He couldn't wait to tell Lisa.

Oh, wait. He couldn't tell her.

She didn't know about the food, the guns, or any of the other "survival" stuff. This secret life he had been living was draining him. The most important thing in the world (other than his family) was something he couldn't talk about with his wife. His fears about the future and his plans for taking care of his family… he had to keep this huge part of his life secret. This secret that he couldn't talk about made him feel their marriage was incomplete. They were such a great couple on so many levels — all their friends always said they were the perfect couple — but that was only because Lisa didn't know Grant's big secret.

On the way home from the range, he seriously considered telling Lisa about everything. She would understand that he was doing this as a precaution against all the things that were going wrong in the world. She and the kids were the most important thing to him, and prepping was second. Prepping meant he could take care of his family in a crisis; what wife would be against that? He needed a full relationship with his wife so he would tell her. He spent the twenty-minute drive getting his courage up.

He got home and she was there. Here goes. The stock market had just fallen a few thousand points over the past few weeks. Surely this would be evidence that things were going poorly and having a little extra food, a comfortable place to go outside the city, and a few guns would be welcomed.

She was in the kitchen. "How was your shooting thing?" Lisa asked. She thought it was bull's-eye shooting with .22s at paper targets.

"Oh, great," Grant said. "I met some cool guys. We'll be shooting together again." He paused. He was going for it. He didn't want to waste twenty minutes of rehearsing and then chicken out.

"You know, the stock market took a huge beating the past couple of weeks," Grant said. "I haven't been saying anything because I didn't want to stress you out, but I see plenty more of this happening." He went on to describe how the federal debt was unsustainable and could never be paid off without crushing taxes and economic collapse. He explained how the Federal Reserve creating trillions of dollars would lead to inflation. He described all the things the Administration did to control the economy, like taking over the auto industry and health care, and the new controls on the financial industry, not to mention a frightening call for a "civilian security force." Grant told Lisa what Venezuela was like and how they had a "civilian security force" just like what the American Administration seemed to be describing. He gave Lisa a very logical and somewhat understated description of what was going on in the country, all based on things he knew she had read in the newspaper. Then Grant said the "F" word.

"Honey," Grant said in summation, "there is a term for when the government and corporations work together for their mutual benefit and restrict liberties. That word is 'fascism.'"

"Are you out of your mind?" she yelled.

This was not going well.

"What's wrong with you?" She just stared at him.

He started to explain that "fascism" is not necessarily Nazism, but that Nazism was one form of it. He was about to describe Italian fascism under Mussolini before the mid-1930s when Italy entered into an alliance with the Germans, but it was obvious Lisa thought "fascism" meant men with little mustaches and genocide. It couldn't possibly mean America. We are the land of the free; didn't Grant, who was an American History major in college, know that? He must have gone insane.

Grant said, "I've been right about everything so far. About the Dow falling, about the price of gold going up, about the size of the debt...."

"Shut up!" Lisa screamed. She never said that. She was furious.

"What?" Grant was stunned. Then he realized that he had just said "I've been right about everything so far." Big mistake.

Grant continued. "I'm not mad at you, honey. I just want to make sure nothing bad happens to our family. This isn't an 'I'm right' thing. I'm a man and it's my job to take care of my family and I see some things happening, and more to come, that mean we need to take some steps to...."

"Shut up!" she screamed. "I said shut up." He hadn't seen her so mad in years.

"Stop talking," she said. She put her hands over her ears and said screamed, "I can't handle this. I don't want to hear it. Don't talk about this." She calmed down a little and looked at him half-apologetically and said much softer, "Please don't talk about these things. OK?"

Grant realized now that Lisa knew things were going badly in the economy, but she just couldn't handle thinking about it. She didn't know about all the food and other preparations Grant had, so an economic collapse seemed much scarier to her.

Well, now she knew things weren't rosy. Grant could at least work on her not wanting to hear about it.

Then it hit him. Grant had a new plan: build up an undeniable track record. Make predictions that end up coming true, so not even Lisa could deny that he's onto something.

One little problem, though. This meant he needed to tell her all the predictions. How would that work if she didn't want to hear about any of it?

Right then Manda walked downstairs. "Hey, Mom and Dad, whatcha talkin' about?"

That was it. Manda. She was the solution. Grant would tell Manda what was going on, making sure not to scare the fourteen year old. He would build up a track record of predictions with Manda, and then, when he needed to, have her tell Lisa all the things he had correctly predicted way back when. He would turn Manda into a junior co-prepper with him and they would work on Lisa when they needed to. Not a bad plan.

"Nothing, Manda," Grant said. "Have you done your homework?" He asked, changing the subject.

Grant had a huge advantage when it came to Manda. She was already a right-wing whacko. During the past election season, Manda told some friends that she was a Republican and they ridiculed her. When some of her friends found out she was a Republican, they wouldn't talk to her anymore. She was stunned. It pissed her off. She had the fighting spirit — she did have red hair and it's true how fiery they are — and thought if people would be mean to her because of her beliefs, then she would get in their faces about it because they were stupid. That's my girl, Grant thought.

Grant took Manda and Cole to school most mornings. He had Glenn Beck on the radio for the ride. Grant found out how well Beck was explaining things when he brought up the topic of economic collapse with Manda the next morning on the way to school.

"Hey, Manda," Grant asked, "What do you think will happen with the economy?"

"Oh, it will collapse," she said plainly.

This was going to be easier than he thought. "What do you think will happen?" Grant asked her.

"The government is spending way more money than they," Manda said and then corrected herself, "well, actually, *we* can ever pay back. They're taking over stuff like those companies. ."

Wow. This was going well.

They talked about it more. Grant had several more conversations with her about what was happening. He asked her if she remembered the things Beck had predicted.

"Yeah, pretty much," Manda said. "He has been right about most things. No one on TV has been saying these things and they've all been surprised by what's happening. But not him."

Now that Grant had credibility with Manda on the issue of whether there was a problem out there, the next step was to establish that something needed to be done.

Grant tried not to alarm her but asked, "Manda, what do you think will happen to Americans?"

"Bad things," Manda answered. "I think food will cost a lot and we won't be able to afford other things. I think I will have to work really hard the rest of my life to pay for all the government stuff."

Grant decided to go further. "What do you think happens if food prices go up?"

She thought. "People will get mad."

"Yes, they will," Grant said, thrilled that she got all of this. "You're smarter than most adults. You know what happens when people are hungry and get mad?"

Grant proceeded to describe what a riot was. He told the story about the LA riots. Her eyes were huge. She had never heard such things, but she was smart enough, and open-minded enough, to realize that this could happen right here in America.

"Dad," Manda asked, "what can we do to be safe if this happens?"

Perfect. "We're at school now," Grant said. "I'll answer your question on our next ride." He was so proud of her.

Grant dropped her off and then took Cole to his elementary school. As usual, Cole didn't say much and didn't seem to understand what they were talking about. He was doing so much better than when they first started going to the elementary school for kindergarten. Back then, he only knew about ten words.

But, now he had a few hundred words. It took a lot of speech therapy, but he could get by with the words he knew and hand gestures. He was doing OK in the regular classes at school. He was pretty good at math. With his incredible photographic memory, he would just memorize the multiplication tables. He had some trouble with reading comprehension, but he was getting it. He was in the bottom quarter of the class, which was respectable given how hard it was for him to process language.

Cole was the happiest kid in the world, though. He was extraordinarily polite. People always remarked about that. He was the most caring little guy and especially liked little kids. He could talk to them because they had the same vocabulary, and the little kids didn't talk too much for him to process. He would play with them and help them. He was like a little day care worker, getting them food, hugging them when they fell down, and helping them potty. Grant knew what Cole would do for a living when he grew up, and he'd be darned good at it.

Very little bothered Cole, except that he had to have a routine, which was very typical for people with autism. For Cole, that meant bed at the same time and the same food for every meal. He didn't melt down if the routine was altered like he did a few years ago, but he didn't like any changes.

This worried Grant. What if there were a collapse, or, as they said in the survivalist world, the "shit hit the fan?" (SHTF for short.) How would Cole deal with all his normal routines — one kind of pancakes and one kind of syrup for breakfast, video games after school, hotdogs for dinner every night — when he had beans and rice to eat out at the cabin and there was no school, and possibly no electricity for video games?

Not only would it be hard on Cole, it would be hard on Lisa. She tried so hard to make sure he was always happy, which was very understandable. In fact, when one of Cole's routines was disrupted, like when they ran out of pancakes, Lisa would get agitated and extremely focused on getting the routine back on schedule. She was a loving mother. If Cole ran out of his pancakes, Lisa would drop what she was doing and go get them. Cole needed the routine and Lisa needed Cole to have his routine. Grant couldn't fault her for being a loving mother, but he could see how disastrous it would be when things broke down and there were no more pancakes in the stores. Lisa might freak out more than Cole. Lisa had a bad case of normalcy bias.

For Lisa, normalcy bias probably meant when the grocery store was out of pancakes, which would be the first day of the crisis; she likely would not believe that the stores were completely out of them. It must be just this particular store, she would think. She might drive around town in dangerous conditions just to find the store that has those pancakes. And she was beautiful and defenseless and....

Another part of normalcy bias was that when there is a crisis, people are so comforted by the normal pre-crisis things in their lives that they do irrational things to have the normal thing back. That would be another reason Lisa might drive around during dangerous conditions to try to find Cole's favorite kind of pancakes; it would be her way of coping with the disaster.

You have to understand this. Lives will depend on it.

Chapter 25

Cabin Neighbors

Work at the State Auditor's Office was starting to suck. At first it was great. Grant got to do things like help the Joe Tantoris out there. He was able to help people from inside government, with the full weight of the State Auditor's Office behind him.

But, after only less than a year in his position, he was being thwarted by his co-workers. He would ask for information from the Auditor's Office staff on a particular agency or a past audit and would be told the file was "lost." That was hard to do because everything was on a computer which was backed up and could be searched by terms. So Grant would have to take the time to find the information himself, which was time he couldn't spend working to help the citizen. He was now spending most of his day finding information that the old staff of the Auditor's Office could have found very quickly — if they wanted to do their jobs instead of helping their government buddies get away with screwing people.

One thing did not suck, though. The cabin. It was a magical place. Sometimes, when he was there he felt an actual buzz of euphoria. He had worked extremely hard his whole life and, thanks to the miracle of an early inheritance, now had exactly what he'd always wanted. His stress would melt away the closer he got to Pierce Point. By the time he drove up to the cabin, he was completely relaxed. The smell of the place, which was a combination of the sea and evergreen trees, instantly put him in a good mood. He actually measured his blood pressure before and after coming to the cabin. It dropped by ten points.

Sometimes, Grant would go to the cabin for just a few hours. It was only forty minutes from his house, so he could swing out there, sometimes at lunch time. He got to work at about 6:00 a.m. and often stayed late, so he figured he could take a two-hour lunch. Besides, no one really kept track of what he did all day. Other times, he'd stay most of the weekend out at the cabin.

Manda loved coming out Saturday afternoons and staying

overnight. Cole liked coming out, too. He loved throwing rocks into the water for hours. He also liked playing his handheld video games there. Grant refused to get a TV at the cabin, so Cole couldn't bring out his bigger video games that used one. Manda loved the campfire and cooking things in the cast iron pie irons on the coals. It was great to have a place where his kids could make such lasting childhood memories. Sometimes Grant thought about how much better his kids had it than he did as child, and he would tear up. He was being a good dad. He was taking care of his family.

But, to completely take care of his family, Grant needed to prep. This meant food storage, the cabin, guns and training, and creating networks of people with skills they would need to survive when the normal things no longer worked.

When it came to prepping, people are more important than stuff. The Team was an example of how important people were when planning for shit hitting the fan. One person couldn't know everything, but someone in the group probably knew how to do whatever it was that needed to be done. The idea that a "survivalist" is some weird guy alone in a bunker with cases of military rations MREs was a Hollywood creation to sensationalize a story. There was no way to pull off survival completely independently; trusted communities were critical.

During peacetime, for example, a person would just take their car to a mechanic. But during a collapse, mechanics might not be around, or there may be no way to pay them. To accomplish everyday things, like repairing a car would require people to develop the skills themselves — or, more likely, developing relationships and trading with others.

Grant's cabin neighbors were a natural starting place for creating a trusted small community. He needed to get to know them and see if he could trust them with his life and his family's life. It could take years to build up these relationships, and Grant worried he didn't have years before a collapse hit.

Grant had a few neighbors out there at the end of the Pierce Point development. His cabin was relatively isolated but with a few people around; the perfect combination for a bug out location.

The cabin was almost at the end of a little gravel road called Over Road. There were four houses and one RV before Grant's cabin, and then two more cabins past his. The four houses and RV were owned by part-time residents like him. The two houses past his were owned by year-round residents.

One of the two houses past his cabin, and the house closest to him, was owned by Mark Colson. Mark's place was across the road from Grant's on the hill overlooking Grant's cabin and the water. Looking down Over Road, Mark's house was on the right up on the hill and Grant's was on the left down toward the water.

Mark lived there year-round, unlike most of the people down by the water in Pierce Point. He was a great guy. He was in his fifties, owned real estate in the area, and was semi-retired. He was a hillbilly, though, a country boy through and through.

When Mark first met Grant, he assumed the new owners of the cabin would probably be uptight city people. Grant driving up for the first time in an Acura didn't help. The first time they met, Grant saw the USMC sticker on Mark's black Silverado pickup and the conversation went to guns. It turned out that Mark was a former Marine sniper. Could Grant have a better neighbor?

Grant started to chalk this up to the many "coincidences" he was experiencing. But he stopped himself. It wasn't that unusual for a guy living in the country to be a country boy. Grant considered Mark to be luck instead of a full-on "coincidence" indicating that Grant had been placed in a particular place at a particular time for a particular role. Grant was always on guard, telling himself not to consider every good thing to be a full-on "coincidence" that pointed to something bigger. That would dilute the real "coincidences" and cheapen their impact. You'll know a full-on "coincidence" when you see one, he told himself. Inheriting the cabin was one.

Mark really liked Grant and thought it was refreshing that a lawyer could be a fellow hillbilly. Mark watched Grant's place when Grant wasn't there. He invited Grant out hunting and fishing with him; Mark loved to seed Grant's beach with oysters. Grant was more than happy to have him do that, and let Mark dig all the clams he wanted on Grant's beach. Grant borrowed tools from Mark.

The first Christmas at the cabin, Grant got Mark several bottles of "Jar Head Red" wine for the former Marine who, Grant noticed, liked to drink wine. That sealed their friendship.

Mark lived there with his wife, Tammy. She was nice; a basic country girl. She worked for the local power company. Their son, Paul, lived with them. He was in his mid-twenties. Paul was recently divorced and had custody of his daughter, Missy, who was in kindergarten. From what Grant could piece together, Paul's wife was a druggie.

Paul was fat. Not heavy, but obese. He must have weighed 300 pounds. He got winded walking around. He was a very unhappy guy.

Although he was really nice, Paul had been beaten down by life, mostly by his wife and being a male trying to get custody of a child in the courts. He was in the local community college in the welding program.

The next house over, and the last house on Over Road, was owned by the Morells. They lived there year-round, like the Colsons.

John Morell was a retired millwright for the local lumber mill, which was now closed. Grant had never heard the term before, and he learned that a millwright is a cross between an engineer and a construction worker. The term came from when a mill needed to be moved. A millwright would figure out how to take apart the mill, move it, and put it back together.

John was a master carpenter, a good electrician, could weld, and knew heating and cooling systems. He was another amazing neighbor with incredibly valuable skills. This was getting weird, Grant thought. He smiled at his luck. Then he got serious. He started to think about all the help he would need for what could be coming. He was grateful for all the amazing coincidences, but he realized how hard it would be to do what needed to be done. The coincidences just made it possible, not easy.

John's wife, Mary Anne, was a retired school teacher. She was a country girl. She loved canning and baking. She had a nice little garden. It was more decorative than food producing, but it was a garden, nonetheless.

John began to view Grant as the son he never had. He loved teaching Grant how to fix things. After Grant had owned the cabin for about a year, they had "the conversation."

Grant was at John's house having a beer with him after he had shown Grant how to turn off the water meter at the cabin. John looked at him very seriously and said, "You know, Grant, we're living in a false economy." Grant knew exactly what John was saying.

"We sure are," Grant said, lifting up his beer to emphasize the point. "The size of this government is completely unsustainable. People are so dependent. They have no idea how to take care of themselves." That was about the extent of the normal political conversation a person could have without showing they were a "survivalist."

Grant decided to take the conversation one step further than the usual "safe" conversation. He looked at John and said, "I wonder what people would do if semi-trucks quit delivering things for a week or so." Grant waited for the reaction. It was like speaking in code.

"Starve, probably," answered John. "They would be shocked that the government wasn't driving around feeding them. They would demand that the stores just give them food. Gasoline would be more valuable than gold. They would realize there weren't enough cops to be everywhere and they'd start stealing from each other. And probably worse. There are a lot of shitbags out there just waiting for an excuse to hurt their neighbors."

Perfect. John understood the situation. Grant hadn't seen that John stored food and guns, but at least John had the mindset. That was more important than material things. Grant wanted to see how far the mindset went so he asked the next level of questions.

"I try to be prepared for anything," Grant said. "Nothing crazy, just some simple things. I have an extra five gallons of fuel out here." Of course, the extra five gallons of fuel was just a drop in the bucket of his preps. Mentioning it was just to show John that Grant had made some minimal preps. Grant didn't want to give away too much information. He liked, and basically trusted John, but didn't want to tell him about the food and guns out there.

"Five gallons of gas is great, but I've got some other things that will come in handy. Wait here a sec." John got up and went into another room.

He came back with a rifle. "A Remington 700 in .270. I can hit anything with this out to 400 yards." John was smiling.

Great. They were at the "show me yours, I'll show you mine" level of the relationship.

"Cool," Grant said. Grant asked to hold the rifle, which showed respect and that Grant knew how gun owners operate. Grant opened the bolt to make sure it was unloaded; another sign to John that Grant was a knowledgeable gun guy. It was also a habit Grant had of always checking a gun to make sure it's not loaded.

"I got quite a few more," John said, with yet another smile. He went back into another room. He showed Grant lots of nice hunting rifles and shotguns and a few revolvers. John liked good guns. He was a hunter, not a tactical guy, but that was fine. He had plenty of firepower and, more importantly, knew how to use it.

"I've got a couple rifles out here," Grant said. By now Grant was keeping a few guns out at the cabin that could get stolen and he wouldn't cry. A beat up (but highly accurate) scoped .223 bolt action and a .17 HMR that was his "crow" gun. He kept his AR and AK and the rest of his guns at his house in Olympia for a few reasons. First, he went shooting on the weekends and needed to have them handy to take to the range; he didn't want to drive out to the cabin each time he wanted to go shooting.

Second, Grant knew that he might need to fight his way out of his Olympia neighborhood and he'd need all those guns for that. Besides, if he couldn't get out of the Olympia neighborhood for a while, he'd probably need to supply the neighborhood people with weapons to fight off looters.

Finally, his house was much more secure than the cabin. He was only out at the cabin on weekends. His Olympia neighborhood had an extremely low crime rate, at least in peacetime.

John and Grant talked guns over a second beer. Mary Anne joined them and showed them her guns. She had a concealed weapons permit and frequently carried a pistol. Then the talk turned to food.

"I keep telling myself every spring that I need to start planting food instead of these pretty flowers," Mary Anne said. "I'm going to do it this spring, for sure. You know, with the way things are going in the economy."

That sparked a conversation about government spending and the millions, actually, tens of millions, of Americans completely dependent on government money to live. Then John nailed the big one.

"Do you know about the Federal Reserve?" he cautiously asked Grant.

"Don't worry," Grant said with a smile. "I don't think you're crazy." They went on to talk about how the Fed purposefully caused inflation, propped up the economy to be a constant orgy of spending, and kept everyone in debt.

The conversation turned to the parallels between modern America and the Roman Empire. Wow. The Morrells were great. Guns, gardening, skills, and an understanding that the collapse was coming. What great neighbors. Grant thought to himself that the Morrells were a full-on "coincidence," meaning a miracle. Right as he did, he heard the outside thought.

You have been placed in the right place with the right people. You will have a job to do here.

Chapter 26

That's Our Money. We Need It.

Even before he was sworn in as the State Auditor, Rick Menlow was thinking about his next step. After all, there would be an election for Governor in four years.

Many Republicans who were stunned and thrilled to actually have one of their party in a statewide office of some kind, constantly told Menlow that he should run. Day in and day out, all Menlow heard from people around him was how he should be the next Governor. He could save the state of Washington from its current problems. He could do it, they kept telling him.

During one of the transition meetings after he won the Auditor's election, Menlow brought up the subject with Grant and the other WAB staff.

"Should I run for Governor in four years?" He asked them.

"Of course," said Ben. "You'd make a great Governor. You'll have to kick ass during the next four years as the State Auditor, but it could be done. The next election should be a good time to be a Republican, at least nationally. The Ds run everything now so they'll get the blame when all of this stupid socialist shit quits working."

Brian and Tom agreed, and talked about things Menlow could do as the State Auditor to improve his chances for getting the governorship.

Menlow looked at Grant and asked, "If I'm the Governor, what role would you like in my administration?"

Grant thought a while. No one had ever asked him that question. "I wouldn't mind being a judge," Grant said finally. "That way, I could help get things back to the Constitution."

Menlow smiled. "I will keep that in mind." Now Grant's career was linked to Menlow's fortunes, exactly as Menlow wanted. It was the oldest trick in the political book: obtain loyalty from a subordinate by promising career advancement to the subordinate when the higher-up wins the next election. Subordinates had been known to do amazing things for that promised plum position after the next election.

There was one non-WAB person in the room when Menlow started charting his course to be the Governor. Menlow made his campaign manager, Jeanie Thompson, his communications director. She handled the press and ran the Auditor's communications efforts. She was in charge of publicizing the good things the office would be doing.

Jeanie was very young, in her mid-twenties. She had just graduated from college. She was an attractive woman, with black hair and green eyes. She tastefully used her good looks to charm the men and get her boss's agenda out to the public. She backed it up by being smarter than hell.

Jeanie was a conservative true believer. "Conservative" was the term people used for people like Jeanie and Grant who simply believed less government was better; conservative didn't necessarily mean a social conservative. There were almost no social conservatives in the Seattle area. Conservatives like Jeanie and Grant simply wanted less government. They had strong views on social issues, but didn't want the government imposing social views on people because they had seen how abusive government was.

In fact, it would be more precise to call people like Jeanie and Grant "libertarians." They were moderate libertarians who weren't all the way out there on privatizing fire departments and cutting the military by 95%. People like Jeanie and Grant just wanted to return the government to its past role of carrying out limited and well-defined powers as provided in the Constitution. Was that so radical?

Of course, the liberals used the term "conservative" as an insult. They fully wanted people to think that a conservative was a social conservative because social conservatism was so unpopular in the Seattle area. Oh well. Let them use whatever phrase they wanted, Grant thought. People like Jeanie and Grant knew what they believed, even if the liberals were trying to define them as intolerant people.

Because she was so young, Jeanie realized the problems big government created. She hadn't lived through a few decades of watching government slowly build up. She hadn't had decades of being told how necessary all of these programs were. In her short life, she saw a snapshot of how America was.

And it had way too much government. Unsustainable amounts of government. Baby Boomers were voting themselves benefit after benefit — and handing the bill to her generation. The younger the people were, the less they bought into the big government viewpoint. But that didn't mean that younger people were libertarians. Most were apathetic. Government was huge and stupid and that's how it was. They would rather play video games.

Being a conservative in the Seattle area was hard. The socially intolerant connotations of the term conservative equated to being a hateful person. This meant that a conservative had to be his or her own person.

For Jeanie, this meant being herself and not giving a damn what people thought. Since she was far more libertarian than socially conservative, Jeanie partied her ass off. As she put it, "I put the 'party' in the 'Republican party.'" Grant was the same way so they got along just fine.

Grant would have beers with Jeanie, and the handful of other conservatives in Olympia. Jeanie would come over to the Matson house. She didn't have kids so she loved seeing Manda and Cole. Grant even invited her to the very special WAB Super Bowl and Fourth of July parties. She fit in perfectly into the tiny, tiny conservative social circles of Olympia.

Jeanie had a boyfriend, Jim. He was in early thirties and worked for the Department of Revenue, or "DOR" as everyone in Olympia called it. He was DOR's database expert who kept the state tax computer system humming along. Jim was also an officer in the Washington National Guard and worked on their computers.

Jim and Grant worked out at the same time at the gym and they got to know each other well. Jim must have trusted Grant because one day, after a hard work out, he used the "R" word with Grant. It wasn't "Republican."

Jim looked around to make sure no one in the area could hear him. "You know, Grant, things are getting so bad there might be a revolution in this country. People won't take all the taxes and bullying."

Revolution? Grant had thought it but never heard anyone else say that word.

"Don't get me wrong — I don't want a revolution," Jim said. "I'm in the Guard. I will have to put anything like that down. I have an obligation to." He paused and looked Grant right in the eye. "It's coming."

Jim looked away because he couldn't handle how serious this conversation was getting. He resumed a normal conversational tone. "The things I see at DOR would blow your mind. They just make up rules and nail people for cash. It's a racket. Unreal. I can't believe people are just taking this. They can't keep on getting screwed like this for long. They will rise up at some point." Jim appeared relieved by getting this off his chest.

"I'm trying to find another job," he whispered. "I can't stand what DOR is doing. But I know the DOR computer systems like the back of my hand. I run them. That knowledge doesn't transfer easily into any other job. What I do is too specialized."

A guy who thinks there will be a revolution is the guy in charge of the state tax computer system? That seemed like a bit of a security breach.

Grant wanted to help Jim but knew he couldn't really. "I'll keep my ears open for you, Jim." Then talk turned to "safe" topics like sports and celebrities that were destroying their lives.

On the way back to the office, Grant drove by Nancy Ringman, the old Auditor's Chief of Staff. She hadn't been immediately fired by Rick Menlow, but after a few months, she finally left the Auditor's Office.

Nancy landed on her feet, though. Her good friend, the Governor, appointed her to be the head of the Campaign Finance Commission. That agency, commonly called the CFC, was the one that enforced the state's campaign financial disclosure laws. This would give her the power to investigate candidates and political contributors for not reporting contributions. The CFC was famous for investigating Republicans but looking the other way at Democrats. Great, Grant thought. Nancy's experience at the State Auditor's Office covering up Democrats' illegal activities makes her perfectly qualified for the CFC.

Running the CFC was about the same level of job she had at the Auditor's Office. In fact, she was probably making more money. But that's not what she wanted. She wanted to run the Auditor's Office the way she wanted to run it. She didn't want to start again in some other agency. She had been pissed for weeks.

Nancy was cold to Grant the few times he saw her in the neighborhood where they both lived. Vicious was actually a better word. One time she couldn't hold it back and ripped into Grant about "Republicans not caring about the work we do" or something. Grant thought she might try to hit him, which was a pretty silly thought, but she seemed that mad. How weird, Grant thought. What a hateful little monster. Oh well. Grant could care less what she thought, but he was struck at how angry she was. He figured he better steer clear of her for a while.

As a government insider at the State Auditor's Office, Grant now got to see it close up. It was even worse than he knew when he was on the outside.

Grant spent most of his day going to meetings at which nothing got done. During one all-agency meeting in the Governor's Office about what state agencies would propose to the Legislature in the next legislative session, there was a request for suggestions to deal with the ballooning public employee pension crisis. The Governor's legislative director, Sean Patterson, kicked it off.

"Well," said Sean, a distinguished looking fifty-something man with silver hair and an impeccable suit, "our state and local government pension funds are $16 billion in the hole. The unions won't budge. The Governor doesn't want to ask any more of them. You understand." They all did, except Grant. Well, he understood why, but he didn't agree.

Grant blurted out, "How is this sustainable?"

Silence.

Most people in the room didn't know who Grant was, let alone that he worked for a Republican. They assumed he was some uninformed staffer covering a meeting for his boss.

Sean, who knew that Grant was an opponent, said coolly, "The system was set up when times were better."

"But didn't anyone have a plan for if the good times didn't last?" Grant asked.

More silence. Now Grant was getting some glares.

"Let me be honest, Grant," Sean said in a mildly condescending voice. "The system wasn't designed to last. It was temporary. It got us through some elections, OK? We all knew it wouldn't last, but the end came quicker and harder than we thought. OK?" He said "OK" as if to say "you made your point, you little snot nose, now let's move on to the meeting that I'm in control of."

"Understood," Grant said. He had to show some respect, or he'd be thrown out of the meeting. He needed to stay in that meeting to gather more intelligence; political intelligence.

The main subject of the meeting was the recent revenue shortfall. For some reason that no one in the room could understand (except Grant), raising taxes had resulted in less economic activity and therefore less tax revenue. They were baffled.

"We need the money," Sean said. "That's the bottom line. How do we go get it?"

"Let's raise the income tax on high-end earners," was someone's predictable suggestion.

"Well, we've done that a lot lately," said the Governor's

political director, whose name Grant had forgotten. "The 'high-end' earner is now getting down to the upper ends of the middle class." The political director did not want her boss, the Governor, to run for re-election after raising taxes a zillionth time.

Sean shot back, "That's our money. We need it."

"Your money?" Grant said with obvious anger. "It's not your money, it's theirs." Grant looked Sean right in the eyes.

Silence.

Everyone stared at Grant. That was twice now that Grant had said something inappropriate. Grant wanted to leave the room but knew he couldn't. He had to be there for all the Ed Oleos, Big Sams, and Joe Tantoris. But he had nothing more to say. He had just said all he needed to.

After Grant recovered from saying something that stunned the whole room into silence, he started to think about what had Sean had just said. Oh God, Grant thought. It's true. These people really think the people's money is the government's money. The people work for the government. The people need to work harder so the government can get more. Grant had always thought they believed it, but there in that conference room they had come right out and said it. It was true. He was seeing it with his own eyes. It was frightening.

Right then and there Grant decided that he couldn't be part of this. He also realized — with absolute certainty now — that the government was worse than even he had thought. These people were thieves.

How could these thieves keep doing this and not get caught? Grant had a second epiphany: the idiot sheeple kept voting for the thieves. The sheeple got scraps from the thieves and were too scared to stand up for what's right. It was kind of like his mom letting his dad hurt people because she was too weak to stand up. Same thing, bigger scale.

Grant struggled to stay in his chair and make it through the meeting. When the meeting was finally over, he walked back from the Governor's Office to the nearby Auditor's Office on the capitol grounds. All the post-election euphoria about getting to help people from the inside had thoroughly worn off by now. Little by little, the old staff that remained in the Auditor's Office were thwarting the new Auditor's reform agenda. Grant knew this would happen. Now the old staff was rallying and making it impossible for the new Auditor and the handful of his new people to get any reforms done. It was getting ridiculous. Grant needed to do something about it.

He walked into Menlow's office, and closed the Auditor's door.

"Rick," Grant said to Menlow, "you need to fire some people or they'll derail you."

The Auditor did not like this. Before Grant had made it back to the office, Sean had called Menlow to tell him about Grant's "divisive" remarks at the meeting. Menlow needed Grant to quit causing him problems. Grant's "helping the citizens" thing had gone a little too far.

Menlow calmly replied, "Grant, I need to govern. I'm no longer running for this office when I needed to promise reforms. I need to be practical now. Maybe you could be a little more cooperative with the staff here."

Grant understood perfectly what Menlow was saying. "Play ball" was the message he was sending to Grant. This was the beginning of the end of Grant's government employment. Good riddance.

There was no reason to be a jerk to Menlow; it wouldn't change anything. "I will try, Mr. Auditor," Grant said. There was some silence and then Grant added, "I'd better get back to work." Time to start the exit from the Auditor's Office and get back to WAB. Grant had tried to reform the system from the inside. At least he tried.

Grant looked for Jeanie so he could vent to her. She was a hardcore conservative so she would see his point of view.

Jeanie seemed to have been expecting Grant to talk to her. Had Menlow told her about the meeting?

Grant told her what had happened and that he needed to leave the Auditor's Office. "Jeanie, how can you stand all this?"

"I dunno, Grant," Jeanie said with a sigh. "I need this job. There aren't too many slots for a Republican communications director in this state." Her voice turned jokingly sarcastic to make the point, "Oh, wait, there's only one and I already have the job. I need to keep it."

Grant could see where this was going. He had stupidly put his faith in a politician and a political system. This system was not fixable. At least not without massive change. An election here and there couldn't do it. It would take something bigger. That terrified him.

Chapter 27

Glock

Grant had one hole in his preps: a sidearm. He had a revolver and a pocket pistol. They were fine for what they were, but he needed a tactical side arm. Or two. Like the Glock he borrowed from Pow. He went to Capitol City Guns.

Chip was glad to see him, as usual. "Care to buy anything today, Mr. Matson?" He asked.

"You got any Glocks?" Grant asked. Of course they did. Several dozen.

Grant tried a Glock Model 22, the full-size Glock in .40 just like the one he had borrowed from Pow. It fit perfectly in Grant's hand. It had substance to it, but wasn't too heavy. It was the perfect balance. The one he was handling had glow-in-the-dark night sights. Night sights are a must, Grant presumed.

"Special deal for you, my friend," Chip said. "This is a gently used law enforcement trade-in. Just $399. Night sights and all." Grant looked it over; it was in great shape. It seemed like most police only shot their pistols once a year to qualify. This thing was practically new. "And, of course, we have a liberal return policy here for our favorite customers," Chip said.

"Sold," Grant said. "I'll need a few magazines, too." Grant checked his envelope of cash he brought in from the car. He had been driving all over the state on State Auditor business so he had some pretty decent expense checks from all the reimbursements. "How about ten magazines?" Grant said. Glock magazines were relatively cheap, about $20 each, which was half of what some other pistol magazines were. Grant had at least ten magazines for every gun he owned that used magazines. A gun is useless without a magazine, and magazines break and get lost. Pistol magazines were a good investment, too. A $20 Glock magazine would be worth ten times that during a collapse. There were likely half a million Glocks in .40 out there. They were standard issue to most police departments. There would always be demand for them and for their magazines in a barter situation. With so many of them out there, there would be parts (although Glocks almost never broke) and there was always lots of .40 ammo available. With all those cops with Glocks in .40, they would have guns, magazines, and ammo to sell if they needed spare cash. It scared Grant that his vision of what was coming included some cops selling their weapons.

Grant needed some ammo. At first, he bought ammunition in fifty-round boxes. Now, he bought ammo by the case. Capitol City gave him a "volume discount" on cases and basically sold them to him for their wholesale cost. He would use roughly half a case at a time on training.

Grant would take the other half case and stockpile it. He put the ammo in .50 ammo cans like the ones he had in the storage shed and now out at his cabin. At this point, he had about two dozen ammo cans, each holding several hundred rounds, depending on the size of the cartridge. About a dozen ammo cans were at his house. He couldn't believe his wife didn't wonder what was in all those Army green square cans with little blue painter's tape labels on them marked "5.56" "7.62" "12" "38" and "380." Now ammo cans with "40" on them would be appearing.

Grant used reloads for training. These were cartridges that had been fired once (or more) and then a new bullet, primer, and powder were put on. Some guys, like Pow, reloaded their own ammunition. Grant wanted to reload his ammo, but he didn't have the time to do it and didn't shoot enough to justify the cost of the reloading equipment. Reloads were about half as much as new ammunition. They weren't as accurate, but they were still plenty accurate for clanging a steel plate. They would certainly work for defensive purposes, too.

"I'll take a case of .40 reloads," Grant told Chip. He had plenty of cash in the envelope. "Oh, hell, two cases" Grant said.

There was nothing more comforting to Grant than buying cases of ammo. A case of ammunition is a very comforting thing for someone who thinks the country is spiraling toward a collapse. Ammo would never be cheaper than it was then, he would use it and have fun, and it was literally a precious metal that was an investment. Most importantly, a case of ammo could save his life and many others'. There was no downside. It was better than spending the money on something like golf clubs.

When Grant was a kid, getting a new pair of shoes before school started was a really big deal. It was his only pair for the year. It meant going to Grossman's, the "department" store in Forks that was really just a store with a few different things. Grossmans would give him a plastic Easter egg with candy in it when he bought a new pair of shoes. That candy was an event for poor people. And with new shoes, it was easy to forget he was poor.

Grossman's would give Grant the chance to wear his new shoes out of the store after his mother paid for them. Grant would always say yes. It was such a great feeling to walk out of the store in those new shoes. The thrill of getting something new was magnified by using it right away.

The same was true of guns. Grant took the new Glock to the range immediately. It shot just like the one Pow had loaned him. It was so smooth. And accurate. The holster worked flawlessly; he was getting very fast at drawing that thing. He fired the Glock 22 as fast as he could to see if it jammed. Never. Not once. In the thousands of rounds he put through that gun, it never jammed once.

Grant was ready for the next Sunday afternoon with the Team. Chip would come by the range every couple Sundays. Chip was pretty good with a carbine and pistol.

The guest instructor on some Sunday afternoons was Special Forces Ted. He would teach the guys basic small arms skills. How to move. How to shoot. How to move and shoot. And communicate. Nothing fancy. No complicated gear or advanced tactics. Ted realized that the Team members were civilians who did this every other weekend.

Special Forces Ted loved it. These young guys worshipped him. Teaching these basic small arms tactics was exactly what Ted had done in the Army. The primary mission of Green Berets was to train allied indigenous fighters behind enemy lines to be guerillas and harass whatever enemy army the U.S. was fighting. Special Forces spend most of their time training raw indigenous recruits in very basic skills. That's what Ted was doing with these guys. And he had some very good students.

Training with the Team was going great. Grant was getting better with every session. He became so comfortable with an AR and a Glock that they started to seem like pieces of clothing. Comfortable clothing he loved to wear.

Grant was bonding with these guys. They started working on shooting together as two-man and larger teams. They all started watching the Magpul Dynamics training DVDs in between their time out on the range. These DVDs had several hours of expert training on handguns and carbines (a term for short tactical rifles like an AR). They were invaluable. Another fabulous, and free, resource was the availability of hundreds of YouTube videos on shooting, guns, and tactical gear. A particularly good YouTube channel was the one by a guy who went by "Nutnfancy."

The Team did one thing differently than lots of guys who watched the Magpul DVDs and Nutnfancy videos: they practiced. Instead of sitting in a warm, dry house on a couch and watching people doing tactical things on a TV or computer screen, the Team took what they saw on those screens and went out and practiced. Every other Sunday afternoon they went to the range and coached each other. The DVDs and YouTube videos were a basis for it, but the practice, with live rounds, was how they got good. Really good.

The most valuable training came from Special Forces Ted. Realizing that these guys were civilians and only had ARs and pistols — instead of grenades, machine guns, and air cover — Special Forces Ted kept the training at what he called the "law enforcement level," which was short ranges like point blank to about fifty yards, maybe 100 for some situations. With a potential urban battlefield in mind, Ted trained the Team on picking cover, changing out magazines, switching from rifle to pistol, moving, communicating, and shooting, shooting, shooting.

On the range, the Team worked on their communications. They had standard terms they would yell to each other. "Check" meant they were reloading a magazine or had a jam (very infrequent), so they were temporarily out of commission. They didn't use the term "Reloading" or "Jam" because, at these short urban warfare distances, an enemy may hear that and know one of the Team was temporarily out of action.

If a member of the Team heard one say "Check," that meant that the other guy would cover the first member while he fixed the problem. The other guy would yell "OK" to signal that he heard the "Check." If a member's rifle ran dry and needed a new magazine, he would usually transition to his pistol, get to a place like behind cover where he could put a fresh magazine in his rifle, holster his pistol, and keep going with his rifle. If a Team member needed to move to another position, he would yell "Moving" so the other guy knew he was moving and could keep track of where he was and wouldn't shoot him by mistake. The other member would yell "Move" to let the moving member know that he heard him (it was hard to hear when guns are going off). The moving member would go behind the member who yelled "Move" and tap him on the shoulder so he knew the moving member had cleared him, and then take the next position. They were always assessing the scene to find the next piece of cover.

There was a lot of thought that went into gun fighting. The shooting part, the marksmanship to hit a target, was just a small piece of it. Thinking about transitioning between weapons, realizing when one magazine was getting low, changing out empty magazines, communicating, and moving so that they didn't shoot each other took lots and lots of practice, but it was worth it. And it was the most fun they could have with their pants on.

The Team started incorporating movement into their drills. Moving around while people are shooting live ammunition is something that must be done with great care. Trust was very important among teammates. No one even came close to doing anything — ever — that was dangerous. They always knew exactly where their teammates were and never fired in a dangerous direction. They practiced the movements dozens of times without firing to get a rhythm down.

On those Sunday afternoons, the Team practiced leap-frogging so at least one guy was firing on a target as the others were moving. They practiced sustained fire, which was firing a round every so often to keep the bad guys' heads down while a teammate reloaded, advanced, or retreated. Communicating all the while. Finding cover and constantly moving, if possible.

After one particularly good training session, Pow seemed a little choked up. He said, "I'd go into a fight with any of you guys." It was weird and totally understandable at the same time. It was weird because they were civilians and it was peacetime, so there was no logical reason to think there would be a gunfight anytime soon. But it was also understandable because all of the guys knew they were training for something. Some, like Grant, knew exactly what they were training for. Grant knew he wouldn't tell the Team he was a "survivalist" until later. He didn't want to seem like a weirdo and have the guys shy away from him.

Scotty had a feeling things would be going downhill in the country soon and that they had better learn how to take care of business if there were no cops around.

Others, like Bobby and Pow, had an inkling of what looting and gang warfare could look like, but they were training primarily because it was fun.

Wes was hard to read. There was something complex going on in that guy's head. Grant decided to find out. If Wes were crazy, Grant needed to know so they could kick him off the Team. Crazy people can't be trusted to be around live fire exercises.

"So what's the life story of Wes Marlin?" Grant asked one day when they were cleaning their guns and were the only ones left on the range. There was something about cleaning guns that leads guys to have deep conversations.

"Not much," Wes said in that southern accent. He paused.

"I grew up in North Carolina mostly," he continued. "My dad is in the Army and we went all over, but he spent a lot of time at Bragg and Benning," two Army bases for special operations forces.

"What does he do in the Army?" Grant asked.

"He's a Ranger," Wes said. "Just about to retire. He's out at Ft. Lewis now. That's how I got out here to Washington State." Wes was kind of quiet.

"Do you like it out here?" Grant asked.

"Yeah, it's OK," he said with a shrug. "It's a little cold up here and the people are a little weird. There are too many leftist, bleeding heart stickers on Subarus up here, y'know?" They talked about all the liberal whack jobs in Washington State for a while.

"So what do you do at the equipment rental store?" Grant asked.

"Just about everything," Wes said. "I fix all the machinery and maintain it. I show customers how to use all the machines." Wow, Grant thought. This guy knows how to fix machinery. What an asset when equipment breaks and there's no one to call. Wes was still holding something back. Grant thought there was a disconnect between Wes coming out to Washington State and spending the past few years working at the rental place.

"What's your dad like?" Grant asked.

Wes straightened his posture, looked Grant in the eye, and said, "He's an asshole."

That's what Wes was holding back.

"He's a gung ho Ranger and always pushed me to join the Army," Wes said. "I wouldn't mind being in the Army, but he said I needed to be a Ranger or something equivalent or I would embarrass him. He actually said that. He was constantly deployed when I was a kid and when he was home he would ride me pretty hard. I just didn't want to deal with his shit anymore so I graduated from high school and went to work out here. I see him on occasion, but we're not really close. He can't understand why I didn't join the Army."

Grant and Wes had something in common: asshole dads.

"Is your mom out here?" Grant asked.

"Nope," he said. "Divorced a long time ago." Wes looked off. "Not sure where she is now."

"What kind of equipment do you work on?" Grant asked, to both change the subject from asshole dads and to get an inventory of Wes's skills. He described how he worked on power tools; small gas-powered things like chainsaws, trucks and trailers, and things all the way up to small bulldozers. Like so many others Grant was coming into contact with, Wes didn't really have a family. He would need a family when a collapse hit, and Grant would provide it.

The conversation wound its way to guns and women, as conversations between men cleaning guns often do. Then they went home; Wes to his apartment alone and Grant to his family who had no idea about the guns, the Team, the stored food, or his thoughts on the coming collapse. In a sense, Grant was as alone as Wes was.

Chapter 28

Spiders in the Shed

Coming home from the range after a session with the Team was always a weird experience. Grant went from being one hundred percent himself with the guys, with an AR slung over his shoulder and a sidearm, to being a typical suburban father and husband. That twenty-minute car ride from the range to home was a forced transformation process. He had to go from gunfighter to suburban conformist.

It was bullshit. Why did he have to keep hiding what he was doing? He wasn't hurting anyone. In fact, he was doing things that could very easily save all their lives. Most of his friends from work had habits and hobbies that were a lot worse; drinking and overeating, trips to Vegas where who knows what happened, a new car every few years, and spending money on totally useless things like golf. A year's worth of prepping cost about as much as a trip to Vegas or playing golf, and a lot less than new cars every couple of years. At least with prepping, he actually had tangible things to show that were slightly more useful, like food to feed his family and weapons to defend himself and the ones he loved most.

Yet, Grant was the weirdo for being a "survivalist." It wasn't weird to waste money on Vegas or clothes or cars. Nope, that was normal in suburban America, where people didn't worry about how they would survive and protect their family if an unexpected event changed their lives.

The outside thought had been telling Grant for a few years that it wasn't normal for people to just consume things and live in comfort and peace. Maybe it was normal for these suburban people, but Grant had lived the way most other people in the world had to: poor and scared. He knew that this current affluence in America was not "normal." It would end soon. It had to.

Grant pulled into his driveway and hit the garage door button. Time to be a suburban guy again.

"Did you have fun shooting?" Lisa asked when Grant got

inside the house. She thought it was fine that he went and shot a .22 at paper targets or whatever it was he did. A .22 and paper targets was the impression he had left with her.

"Yep," Grant said. "Good times." But he didn't want to dwell on how much fun he had; he needed to be a good suburban dad. So he asked Lisa, "Do the kids have any homework I need to help them with?"

Whenever Grant came home after prepping and saw Lisa, he would think about how unfair it was that he couldn't share his whole life with her. He couldn't talk to her about his greatest hopes and fears. That would involve a topic that was off limits. He had to hide expense check money from her and literally hide things like guns and stored food. He felt like a wimp for not telling his wife.

But he couldn't. Grant remembered the conversation about the stock market and the coming collapse. She literally put her hands over her ears. She would not hear about it. He needed to control his emotions. A survivalist who gets his family through the worst possible times will have to keep his emotions in check. Start practicing now, pal, Grant thought to himself. Emotionally you want to tell her all about the prepping and to have her accept you as you are. But telling her won't accomplish that. It will just get her mad, especially that you've been hiding things from her. She'll tell you to get rid of all this stuff and start golfing like a normal guy. And you won't. This will lead to…

OK, Grant told himself, there is no upside to telling her except to feel better. Feeling better is for pussies. Toughen up. You have a job to do.

Manda was the bright spot in the family. She got it. Grant had an idea to bring her into a closer orbit with him on the prepping stuff. An idea that would also make him feel better. If he couldn't share his prepping with his wife, at least he could with his daughter.

Grant briefly thought about getting Cole involved with prepping. He wouldn't understand the words. Grant could involve him by taking really good care of him when disaster struck. That's what drove Grant to prep when it came to Cole. He wanted to make his life as good as possible. It was all about pancakes and safety.

Grant popped his head into Manda's room when Lisa was downstairs. "Hey, Manda," he whispered, "next time we're out at the cabin I'd like to show you something. Do you promise not to tell your mom?" Nothing drew people closer together than sharing a secret.

"Of course, Daddy," she said back in a whisper. When she said "Daddy" sweetly, Grant could not say no to her. She knew it and used the word sparingly, only when she wanted something. She wanted to be in on a secret her mom didn't know about. Grant knew he was getting played but he was OK with it. Dads are supposed to be that way.

The next Saturday, they went out to the cabin. Grant told Manda that they would be stopping at a store first. They went to Cash n' Carry, the discount food supply store.

Manda had never been there. Suburban people shopped at the fancy grocery stores. As they pulled in to Cash n' Carry, which was in a bad part of town, Manda asked, "Why we going here, Dad?"

"You'll see," Grant said. He wanted to make a big impression on her when she saw all the food stored out at the cabin for the first time. He wanted her first memory of what's in the shed to be a big one. Going to Cash n' Carry and getting more bulk food would add to that impression. Plus, he had some more money and needed to increase his food storage.

Grant got a big cart and started filling it up with food. "Hey, these are the garlic and herb mashed potatoes you like, right?" he asked Manda.

"Yeah," Manda said. "Wow, they have everything here and in huge packages," she said. Manda thought her dad was doing some grocery shopping in giant quantities. She had no idea where this food was really going.

"Dad," Manda said, "could we hurry up with this grocery shopping because I'd rather spend as much time as possible out at the cabin."

"We're taking this out to the cabin. You'll see." Manda looked puzzled.

The whole cart of food, which was enough to feed the family for weeks on staples like mashed potatoes, pancakes, beans, and rice, came to a little less than $100. Grant put it in his car and they headed to the cabin. He could tell Manda was wondering what he was up to.

When they got to the cabin after the forty-minute ride, Grant got out and motioned for Manda to follow him to the shed.

"Do you know what's in here?" he asked.

"Spiders?" she said.

"Something better," Grant said. "You know our conversations about how the U.S. is collapsing?"

Manda nodded. Her dad was being very serious.

"Do you get a little scared when you think about the stores being out of food?" he asked.

"Not really," she said.

"What?" Grant said. "Why not?"

"Because I know you'll take care of us," she said with a shrug. "Not sure how, but you will." That was the nicest thing anyone had ever said to him.

Grant was beaming. He unlocked the padlock on the door to the shed and said, "This is how."

Inside the very clean shed were big plastic tubs. They were the big thirty-nine-quart jumbo storage containers they kept their Christmas decorations in. He opened up the nearest one and motioned for her to look inside. There were vacuum sealed packages of pasta, big cans of spaghetti sauce, tuna, sealed packages of mashed potatoes, oatmeal, hot chocolate mix, and a case of the canned chili Manda loved so much. He was smiling.

So was she. "Wow, Daddy, you are really taking care of us." Grant was so proud he couldn't contain himself. Finally! Someone understood him.

Grant started to explain how each tub had a number and then showed Manda the sheet of paper with the contents of each tub on it. Everything had an expiration date on it. For the things that were vacuum sealed and not in the original package, Grant wrote the expiration date or the "Best by" date in big numbers. Many things had no expiration date, which was even better.

He showed her the next tub. It had cases of canned refried beans, five pound bags of instant corn grits, bottles of maple syrup, gallon jugs of honey, biscuit mix, cornbread mix, and instant gravy mix. There were also No. 10 tins of canned fruit, more chili, and barbeque beans. A few cases of tuna fish and canned chicken were in there, too. There were also gallon jugs of cooking oil and big jars of peanut butter.

The tubs contained sugared drink mix because people will need the extra calories of sugared drinks and they were way cheaper than diet mixes. Grant even got Gatorade mix because dehydrated people would need electrolytes. He also had big containers of salt, spices, and flavorings. They were so cheap. A big restaurant-sized container of cinnamon for $4.00 would last for months of flavoring oatmeal, pancakes, and biscuits. He had sugar, too, both in bulk and in little packets. The little packets could be given out and would travel well; Costco had a 1000 sugar packets for $5.00.

Grant had fourteen tubs in the 10' x 10' shed. All the food in the tubs met Grant's four criteria: It was storable for long periods of time, his family would eat it (after an adjustment period), it was cheap, and could be eaten without cooking, or with just heating water.

Manda asked, "Daddy, is there any brownie mix?" She loved brownies.

"Nope, dear," Grant said. "Brownies need milk and eggs. Storing milk and eggs requires electricity to keep them cool." Grant knew that he could store dried milk and eggs but thought that they wouldn't make the brownies just right like fresh milk and eggs. Besides, he was really trying to stretch his dollars to get just the staples, and lots of them.

Grant expected the resourceful people out at Pierce Point would be milking cows and raising chickens after a collapse, but that would take a few months, or maybe a year. The food in the shed was to get them through the beginning of a collapse until they could get some gardens and livestock going. It was to tide them over, not to feed them for years. Grant didn't want to tell Manda this. He needed her to get the information about something as terrifying as a collapse in little bits, not all at once.

Grant also had five cases of MREs in the shed. He explained to Manda that these are Army meals, which she had seen in movies. Each case had 12 meals. Actually, one MRE was a full meal for a big guy like Grant when he was working hard. Each one had about 1,250 calories. One MRE could last a normal sized person who wasn't working hard maybe a whole day. MREs were great for eating while in the field or moving. They were all in one container, ready to eat, and had everything required to eat them right there. They had an entrée that usually had some meat, a couple of side dishes, and a dessert. The crackers and tortillas were amazing. Most of the MREs came with cheese and jam packets. There were a few dozen side dishes and desserts: rice pilaf, clam chowder, BBQ beans, pineapple, fruit cobbler, Skittles, milkshake mix — the list went on. There was even cappuccino mix in some MREs.

Each part of the meal was in a separate package so they could be eaten separately, which was important in dangerous, on-the-go situations. They thought of everything when they invented MREs.

Despite their reputation, MREs tasted great. There were horror stories about the first generation ones, but modern MREs tasted pretty good. There were twenty-four different meals. A few weren't great but the vast majority were. Grant usually ate an MRE when he went shooting because he needed to pack a lunch, and MREs were cheaper and healthier than drive-thrus. Plus, he got to try each meal this way. It was an adventure every time he tore open the package. Actually, he didn't eat a whole MRE because it was too much for one meal. He would save leftover side dishes and desserts. He had several big Ziploc bags of them. They would last for years, which was maybe the best thing about MREs: They lasted about fifteen years if stored out of the heat. Grant's MREs had been made within the past few years.

Manda read the side of the MRE boxes, which said "Commercial resale is unlawful." "Dad, where did you get these MREs?" she asked. "You're not in the Army." These were the real MREs, not a commercial knock offs.

"I have some friends." Grant said with a smile. He wanted her to think he was magic, which was what every dad wants. There was another reason to make her think he was magic: it would give him credibility when a collapse hit and he needed her to trust him.

The truth was that he got three cases at a Ft. Lewis surplus store where soldiers sold extra MREs. Apparently, there was no real restriction on selling to civilians, or everyone just looked the other way. A case was $60.00, so that was $5.00 for a big, complete, portable, pretty tasty, and highly nutritious meal that stored for fifteen years.

The other two cases were a gift from Chip, who got them from Special Forces Ted. While he was on active duty just before he retired, Ted taught ROTC cadets during their summer training camps out at Ft. Lewis. These college kids would be issued MREs to eat out in the field but they didn't eat them all. Ted said that some of them were spoiled little brats who wanted the scholarship money from ROTC but didn't want to eat "Army food." So Ted got dozens of cases of leftover MREs each year. Ted, who knew how valuable the MREs would be when things got bad, stored them at his bachelor pad after his divorce. He would hand them out by the case to friends. The Army issued them to people, it was a paperwork pain to turn them back in, and Ted was putting them to good use. One day, Grant was in the gun store and a big shipment of guns came in. Grant, who had a suit and tie on, helped Chip unload the truck. Chip thanked him with two cases of MREs.

The shed had more than just food in it. Each tub had a can opener in it. Grant also put medical supplies in some of the tubs. He didn't stock complete trauma kits; they were expensive and he didn't know how to use them. He knew first aid well, but didn't want to waste money on fancy medical gear he couldn't use. He thought he'd stretch the money he had on things that are more likely to strike people and were cheaper to remedy. He watched YouTube videos by "Patriot Nurse" who provided valuable insight on field medical issues.

A small sample of the medical-related things in the shed included lots of electrolyte pills from a running store to supplement the Gatorade mix. He had Imodium for diarrhea. He hoped the water supply would be OK when the collapse hit, because he saw a partial breakdown rather than a total one, but knew that a dollar's worth of electrolytes or Imodium could save someone who is dehydrated from drinking bad water.

Grant also got many one-quart containers of rubbing alcohol. They were $4.00 each at Costco. For about $5.00, he got a few 250-packs of cleaning wipes for glasses in individual packets; they were made of rubbing alcohol. The wipes and jugs of rubbing alcohol would come in handy for sterilizing instruments and dressing wounds. And they were very cheap and stored for years.

The medical tub also included the caffeine pills and the non-drowsy allergy pills he needed for his hay fever. It was thinking of little things like this and acting now that would make life so much better later.

Manda noticed that all the receipts were in the tubs and asked why.

"So," Grant explained, "during a collapse, we can look back at the receipts and realize how little all these things cost beforehand. It will make it even more apparent to people how much sense it made to spend a little money now." Grant grinned.

At the very beginning of his prepping, when he was frustrated that Lisa wasn't on board with it, Grant dreamed about the gloating he could do when she realized how right he had been all along. Then he realized how stupid that was. He decided that he would not gloat at all; that would only drive her away from him and turn prepping into an "I told you so" instead of what it was really about: taking care of his family, which is a man's first and most important job. No gloating. But, he might need a little bit of credibility with her. Why he felt he would still need credibility with her after his family was eating and was protected while others weren't, he didn't understand. She would see that fifty pounds of pancake mix was just $35 in peacetime, but was twenty times that much during the collapse. The receipts would increase his credibility with her right when he needed her to trust him with her life in circumstances that she could never imagine. This trust would be a matter of life and death, and if a little thing like a peacetime food receipt helped with that, then he should do it.

Grant finished showing Manda all the tubs and then asked, "What do you think?"

"Awesome, Dad," she said with a big smile. But she was very practical, so she asked, "How much did all this cost?"

"About one ounce of gold when I wanted to buy it and your mom said I couldn't," Grant said. "I decided to take the money I would have spent on one ounce — about $900 — and invest in some assets that would be far more valuable later." Grant was trying not to scare his lovely, bubbly innocent daughter with all this gloom and doom talk. That's why he didn't show her the guns or the twenty or so ammo cans in the cabin basement, or the tubs with the fifty-five bricks of vacuum-sealed .22 ammo. No, he would just show her the food for now.

"You can't tell your friends about this, Amanda," Grant said, using her full name to emphasize the seriousness of the point.

She nodded. "Not even Emmy?" She was Manda's best friend.

"Not even her," Grant said. "Sorry, dear, but if you tell her, she'll tell her parents. And when a collapse hits, they'll try to come out here. We don't have enough for everyone."

"They could have bought food like you did," Manda said, "but probably didn't."

"Exactly," Grant said, thanking his lucky stars that his daughter understood all this better than most adults.

"What would you do if Emmy and her parents came out here and asked for food?" Manda asked.

Time to tell her straight, like she was a grown up.

"Turn them away because this food is for my family," Grant said. "I spent my time, money, and stress of hiding this from your mom when Emmy's parents were playing golf or whatever."

"What if her parents wouldn't leave or got angry?" Manda asked.

"I'd make them leave," Grant said.

"What if they wouldn't leave or tried to take the food?" Manda asked.

"I'd give them another chance to leave before I resorted to force," Grant said. He looked her right in the eye when he said that. He wanted her to understand how serious this was. Manda just stood there, trying to take in the thought that her dad would use force against her best friend's parents.

"People knowing about our food could get us killed," Grant said. "Those hungry and desperate people could try to hurt us for the food or they could tell other people we have food and the other people, maybe even a gang, could try to hurt us."

174

Manda nodded.

"New friends are easy to come by. Resurrecting your family from the dead isn't," Grant said.

"That's a pretty good reason not to tell Emmy," Manda said, "because if she doesn't know about the food, you won't have to hurt anyone."

"Exactly," Grant said.

Grant wanted to ease his sweet teenage daughter's fears about the terrible topic of shooting her best friend's parents, so he tried to change the subject back to the reasons for having the food.

"Assume that there is no collapse," Grant said. "Worst case scenario is that in a few years as the expiration dates start to come up, I donate the food to a food bank." He was trying to act like he thought that would happen.

"That won't be happening, Daddy," Manda said. She looked at Grant with the most serious look he had ever seen from her. "I know what's coming."

Chapter 29

It's Going to Get Ugly

Grant was sick of the government assholes at work. It was getting ridiculous. Jeanie was trying to fend them off and get Menlow pointed in the direction of reform, but she wasn't willing to do anything that jeopardized her job.

Menlow had secretly started running for governor long ago. Although election day was still years away, his actions were already becoming calculated, as he prepared for the race. There is nothing more spineless than a politician running for a higher office. Menlow was so busy trying to make all the government people, and all the other left-wing Washington State voters, happy that he had long since abandoned his pledge to reform the State Auditor's Office into a force for exposing corruption. It was pathetic. Grant felt stupid for believing in him.

Grant was looking for a way out of government employment. He had toughed it out for longer than he expected to be there. He had helped many citizens when he was there. He got so much more done on the inside of government, even for that short period, than he could have from the outside. But, he'd been thwarted. It was time to go back to WAB.

The Matsons were hosting the annual Fourth of July party with Tom, Brian, and Ben from WAB. When Menlow found out that Grant was having the WAB people over socially, he was a little concerned.

"Do you think that's a good idea, Grant?" Menlow said with grave concern. "I mean, WAB is pretty partisan."

"Yeah, partisan for your party," Grant said. "You are a Republican."

It was becoming increasingly socially awkward to be a "conservative" in this liberal town. The liberals weren't screaming or throwing things, but there was definitely a separation between them and those who were conservative. Only fellow liberals were allowed into this mainstream world. The WAB guys talked about this over too many beers at the Fourth of July party.

This was the perfect time for Grant to ask for his job back. After they started talking about what a piece of shit Menlow had become, Grant simply said to Tom, "Can I come back to WAB?"

"About time," Tom said. "Same salary and everything?"

"OK," Grant said. "You drive a hard bargain." That was it. Grant was no longer a state employee. It felt liberating. They celebrated some more.

Now that they were good and drunk, Ben had an idea. A conservative think tank in town (the only one) had a full studio for making political podcasts and doing radio shows. WAB knew them well. Ben suggested that WAB get together and start a podcast called "Rebel Radio" to begin describing all the corruption they were seeing. It would be more than just a show about state politics; it would have an edge. A "Don't Tread on Me" edge.

"How about a show on the coming collapse of California?" Tom offered.

"Yeah, and how public employee unions are looting the treasury of this state," Brian suggested.

"We need to have a show on Baby Boomers and how they voted themselves tons of shit and now the rest of us need to pay for it," Ben said.

The show topics started flowing like all the beer. Brian was writing them down.

The conservative think tank was happy to produce the podcast, but secretly. Their sound engineer could easily electronically alter each speaker's voice to make them unrecognizable. It didn't sound like an artificial robot, just like another person. It was amazing. The sound engineer made Grant's average radio voice sound rich and deep. Hiding their voices was important because the identities of the podcasters and the think tank had to remain a secret.

They knew that Rebel Radio was going to say some unpopular things that would make some very powerful people mad. The WAB guys still had to lobby legislators for their small-business members. This "Don't Tread on Me" edge to Rebel Radio would terrify the spineless Republicans they had to lobby. The think tank was especially interested in not having anyone know they were involved with Rebel Radio because they had a tax-exempt charitable status. They knew the IRS would yank it if they put out opinions like this. Of course, it was perfectly legal for them to do this but the IRS had been "interpreting" the tax-exempt laws pretty harshly against conservative groups.

A few days later, Grant resigned from the State Auditor's

178

Office. The resignation was anti-climactic. He didn't even go into Menlow's office and talk to him like he used to. He just wrote a letter and put it on Menlow's desk. The letter was polite and didn't go into all the details. It just said that Grant was going back to the private sector after he had assisted the Auditor with his reform goals. It was bland but Grant didn't care. He just wanted out.

The two-week period at the State Auditor's Office between resignation and his last day was weird. The bureaucrats there started unloading on him since they knew he was leaving. All kinds of little things that had been festering for a while came out. A few of his soon-to-be former co-workers actually raised their voices with him. He couldn't wait to get back to helping people for real again. He also couldn't wait to start broadcasting Rebel Radio.

A few weeks later, Rebel Radio was taped. The show consisted of the WAB guys knocking back a few beers on the air and just saying whatever they thought. No holds barred. Exactly what they thought. WAB knew things that no one else knew because they were insiders. They knew exactly how bad the state's finances were because they got the briefings. They interviewed citizens getting screwed by government; the stories were amazing. No one else was saying the things they were saying.

The number of downloads grew each week. It was becoming a pretty big deal. Most of the listeners were in Washington State because they described facts specific to that state, but they were noticing downloads from computers in other states, too. Rebel Radio tapped into something out there: rage at increasingly unjust government. They had fans, at least among the little people out there getting screwed, who had no one else telling them exactly how things were.

Rebel Radio wasn't loved by all, however. It made the State Auditor's Office look bad because that agency was supposed to be helping people, but Rebel Radio described why they weren't. The people in the State Auditor's Office made no secret that they would shut down the podcast if they could. It frustrated them that they couldn't. They were so angry at the criticism that it was a little creepy. They really, really hated the people doing Rebel Radio, especially Grant. Despite the voice synthesizer, they suspected that Grant was one of the podcasters and hated him for sharing his inside knowledge of their failures.

The Governor's Office openly talked about how they could legally shut down Rebel Radio. No one in state government could come up with a way to shut them down. Things were getting mean. In the past, it would have been absurd to say that the Governor's Office would be talking about how to silence criticism, but things were getting nastier and nastier.

The state budget deficit was ballooning. The "recession" meant less economic activity, which meant less tax revenue. Despite far less taxes coming in, the state kept spending money. And more money. Washington State was a smaller version of California: chasing out businesses, falling tax revenue, and massively increasing spending. The people doing it were being re-elected by huge margins. The voters loved having more stuff. They could not comprehend the debt they were running up. Besides, the "rich" paid for it all, right?

In these tough times, the government employee unions demanded more money. They insisted on pay raises. They even wanted more for their gold-plated pensions. They said that with the losses in the stock market that had previously paid the interest on their pensions, the state must put in more money so they would not suffer a decline in pension payments. In the mind of government employee unions, the taxpayers needed to pay more to them so they wouldn't suffer any losses from the stock market — like all the taxpayers had. The Legislature and Governor, all elected with the money donated by the unions, were happy to do so. The voters, at least enough of them to swing an election, seemed to be OK with it. Actually, voters in the largely agricultural eastern half of the state were not OK with it. But the conservatives in Eastern Washington were just a small part of the population, so they didn't count when it came to politics. Most voters in Washington State had been told for several decades how underpaid public employees were (which was no longer true), so many of them thought the recession was a chance for the unions to "catch up" with the private sector on pay and benefits.

Of course, with unemployment going up, the government scrambled to create more "safety net" programs. State unemployment benefits were increased. The federal government was handing out several billion dollars in aid to the state. That would allow all this spending without any consequence. For a while, until eventually even the feds realized they couldn't keep shoveling money to the states and started cutting back on aid. Now what? The state budget deficit would be about half of all the money they had control over. About half of the state budget was spent on federally mandated things like Medicaid, and the state portion of other entitlements that couldn't be cut. Half of all the money? No more federal money and no more accounting gimmicks. The state had to, for the first time ever, actually consider cutting.

State workers were asked to take furloughs, which was a week or two off each year without pay. "Essential" services, about 40% of the employees, were exempt from the furloughs.

Union representatives responded as if state workers were being executed in the streets. They ginned up huge protests and angrily demanded a stop to the cuts. Most people in the dwindling private sector looked on in amazement. They had either been laid off or knew plenty of people who had, but these government employees were going nuts over taking a tiny pay cut.

Instead of making real cuts, the government demanded more money. It raised every tax it could. It started charging "user fees" for the most absurd things. Every government permit — and there were hundreds of them needed to conduct daily life — came with a price tag. Registering a car now had a new fee of several hundred dollars. Fire departments started to charge to respond to 911 calls. Counties started to require inspections of appliances to ensure they were energy efficient and charged a hefty "inspection fee." Cities started charging a license fee to owners of dogs, threatening to take unlicensed dogs and euthanize them. It was like the government thought it was entitled to as much of the people's money as it demanded. Grant remembered the meeting at the Governor's Office when they said exactly that.

But the people, for the most part, just stood by and watched. They didn't want to get involved. A surprisingly high number of them were getting government money in one form or another. Almost half of households were dependent, in whole or in part, on government benefits. They wanted to keep theirs.

The rest of the people who weren't getting government benefits didn't want to rock the boat because they didn't want to be "extremists" or be called "greedy." Besides, they had enough to eat (actually, too much, in most cases), there were plenty of good reality shows on TV, and they didn't really understand politics, anyway. All they knew is what they learned in school: government needed more money to do great things for the little guy and business was greedy.

People assumed that the WAB would be looking out for big business. Not true. Big business and small business had radically different interests. Big business could get the government to write regulations and tax laws to put their small-business competition out of business. Big business was run by CEOs who, by and large, were products of the liberal education system and the Seattle cocktail party circuit where one chats about how awful Republicans are.

Small business, on the other hand, actually wanted government to be limited. The taxes, regulations, and stupid paperwork requirements were killing them.

Big business and government got even cozier during the "recession." At the federal level, the Administration, with ample help from the Republicans, bailed out GM, Chrysler, AIG, Goldman Sachs, and just about all the other big corporations.

The same was true at the state level, but the help was in different forms. Big business in Washington State got all kinds of state contracts for "stimulus money" projects to build roads and government buildings, and to buy many things big business sold. For example, the big car dealers' association got the state to buy millions of dollars of "fuel-efficient" cars for the state motor pool, which didn't actually need any new cars. Big business returned the favor, donating almost all their corporate contributions to the ruling Democrats and the few Republicans in office. Big business would help the politicians in other ways, like PR stunts disguised as meetings between business leaders and the Governor with the business leaders praising the Governor. The state returned the favors by imposing requirements on businesses that only large employers could afford to comply with, thus reducing the number of small businesses and thereby reducing the competition big businesses faced.

This was soft fascism; government and large corporations helping each other to the detriment of everyone else. It was still fascism though — just without the little mustache and the genocide.

"Are we the only ones who see what's going on?" Grant asked Brian one day.

Brian sighed. "Pretty much. Most people don't know or care what's going on. They're pathetic. But they'll get what they deserve."

Grant decided to have "the conversation" with Brian.

"You know, Brian, this whole thing is going to come crashing down," he said. "Soon, too. Maybe a year, maybe five. But, soon."

Brian looked relieved. Finally someone was saying what he was thinking, but he thought it was too outlandish to say out loud. "I know," Brian said. "The government is out of money and they can't stop spending. The only thing that will stop them is bankruptcy. It's going to get ugly."

They talked about the civil unrest that would come from the cuts and the protests of all the people dependent on government money. They talked about how the government would crack down on dissenters like them. Not haul them off or anything, just start auditing their taxes and that kind of thing. Soft fascism; not the little mustache stuff.

Grant didn't tell Brian about the preparations he had been making. It wasn't time yet. But he did say to Brian, "If things get crazy, we need to stick together. You, me, Tom, and Ben and our families."

Brian nodded, solemnly. He couldn't believe they were having this conversation, but he was glad they were.

Chapter 30

Foreign and Domestic

Grant had two ARs; the standard A2 and his customized M4. What to do with the A2? Having two ARs was important. There was a phrase among preppers that "one is none and two is one," meaning that a backup is always necessary.

At Capitol City Guns, Grant saw a .22 conversion bolt for an AR. Just by popping out the bolt and putting in the .22 bolt, an AR became a .22 rifle. This allowed cheap and realistic training, and provided a lot of fun.

Manda didn't know about Grant's guns. She knew he had some but had never seen them. He needed to get her proficient on the AR. "Every girl needs to know how to use one nowadays," Grant told her.

Cole was still a little spooked by loud noises so Grant would wait to get him shooting. The .22 conversion bolt would be perfect for Manda's training. It had no recoil and was quiet. What better way to introduce a fifteen year-old to ARs?

"Hey, Manda, want to shoot a real live Army gun?" he asked her one day.

"Are you kidding?" she asked. "Do you have one?"

That was the beginning of Grant and Manda's Sunday afternoons at the shooting range. She quickly became very good with the AR in .22. The light recoil made it perfect for training a new AR shooter. Shooting the AR with the regular 5.56mm ammo after that was no big deal for her. She even learned how to field strip the AR. She loved the fact that she had a thing to do with her dad, and she could keep it secret from her mom. Lisa would have spazzed out if she knew Grant was teaching Manda to shoot an "assault rifle."

Next, Grant got her shooting the AK. She was good at that, too, but it had more recoil for the fifteen year-old and the folding stock made it harder to aim. However, she could shoot an AK no problem, and she loved it.

It got even better. The AK-47 had a cousin, the AK-74, which was the rifle the Russians used. The AK-74 shot the smaller 5.45 x 39 cartridge, which, like the AR's 5.56 x 45, had little or no recoil. And AK-74s were light, about half as heavy as an AK-47. On top of all that, the AK-74 had a short "European" sized stock for smaller Europeans.

Light, short stock, and virtually no recoil. The perfect gun for Manda, and any other smaller person. It was a "wives and kids" gun.

The AK-74 was cheap. The Russians made millions of them, and they were about $400. A person could put a cheap red-dot sight on and have a fine rifle with an optic for about $500. Magazines were dirt cheap, about $10 a piece. And, to top it all off, ammo was absurdly cheap. A person could get a metal tin, called a "spam can" because it looked like one and was opened with a can opener, of 1,080 AK-74 rounds for $120. All of this meant that a prepper could get an AK-74 with a basic red-dot sight and over 1,000 rounds of for half the cost of an AR-15 without an optic or any ammunition.

Since they were so cheap, Grant got two AK-74s — one for him and a matching one for Manda. She loved shooting it. One time she said, "Daddy, I did all my homework. Can we go shoot the AK-74s? Please."

Grant got one spam can at a time with the expense-check envelope money. Pretty soon, he had four spam cans (over 4,000 rounds) at home and another four at the cabin. He got ten magazines for each rifle. It was the cheapest SHTF battle rifle to be found. And it was so much fun to shoot.

Now it was time to tell Manda what was in all those green square cans in the garage marked "5.56" "7.62" and now "5.45." Grant was glad he gently and slowly broke the news to Manda that her dad was a "survivalist." He could only imagine if he had just announced one day, "I have stored a bunch of food and guns. I think the world is ending."

He now considered Manda a full partner in prepping. They talked about the details of their prepping and planned it out together. They also talked about how the country was disintegrating. At least he could talk to one person about this. Too bad it was a fifteen year-old instead of his wife and friends.

Grant had to make sure there was a check on his emotions and that he was making rational decisions. He was dealing with such heavy thoughts — the collapse of the country, food shortages, protecting loved ones from uncontrolled violence — that he had to have something in place to make sure he didn't overreact. Fear should never rule decision making. Grant figured Manda could be his reality check. Looking to a teenage girl for emotional clarity wasn't the best option, but given that she was the only one who he could tell about all this, it was his only option.

One day at the shooting range, he said to her, "Manda, I want to make sure I'm approaching prepping rationally. I don't want to get emotional and buy a bunch of food or guns every time there's a dip in the stock market. Prepping isn't a crutch; it's a logical plan to handle bad times. So here's the deal. Any time you think I'm not doing something logically, you have permission to say, 'Dad, you're wrong.' But you need to be able to then say, 'Here's why.' Deal?"

Asking a teenager if she wants permission to tell her parent when they're wrong?

"Of course Daddy," she said. "Nothing you've done so far has been weird."

It turns out lots of other people, a few million, were having the same concerns as Grant.

Capitol City Guns was lucky to have opened its doors when it did. During the various recent ammo scares, customers felt they needed more guns, ammo, and accessories. They would return to the place where they got their first guns, as they responded to the Federal Reserve's continued printing of absurd sums of money, the increasing crime rate, and all the other signs of what might be coming scared more and more people. They kept buying guns; lots and lots of guns.

During this time, an estimated one to three million AR-15s were manufactured, sold, and put into American civilians' hands. Some thought that there were about as many civilian AR-15s, or maybe more, than the military's stockpiles of military-version M-16s. Americans bought hundreds of thousands of tactical shotguns and millions of pistols during this same period. Billions of rounds of ammunition were also moved from warehouses to Americans' gun safes, ammo cans in garages, storage sheds, and sock drawers. All of this didn't count the tens of millions of scoped hunting rifles and hunting shotguns already existing in the United States. Estimates were that there were over 100 million firearms in the country. They were in closets, night stands, and attics all across the nation.

Not only guns and ammo, but sophisticated gear was flying off the shelves. Stores like Capitol City were stocked with night vision scopes and body armor. There were millions of extremely well-armed American civilians. Most of them were not trained as soldiers, but they had decent gear and could train later.

The military and law enforcement knew this. The vast majority of them never thought about trying to take over the country. However, a tiny percentage of them — the political ones who wanted to get promoted — planned out how to do it under the guise of "contingency planning." Those planning a takeover realized that it wouldn't be a cakewalk. It would be a nasty, brutal civil war with guerillas killing them for years and years. No army — not even the U.S., which had the most powerful military in the history of the Earth — could possibly take over and occupy the country.

Another reason it would be hard for the military to totally take over is that many in the military and law enforcement hated the politicians who would order them to try to take control. It would be a hard sell for a politician to tell a soldier or cop, "Go kill your neighbors and stand a good chance of getting killed yourself — all so I can have more power." Of course, some in the military or law enforcement would use the "crisis" as an excuse to grab their own power. It had happened for all of human history; America was no exception to the laws of human behavior and history.

Others would be in-between. Some in the military and law enforcement would go along with the politicians at first; there would probably some genuine crises to protect people against. But after a while, they would increasingly refuse to shoot and imprison Americans if that's what they were ordered to do. Therefore, eventually most in the military and law enforcement would probably not be part of an attempted takeover. In fact, a good portion of them would actively fight against the politicians trying it.

Special Forces Ted was one of them. He was a member of Oath Keepers, as were many of his Special Forces buddies.

It would be safe to assume that something as simple as pledging to keep an oath to uphold the Constitution wouldn't be too controversial. But it was. The progressive politicians hated Oath Keepers. They thought Oath Keepers were violent right-wing militia nut jobs bent on taking over America via a coup.

One day, Grant went to Capitol City and found Chip and Special Forces Ted in the shop making some ARs. Now that Ted was retired and divorced, he spent most of his time there. Grant had apparently interrupted them in some deep conversation. Ted wanted to change the subject but Chip wanted to continue with it in front of Grant.

Chip said to Ted, "Go ahead, man, you can trust Grant. Tell him what you were telling me."

Ted paused. He didn't want to keep talking. Finally, he reluctantly said, "I'm organizing an Oath Keepers group in my old unit. There are lots of us who think something bad is going to happen." Ted paused and chose his words carefully, "We didn't sign up to take over our own country. We signed up to protect it. We will. Enemies foreign and domestic. Domestic."

Grant was stunned to hear this. An American soldier saying out loud that he was concerned that the government was thinking of taking over by force and other soldiers would have to get involved to stop it. The part that wasn't surprising, at least to Grant, was that soldiers had to think about this. Grant knew things were collapsing. Those Green Berets knew it, too. They received the briefings on what was happening.

Now that Ted was warming up to the idea of trusting Grant, he got on a roll about Oath Keepers. He explained to Grant that at least half of the guys in his old unit were Oath Keepers, or wanted to join. The other half were either "not into politics" or were so young that they didn't fully appreciate what an unlawful order was. The young guys hadn't been deployed to hellholes around the world, like the older guys had, where it was the norm for power-hungry politicians to use force against the civilian population. Of the half not immediately interested in Oath Keepers, Ted figured about half of them (about a quarter of the unit) would be open to it, especially if the rest of the unit was. The remaining men in the unit were either not interested or, in a few cases, were "ladder climbers" who would follow just about any order to advance in rank. Ted couldn't think of any ladder climbers in his former unit, but he had to admit that when times got tough some guys would just follow orders. Ted explained that the more elite a unit was, and Special Forces was certainly at the top of that list, the more open the unit was to Oath Keepers. Mid-level infantry units would have many good Oath Keepers, but also had a higher percentage of guys who joined for a free college education. The lower level units, especially the non-combat support units, had a majority of guys who treated the Army as just another job. Guys like that would probably follow orders just to keep their jobs. But, a unit full of Army administrative specialists isn't too fearsome compared to a couple of Green Berets.

Besides, Ted explained, America's high-tech military was extremely dependent on supplies and logistics. If semi-trucks quit rolling, the Army would face shortages of fuel, ammo, and spare parts just like everyone else. They had stockpiles but they, too, had fallen for just-in-time inventory. Cost-cutting wizards at the Pentagon had decided to go with just-in-time inventory to save money. Oh, how shortsighted that would be. Just like almost everything else in America. Shortsighted and disastrous.

"Another big problem a unit will face in a domestic crisis is that most guys will want to get back home to their families," Ted explained. "Especially the lower level units. But, with the more elite units, we are each other's family so we'll fight as group. And most of those units will be Oath Keeper units."

"What about cops?" Chip asked. "Those guys come in here all day to buy guns and hang out. They seem pretty solid to me." Ted and Chip talked about law enforcement and how they thought a good chunk of them would choose the Oath Keeper side, either at the outset of a collapse or a little bit into it.

Grant didn't know what it was like to be a Green Beret, but he knew a little about cops. "Hey, I don't claim to be an expert here," he said, "but aren't cops a little more prone to corruption than, say, Army units? I mean, I see a little cop corruption in the cases I work on."

Ted and Chip agreed that cops would be more likely to be corrupt just because cops were in constant contact with criminals, whereas soldiers weren't. The consensus among Ted, Chip, and Grant was that some cops would go bad and maybe steal from people, but that the majority would not.

"Cops are local," Ted said. "They don't move around to a new base every few years like we do. That means they'll think twice about shooting people in their own towns who are their neighbors and relatives, in some cases."

Most cops would probably just quit their jobs. The current round of budget cuts would mean even fewer cops would be around. Those that were might decide that a collapse was a good time to quit, especially when it meant getting killed, or having to kill their neighbors.

Grant was soaking all of this in. He still couldn't believe what he was hearing. It was reassuring. No, actually, it was a huge relief to hear, straight from the horse's mouth, that the military and lots of law enforcement would not turn into an anti-civilian thug force. It sounded like there would be plenty of good military and law enforcement people to keep the bad ones under control. But there would still be plenty of bad military and law enforcement units.

As much Grant had improved his tactical skills, he always knew that his little Team was no match for any competent military or law enforcement opponent. Not even close. He remembered the day at the range with the Team when some Rangers from Ft. Lewis showed up to shoot. The Team was glad to let them use the range to learn from them. Those Rangers were amazing; ten times better than the civilians on the Team. Right then and there Grant and the rest of the Team knew their limitations. They were only able to defend themselves against civilian criminals, maybe up to the sophisticated gang level of civilian criminals. But that was it. Now he realized that his side would have some military and law enforcement backup with the Oath Keepers.

Grant had to head home, which was a short drive from the gun store. He would have stayed and listened to Ted for hours if he could. On the way home, he tried to "normalize" himself by getting back into the suburban world he was returning to. He struggled with making the mental switch from hearing a former Green Beret talk about which of the guys in his unit would fight against the U.S. Government in a coup, to hearing about how ballet practice went and what homework the kids had that night.

When Grant got into the driveway, he hit the garage door button. Hitting that button had become a symbol to him that he needed to go from thinking about the end of the world to thinking about being a suburban dad and husband. It was a hard transition on evenings like this one. Very hard.

Chapter 31

Budget Crisis

The State of Washington was technically bankrupt. Of course, a state can't really declare bankruptcy, although California was considering it.

The official Washington State deficit for the year was $5.7 billion. It was widely rumored to be even bigger. Washington State's budget for the previous year was about $30 billion, but half of that was the state portion of federal programs like Medicaid that the state couldn't cut. That meant the state had about $15 billion it could control, and it was short by $5.7 billion. The local schools got almost all of their money from the state, which was close to $5 billion. The state was required by the state constitution to pay for education, so that meant that $5 billion could not be touched. That left Washington State with $10 billion to pave roads, operate prisons, provide social services, have a state police force, and more.

Of course, a big chunk of paying for those things was paying the salaries, and especially the pensions of the state employees. But, with $10 billion of spending and a $5.7 billion deficit, the state had only half of the money it needed to do those things. Half.

It never should have gotten to this crisis point, Grant thought. The policy wonks at WAB told Grant that if the state would have just spent at historically normal levels for the past six years, there wouldn't be a deficit. But, during the boom years, the state was raking in the tax money — and spending even more than the record-setting amounts it was taking in. Spending kept growing faster than revenue, and when revenue stopped coming in, the spending actually went up. A lot. Besides the increases in "safety net" spending, the other reason that spending kept going up was that, unlike the private sector, government spending was not a one-time thing. Once a program was created, it had to continue being funded, and each year the budget for it went up. It was called "baseline budgeting" which meant that one year's spending was the "baseline," and an increase for the next year was required. To reduce the increase was a "cut." And voters hated "cuts" even if the cut was just slower growth in spending, not an actual cut. This stupidity was only possible with masses of brainwashed people.

The biggest reason spending went up so fast was that the state kept saying "yes" to every state employee union it could. More pension money? Sure. State employees had the most generous pensions of anyone in the state. Want to get out of paying for any real portion of your health insurance? Sure.

In return, state employee unions would take millions of dollars from their members and donate the funds to the politicians who ran the state, and "negotiate" things like pensions and health insurance. It was theft.

But no one cared. Grant could not comprehend why people didn't care that they were being taxed so much, under the threat of going to jail, just so politicians could buy votes and keep their little politician jobs? How was this not obvious? He thought of it this way: If someone came to a person's house and said they needed to pay thousands of dollars a month — and if they didn't they'd be hauled off — so their neighbor can have plenty while they struggled, and they could simply end the monthly knock on the door by voting at the next election, why wouldn't everyone do that?

Because they were brainwashed. They seemed to chant like zombies, "Must fully fund education. Is for the children. State employees are underpaid. Must increase funding...." It was like mass hypnosis. It started in the public schools. Manda would come home and tell Grant what they "learned" in school and Grant would come unglued.

"So, Manda, what did you do at school today?" he asked her one time.

"In History we learned about the Depression," she said.

"What did they say about it?" he asked.

"That some FDR guy saved the country with new government programs," she said. "You need to spend money to get out of a depression. All those people getting the money spend it and that's good for the economy."

Grant gave her a quick overview of why that wasn't true. He found himself quoting Ludwig von Mises to her. It was going over her head.

"Sorry to go off, dear," Grant said, "it's just so frustrating that they're teaching this crap."

"That's OK," Manda said. "I just listen to what I need to know for the test. They've been wrong about just about everything in History and especially Social Studies. Remember when they said gun owners were dangerous? You own guns," she said pointing to Grant, "and you're not dangerous. I'm just trying to get a good grade. Don't worry Daddy. I'm not a little socialist." She smiled when she said that.

Manda got it. Grant remembered how appalled she was when he told her that her share of national debt was $150,000. She said, "That's payments I have to make on a house, except I don't get to live in it." Smart girl. She knew more about politics and fiscal matters than 95% of adults in government-loving Washington State.

Grant thought about the federal "stimulus" money that the feds had just stopped handing out to the state. For the bailout of Washington State alone, the feds created several billion dollars of debt just so the Governor and legislators wouldn't have to be uncomfortable around their union friends. What a great trade. An awkward moment at a cocktail party is such a horrible thing. Better to put another couple hundred bucks on Manda's $150,000 tab that she'd be paying for the rest of her life, with interest. That actually made sense to these people. And, once again, the majority of voters in the state applauded the politicians doing this for their "leadership." It was surreal. How could this be happening?

Grant wondered if this was really happening with the state, or if he was just getting bad information. He called Jeanie. She was still nice to him. She felt bad that she wasn't being principled but was, instead, keeping her government job. She had been dying to tell someone what was happening and was happy to fill him in.

When he called, he made sure she was in a place where she could talk without her co-workers overhearing. Jeanie described how the Governor called a big meeting of all the agency heads. That included Menlow, even though he was the separately elected State Auditor and a Republican (at least on paper). The state budget flowed through the Governor's Office, so they had control over the money. Jeanie went to the meeting with Menlow.

"It was crazy, Grant," she told him. "These people are absolutely terrified of what's coming. One of them, Montoya at Corrections, started crying. She said prisoners would have to be released. Lots of them. Some pretty bad ones, too." Jeanie was scared. She knew what it would mean for these animals to be in neighborhoods like hers.

Grant felt terrible. Not because of all the cuts; they were inevitable and spending never should have gotten so large that devastating cuts like this were necessary. No, Grant felt terrible that he was enjoying this so much.

What kind of asshole takes pleasure in this? Him. That's who. He couldn't control the warm joyous feeling he was having that this beast of government was wounded. It was wounded and couldn't hurt people as much, anymore. No more ruining Ed Oleos, Big Sams, or Joe Tantoris. The collapse was beginning. It was about damned time.

Then he felt guilty. How could he enjoy this? Seriously, prisoners released to terrorize communities. How was this good news? It wasn't. This was why Grant and a few others had been yelling at the top of their lungs for years that the state can't keep spending more and more money. When the federal stimulus money came in, everyone else cheered. Not Grant. He knew that postponing the necessary cuts would only make the day of reckoning harder. Much harder. Which it was. The warm joyous feeling wouldn't go away. Grant needed to try to be sympathetic.

"What about state employees?" Grant asked. "What kind of cuts will there be?" He was trying to keep the topic on things that affected her.

"No raises this year," she said. "No increases for the pensions. Furloughs for five days a year."

"How much will that save?" Grant asked.

"The Governor's Office thinks $98 million over two years," Jeanie said.

"That's a drop in the bucket when you're looking at $5.7 billion," Grant said.

"That's all they think the unions will tolerate," Jeanie said. Taxes would go up — way, way up — but there was a limit to what people could pay.

Jeanie added, "The state can't borrow any more money." Grant, who had become an expert on the state constitution from all the cases he worked on, knew why. The constitution limited state borrowing to 9% of tax revenue. Revenue was down, way down, and 9% of it wouldn't come close to the $5.7 billion.

Grant said, "The State of Washington has maxed out its credit card." That was quite an astounding statement.

It got worse. The $5.7 billion deficit and maxing out of the state's credit card was just the present problem. The problem for the next few years was the pensions as a huge wave of state employees would start retiring and collecting their pensions. The amount of the actual shortage in the state pension system was a closely guarded secret, but the rumor was that the deficit was about $20 billion, which was about two years of the state's entire discretionary spending. In just a few years, the pension checks would start bouncing, unless taxes were raised to levels so high that no one in their right minds would get up and go to work. There was no way to avoid this. Unless, of course, pension benefits were drastically reduced. Everyone knew that wouldn't happen. Retired union state employees were a huge voting block. The politicians would never do it willingly.

But, future events would force their hand. It was inevitable. Those greedy politician bastards created this system, knowing it would fail. They knew it, but they'd be out of office by the time it all fell apart.

After a long contemplative pause, Jeanie said, "Just about everyone I know is a state employee. Jim is. I am. Just about everyone in my neighborhood is."

"Same in my neighborhood," Grant said. He started mentally going up and down the houses on his street. He didn't know most of his neighbors' names, but, strangely, knew what agencies they worked for. The people on his cul-de-sac were the director of the Office of Women and Minority Business, the assistant state treasurer, a recently retired assistant director of the state education department, a biologist with the state game department, the soon-to-retire budget head of the Department of Ecology, and an administrative appeals judge. The only two private-sector families on the cul-de-sac were his family and the Spencers. That was it. Obviously, Olympia was different than other places because it was the state capitol. But still.

Grant started to think what would happen if the state had to lay off a third or half of them or if paychecks started to bounce. What would the people on his street do?

They would freak out. Big time. They would be stunned at first, and then they would get angry at the taxpayers who hadn't allowed taxes to keep going up to fund their jobs. Grant remembered Sean, the Governor's legislative director's statement, "That's our money. We need it."

The people in Grant's neighborhood would get desperate, because all they knew how to do was government work, and if they were unemployed then several hundred thousand others would be too, and the tiny number of private-sector jobs left would have long lines of applicants. If the state checks stopped coming, these people were totally screwed. They would assume that there would be government programs for them like mortgage assistance and utility bill reductions. But that wasn't likely. If there wasn't enough money to pay state employees, there wouldn't be enough to give everyone handouts. This was real. The State of Washington could collapse.

There was that joyous warmth again. Collapse is what is needed. Not wanted, but needed. Grant thought about the years of work he and people at WAB had done to predict that spending was out of control and that something needed to be done or the sudden and drastic cuts would be devastating. No one listened. In fact, they mocked people like him sounding the alarm.

A collapse would be awful, but there was no political way to trim spending and get the government back into the role it was supposed to have: doing a few things well, like police protection, but not becoming bigger than the private sector. However, the system was dysfunctional. It was out of control. Some furloughs and no raises was all the system could do to plug a hole of half the money it could spend. It couldn't borrow any more money.

Grant whispered, "It's finally happening."

Jeanie was still silent on the other end of the phone.

He felt like he was watching a car crash, but smiling at the same time because he told the driver a thousand times not to drive on the wrong side of the road. He was feeling horror and "I told you so" at the same time. Like the impending car crash, Grant couldn't do anything about it; not a thing. All he could do was be sure that he wasn't in the car when it crashed. He couldn't save the people who had decided to do really stupid things over and over again. He had tried. All he could do was watch. Then it would be up to him to render first aid and clean up the wreckage. He would clean up after the mess because he had to, but the whole time he would be shaking his head and muttering, "Dumb asses."

Grant started thinking about the part about him not being in the car when it crashed. He had taken steps, at the risk of his wife finding out and being furious, to take care of his family and shield them from the coming collapse. He thought about the food, the cabin, the guns, and the network of people with vital skills. His family was taken care of because he got off his ass and did it. He was a man. He took care of his family. That made him smile.

Chapter 32

You Done Good

In the middle of this budget crisis and political gloom, Grant had an escape; his cabin. He went out there every chance he got.

The only thing better than being at his cabin was being there with friends and family. Manda came out all the time and Cole was out there pretty regularly. Lisa came out when they had family friends out.

Grant loved having his friends out there, but limited the ones he invited. He didn't want too many people to know where the cabin was. He certainly didn't show them the food and ammo.

One of his first "guy's weekend" guests was Steve Briggs from Forks. Grant wanted to show Steve how cool the cabin was, and drink a lot of beer.

Steve came out one glorious June day. It was seventy-five degrees and sunny.

When he drove up, Steve rolled down his window and said "Whoa. You done good."

Grant gave him the tour and they sat in comfy lounge chairs on the deck and drank for a few hours. They had a long conversation about Forks, all the Civil Air Patrol stories, leaving Forks, and the time Steve saved Grant's life on Goat Island.

During their conversation, the topic turned to the seemingly inevitable collapse. It all started when Steve said the same phrase he said in Forks years earlier that got Grant prepping.

"This is a false economy," he said when he was talking about how all the car parts at his store were made in China and arrived through a just-in-time inventory system. This was Grant's opportunity to have "the conversation" with Steve.

"What happens if the stock market crashes or whatever and people don't have Doritos?" Grant asked.

Steve smiled. "If the shit hits the fan, and Forks isn't safe, we come here. You probably have a firearm or two for me." Perfect. Steve got it. "And if Olympia or this place isn't safe, then you come to Forks. I've got a firearm or two for you."

"Roger that," Grant said as he finished off his umpteenth beer. God, it was great to have friends like Steve. The next day, when Steve left, Grant felt that they were even closer friends than when he had arrived.

Chip was another friend that Grant knew he could trust, and he wanted to invite him to the cabin.

He went into Capitol City Guns and, when Chip was out of the earshot of the others, Grant said, "Hey, man, you need to come out to my cabin. Free beer. There's something I want to show you. How about Sunday?"

"Sounds great," Chip said.

"Don't let this out," Grant said. "I don't advertise that I have this place."

"Why might that be?" Chip asked. "This wouldn't be a hideout, would it?" He was grinning.

That Sunday, Chip drove up in his truck. "This is perfect," he said to Grant. "How cool. Very nice." That was music to Grant's ears.

"Let me give you the tour," Grant said.

Chip motioned to the back of the truck. "I need to get my friends inside." Chip pulled out two cases of beer. "They don't like the warm air. They need to be somewhere cooler."

This was going to be a good day.

They brought the beer inside. Chip looked around. "This place is nice. A guy could live here year round no problem."

"Yep," Grant said with a big smile.

Grant opened a beer for Chip and one for himself. He looked Chip right in the eyes and said, "Can you keep a secret?"

Chip looked back at him very seriously and whispered, "You're gay, too?" And then laughed.

"No, something even more socially frowned upon," Grant said. "I'm a 'survivalist.'"

"No shit," Chip said, pretending to be serious. "You mean all those ARs, AK, and Glocks. All the stories about how corrupt the government is. All your excitement about having a 'bug out location?'" Chip faked surprise and said, "You are a survivalist? Who saw that coming?" He laughed. "So let's see the stash, Bunker Boy."

Grant showed him the food in the storage shed. "Impressive," Chip said. "I recognize some of those cases of MREs. I'll get you some more when Special Forces Ted comes by. I like to see that they have a nice home like this."

Grant showed Chip the basement and took him down to the

beach. They sat in the chairs on the bulkhead and drank beer. Grant brought down a half rack in an iced cooler. They peed off the bulkhead into the water. "That's livin'," Grant said. Chip nodded and concentrated on relieving himself.

After they were good and buzzed, Grant decided it was time to have "the conversation" with Chip. It would be the short version, since Chip already knew what was going on.

"Chip, when the shit hits the fan," Grant started to say.

"I'm coming here," Chip said, finishing Grant's sentence. "I'll bring all the food and gear I can. Done."

That was easy.

"I will have a special role for you and this place," Grant said. He pointed back up toward the cabin. "You know that unfinished basement. It could store a lot of stuff. If they ever try to outlaw guns and you 'lose' some of yours, you could keep them here."

"Way ahead of you partner," Chip said. "Already thought of that when you showed it to me. All I need is a spare key."

"There's one under that big rock," Grant said pointing to a rock near the bulkhead.

"Roger that," Chip said. He paused, realizing the implications of what they were saying. He didn't want to dwell on it. He didn't want to acknowledge to himself how serious this was. He wanted to think things would be OK and Grant's cabin would just be a place to sit on the beach and drink beer, not a hideout when shit hit the fan.

Chapter 33

Conditions Worsen

That summer, things changed quickly. In just a few days, everything that had been building suddenly erupted.

As bad as things were in Washington State, they were worse in California. Their spending was totally out of control. The state had so much debt that it couldn't possibly pay it back.

Finally, reality caught up with the utopians running California. When their latest bond issue didn't sell, it was time, finally, to make cuts.

A third of state employees were laid off. Half of the prisoners were released. They tried to limit the releases to "non-violent" criminals. But many of them went on horrific rampages. Of course, gun ownership was restricted in California, so the criminals didn't have to worry much about decent people stopping them. Too many Californians found out that the ban on magazines holding more than ten rounds was a real problem when four gang bangers were busting down their front door. Those extra few rounds would have come in handy.

There weren't many police around, either. Many had been laid off. It was a summer of crime and disbelief in California. Most people were so oblivious in California that they had no idea what was coming.

One of the biggest shocks was when the welfare payments stopped coming. With the massive budget cuts, many people lost welfare all together and those who still got it had much less on their prepaid debit cards. The well-organized welfare groups started massive protests, and many turned violent. Push-and-shoving kind of violence, maybe a few broken windows at government buildings. That was all (in the beginning).

Grant was glued to the TV watching the California protests. Everything was playing out exactly like he thought it would, which scared him because that meant he knew what else was coming.

It was happening so fast and people were so glued to the TV. Many went to work one day and so much happened by the time they got home that they felt like they couldn't keep up with the all the new events.

Grant didn't even try to talk to Lisa about all this. She might get mad at him again for being an alarmist. Besides, he didn't want to "overreact" and lose credibility with her. The California crisis was the elephant in the room in the Matson household. Grant would turn off the TV when Lisa was around. He didn't want her to know how closely he was following it.

He could watch all the TV he wanted at WAB. No one was getting any work done there. People at the office just stood in front of the TV in Tom's office. They were in shock. While they knew the spending was unsustainable, they still couldn't believe a collapse appeared to be happening. WAB people didn't want to say out loud what they feared. It was weird. It was the biggest news since 9/11, but no one was talking about it much. They were trying to appear calm. They weren't doing anything to prepare; they were just sitting there in shock.

Watching the news at WAB, Grant looked at crowds of welfare protestors on TV. Quite a few of the protesters were minorities. Many of them seemed to be here illegally. Some people were tempted to make this a racial thing.

But the racists were wrong. Grant thought about the whole country, not just California. He realized that just about everyone, including whites was dependent on the government one way or the other. Contractors needed government projects. People of all colors were on "disability" and didn't work. Accountants, most of whom were white, made a living by navigating clients through the bizarre maze of the state tax laws. Engineers were hired to prepare useless environmental impact statements for every little construction or home remodeling project. Farmers collected subsidies. And on, and on, and on.

Not only were the racists wrong, they were part of the problem. The government benefitted by having everyone divided. It wasn't a conspiracy; it was simple politics. Racists, of all colors, fit right into the agenda of dividing people. When the Mexicans were mad at the whites, and the whites were mad at the blacks, who hated the Asians, everyone became distracted by their racial grievances. The color of a person's skin was so much easier to focus on rather than complex things like baseline budgeting or unfunded pension liabilities. It was much easier for one group to say to their people, "Hate those other people." Politicians and fear mongers could use hate to motivate people to keep fighting each other. It wasn't just white racists, of course. Mexican and black racists very effectively stirred up hate against whites. By fighting each other, people weren't looking at the big picture. They were overlooking the out-of-control spending and taking the easy way out of everything. When things got hard, there were new government programs, and new cushy government jobs. People were taking the easy way out so much that they nearly quit being Americans. It was almost like the country decided it didn't want to be America anymore.

Some portion of the population wanted America back. They wanted to work hard and keep most of what they earned. They wanted to be free and were willing to take the bumps in life that came from being free. They wanted to be self-reliant and live honorably. They were the Patriots.

Patriots all across the country were coming out of their shells. Normally, they were a very quiet group of hard-working people who were busy raising families; however the Patriots realized their country was very close to disappearing. They woke up. Fast.

One of the things that woke them up was the fact that Mexico was starting up a full-scale civil war. The drug lords who had been effectively running the border areas of Mexico decided to take over the whole corrupt country. It was bloody. Thousands of killings; many of them beheadings. The drug gangs were extremely sophisticated armies. They were better armed than the Mexican Army (actually, the Mexican Army sold most of its arms to the drug lords so they had the same weaponry). The drug gangs were ruthless and had something the Mexican Army did not: sacks of money. By selling their product in the U.S., the drug gangs could raise billions of dollars, which buys a lot of friends, such as entire Mexican Army units that would defect.

The drug gang leaders were well read. They knew from Mao's writings on guerilla warfare that they had to effectively administer the areas they took over. The Mexican government was a corrupt joke. It couldn't keep the electricity and water running. The drug gangs did. They would behead anyone who got in their way. If they ordered that the people would have electricity and water, and heads would literally roll if that didn't happen.

Taking care of basic government services like utilities didn't mean the drug gangs were nice. They were vicious animals, pure evil. But, they were effective at governing and they had a lot of support from the population. Whether it was fear or genuine loyalty, it was still support. The gangs would provide the government services that a corrupt government could not.

The horrific violence sent a flood of refugees into the U.S. Many went right into California, which was essentially shut down with all the protests and crime waves. Arizona, New Mexico, and Texas were also hit hard by the human tidal wave coming into their states. Grant thought of "human tidal wave" as a cliché until he saw a satellite image on the news showing a literal wave of human beings flooding the U.S. border. They were hungry and needed shelter. They were human beings and had to be helped.

The U.S. Government and a few private organizations set up refugee centers in California, Arizona, New Mexico, and Texas. With so many Hispanics in the U.S., many Americans had a personal connection to the refugees and everyone was trying to help. There were still plenty of decent people in this country.

The images on TV were unbelievable. It reminded Grant of the Albanian refugees in the Balkan War of the 1990s — except it was here in America. Hundreds of thousands of Mexican women, children, and elderly were dying of thirst, starvation, exhaustion, and cholera. It made Katrina look like a mild rainstorm.

Of course, the government screwed it up. It could not act quickly enough. In Texas, FEMA spent time trying to get environmental approvals for shelters while children were dying. A particularly powerful photograph that became famous showed a middle-aged white man in a FEMA truck on a cell phone with a dead child lying on the ground near him. He was apparently on the phone with the EPA trying to get a waiver to locate the food, water, and medical supplies for that child and about two million more people.

People were outraged. How could the government, that supposedly was the solution to every problem, not have a plan for this? The Mexican drug wars had been going on strong for years; the fall of the Mexican government could not have been a surprise. Why didn't the government have a plan for the inevitable wave of refugees? The U.S. was the richest nation in the world, but it didn't have bottled water and tents for people? People paid almost half their money to the government in taxes, but FEMA didn't have money for bottled water? Everyone saw, very graphically, that the government was absolutely incapable of taking care of them in a disaster. It was just like in Katrina, but on a much bigger scale. And, just like Katrina, the government's response to this crisis woke up some people about their incompetence. The Mexican refugee crisis woke up even more people than Katrina did, however.

Hispanics were even more outraged. What they saw was a bunch of white people who weren't helping a bunch of brown people. Hispanic groups charged the government with racism, which was preposterous. It wasn't racism; it was incompetence. Now several million Hispanics in America were convinced that the U.S. Government and all Americans hated them and wanted them dead. Membership in anti-white Hispanic race groups like La Raza, which was Spanish for "the Race," surged. This was exactly how racists of all colors used race and hatred for their political agendas.

Not all the refugees were children, women, and old people. Some were hardened criminals. Some of the Mexican gang members not fit for combat, like young boys and older men went up north with the waves of refugees. There was no better opportunity to transport gang members into the U.S. than by riding the human wave across the border. The criminals preyed on the refugees, raping women and children and stealing supplies. This was captured on TV, too. With the government incapable of doing anything about it.

Not only was the U.S. Government incapable of helping refugees, it was also incapable of protecting its own citizens from some very nasty people. Many of the gang members coming across the border linked up with their brethren who had just been released from the jails. They created "super gangs," which were very large, well-armed, and highly sophisticated criminal enterprises. They were closer to a military unit than a traditional street gang.

In the span of a few days, most people in America realized that they were helpless if something like that happened in their area. But, after decades of thinking nothing bad could ever happen in America, most Americans still could not bring themselves to believe that it would happen to them. The refugee crisis and violence was still far away in California and Texas; not their neighborhoods.

Despite everything going on, many people still did not recognize how dependent and vulnerable they were. Instead, many of them became paralyzed by fear and did nothing. Very few Americans started preparing like they knew they should. They sat around their TVs stunned and helpless.

Texas responded to the crisis differently than California. Texas took its status as a formerly independent republic very seriously. About two days into the mess, the Governor of Texas held a press conference and said what would become famous words, "If the Federal Government can't restore law and order to Texas, then Texas will. We entered this union of states voluntarily and we can voluntarily leave it.

And from what I've seen, the Federal Government can't do much of anything right, so we don't think they can stop us. Texas will take care of Texans. Period."

This secessionist passion had been slowly building for years in Texas, but now, with the Feds screwing up so clearly, it was finally coming to the surface for many people.

One of them was Bill Owens, Grant's friend from law school who lived in San Antonio. He had settled there at a nice law firm and served in the Texas National Guard as a Judge Advocate General (JAG) officer, which is a military lawyer.

Before the Mexican crisis, Bill called Grant periodically and told him how people down there were sick of the federal mandates and the federal taxes; basically, the federal everything. Entrepreneurs and freedom-loving people from all over America were moving to Texas. The taxes were far lower and the business climate was markedly better than anywhere else in the U.S., especially on the East Coast and California where small business was almost impossible. Texas welcomed businesses.

Crime was astonishingly lower in Texas, too. That was because Texas gun laws allowed, even encouraged, citizens to carry concealed handguns. Very often, an armed robber would enter a store in Texas only to be stopped by armed customers and store clerks. The same was true of burglars breaking into homes. Killing one burglar led to dozens of fewer crimes that burglar would have committed. It also led to fewer people who wanted to be burglars.

How did the progressives in the North react? By calling the Texans "cowboys" and Texas the "shoot-em-up wild West." They referred to the armed robbers as "victims of gun violence." It was like there two versions of America: Texas and the North.

Southern and western mountain states were moving in varying degrees toward the Texas model because it worked. Northeastern and upper Midwest states and the West Coast (including Washington State) were moving toward the Northern model. There was a split, which was widening. Confederate flags started popping up everywhere.

Grant never liked the Confederate flag. He respected Southerners' right to fly it and be proud of the many Southerners who served bravely in the Civil War. He knew that the Union Army and the Federal Government during Reconstruction were not exactly the angels that they had been portrayed as in the history books. He knew that Southerners were not all racists. In fact, Grant knew that most Southern whites were generally fine with minorities because they lived among them. Many Southerners (of all colors) were Christians who believed that people of every race were the children of God and should be respected as such. Sure, there was still some racism in the South, but it was nothing like the stereotypes of racist Southerners portrayed by the North.

Grant had never known or even heard of a Southerner who thought slavery was a good idea. But the Confederate flag said something nasty to Grant. That symbol had become a symbol of racism. Try as he might, he couldn't get past the negative image he had of that flag.

The yellow Revolutionary War "Don't Tread on Me" flag was far better. Sometimes called the "Gadsden flag," the "Don't Tread on Me" flag communicated the liberty of the Revolutionary War without any of the racial baggage. The Tea Party had successfully adopted "Don't Tread on Me" as its symbol. Of course, the progressive media tried to make "Don't Tread on Me" into the new Confederate flag and imply that only racists flew the Gadsden.

Bill Owens called Grant from Texas during the refugee crisis.

"Things are getting dicey down here, man," Bill said. "Mexican gangs are doing some pretty bold stuff. People are on edge. I've got all my mags loaded. I sleep with my 12 gauge nearby. People are starting to openly carry handguns and even long guns. All people can talk about is how much the Feds suck. If I need to get out of here, can I come up to you?" Bill was an officer in the Texas Guard so he should probably stay in Texas, but it never hurt to have a backup plan.

"Of course, man," Grant said, trying to take in all this news. It's really happening, he thought. "But I think things will be difficult up here, too. Soon," Grant said to Bill. Then they talked about the logistics of keeping in contact and deciding if Bill's family should come up or if the Matsons should come down. Grant kept thinking about what a hard sell he would have with Lisa. "Hey," Grant would have to say to Lisa, "Let's evacuate to the Free Republic of Texas."

"Have you lost your mind?" she would scream. Oh, what fun times they were in.

Grant had one of those moments when he didn't know if he was in the present or the future. Things were happening exactly as he thought they would. Was it happening now or was he seeing the future? He couldn't tell. Perhaps it was both.

"Who were you talking to?" Lisa asked him.

"Oh, Bill in San Antonio," Grant said as if nothing were wrong. "Sandy says 'hi.'" Bill's wife and Lisa were friends back when Grant and Bill were in law school.

"Are things OK for them down there?" she asked, in her first mention of the Mexican crisis. She must have seen something on TV about it.

"They're taking some precautions," Grant said casually. "I told them they could come up here if need be," he said, wondering what her reaction would be.

"Sure. If they want to," Lisa said. To her, the issue was a visit with old friends instead of people fleeing chaos and violence.

Bill and Sandy fleeing Texas wasn't a visit with old friends to Grant. It was proof that a collapse was happening. Grant wondered if he was overreacting.

Chapter 34

People Get What They Deserve

Grant was driving to work and listening to the radio. At the top of the hour, the news came on. As interested as he was in the California and Mexican crises, he was actually getting a little tired of all the 24/7 coverage of it. He was having crisis fatigue.

He was hardly paying attention to the radio news announcer when she said nonchalantly, "The nation's credit rating has been lowered again. Moodys and Standard and Poors, which rate stocks and bonds, have lowered the U.S. bond rating ..." blah, blah, blah. The U.S. Government's bond rating had been lowered earlier from AAA to AA. This was yet another downgrade, now from AA to A.

The radio news went on, "Experts predict that Uncle Sam's cost of borrowing money will go up yet again. In other news ..." This meant that Moody and Standard and Poors were telling investors that buying bonds from the U.S., loaning money to the U.S. for it to spend on unsustainable social programs, was no longer a safe investment. Grant knew what this meant. Collapse.

The bond rating was a really big deal. It meant that investors, like the Chinese, would be even more reluctant to keep propping up the U.S. Government by buying U.S. bonds, which is, in effect, loaning money to the U.S. Government. It had always been only a matter of time until the Chinese came to this conclusion, but it looked like that day had arrived.

"Today," Grant said to himself. This was it. The lowering of the bond rating would mean a sell-off of U.S. bonds. The question was whether it would be instantaneous or dragged out for some time. The Federal Reserve would create more fake money with a few keyboard clicks to buy the bonds. This meant trillions of fresh dollars would flood into the system. Inflation would go up. Way up; the only question was how high. Would it be 1970s inflation of 10% or 1990s Russian inflation of 300%? Somewhere in between? Even 10% would be devastating.

The lower bond rating had another devastating effect on the

economy. The U.S. would need to raise the interest it paid on its bonds much, much higher to entice investors. Interest on the bonds had always been a percent or two. Now it might be 5%, 10%, or higher.

This meant the U.S. had to pay more (in inflated, made-up dollars) to borrow money. This added fuel to the inflation fire. It also meant the amount of interest people in the U.S. paid would go way up. Many private loans for houses and other things were based on the U.S. bond interest rate; when it went up, so did interest on mortgages, credit cards, and everything else. This alone would grind the economy to a halt.

The stock market crashed about five minutes after the announcement of the second bond downgrade. The downgrade, coupled with the fact that the U.S. Government had basically lost control of its Southern border, led to a massive sell off. The stock market went down 900 points before trading was suspended. Gold went up 50% in about ten minutes. People were in a full panic.

Grant had long ago written off his 401(k). He knew those investments would be worthless; he just wished that Lisa had realized it. Right then, in those few moments after Grant heard the news on the radio, a good chunk of the Matsons' life savings had just been wiped out. Exactly like he knew it would. It was weird. His reaction was a big, fat "I told you so" instead of the horror of losing his life savings. He had known this was coming with such certainty that he had long ago gotten over the anger at potentially losing his savings.

Grant kept telling himself not to gloat. Telling Lisa "I told you so" would only make her more angry. He needed her to view him as resource, not an enemy. He would be asking her to do things she didn't want to do in the next few hours, days, and months. He needed her on his team. Besides, being a dick and saying, "I told you so" wouldn't get their money back.

There was that warm joy again. He had food, a secure place out in the country, guns, and a network of trusted people with skills. They would probably be fine. At least, compared to others. The rest of the country wouldn't be, but a few people like him would be.

Besides — here came that rush of the warm joy — this had to happen. Things couldn't keep going on like they had been. Grant didn't want all the bad things to happen to the mostly innocent people out there, but he knew that it was the only way things would change. Those people had their chance over and over again to stop living like they were. To stop taking the easy way out. To stop looking the other way as other people's rights were taken away. To stop spending money they didn't have.

Grant thought about the people who sat back and let all this happen. Grant tried to explain to them what would happen, but they wouldn't listen. They thought he and others warning of a collapse were crazy.

"People get what they deserve," Grant finally said out loud in the car. He felt guilty for thinking it, but he couldn't deny his sentiment.

It was time to activate the preparation plans. He had already developed two basic plans: one for an immediate crisis like an earthquake, and another for things that would take a few days, or even weeks, to fully unfold. This was a slowly developing crisis.

Given that there was some time to get the final touches put together, there was no need to freak out and start loading guns. That would only scare Lisa and might get him a visit from the Olympia police. No need for that. Stick to the plan, he told himself.

Since he had plenty of supplies out at the cabin, his plan centered on convincing Lisa that they needed to go out there. She wouldn't see any need to go right away. She'd think it was just some dip in the stock market. That happens all the time. Why run off to the countryside over that?

Grant thought about how Lisa would be reacting to this so he could tailor the best approach to fit her concerns. She would not want Grant to overreact; that would be her primary concern. This was no big deal, she would think. The stock market was just having a "correction." It sucked to lose the money, of course, but the stock market would come back. OK, play the hand you've been dealt, Grant thought. Be supportive of her.

Grant thought about Lisa's level of awareness of the situation to decide how to convince her based on that. She did not know how bad things really were. That was probably better for her, given how angrily she reacted to his "doom and gloom." He needed to break it to her slowly; there was no sense overwhelming her.

He called her on her cell phone at work. She answered right away, which wasn't always the case because she worked in the ER.

"Have you heard about the stock market?" he asked.

"No," she said, wondering why he was calling her at work. "Did it go up?"

He told her what had happened. Not the part about the bond rating being lowered. Not yet, at least. He was in supportive husband mode right now.

213

"I'm calling to see if there is anything you think we should do right away," he said. "I'm not suggesting we sell all our stocks, which we couldn't do anyway, given that the market has shut down, but just wanted to see how you wanted to approach this together. I'm at work, but can do things like move money around if you need me to."

He was sure that Lisa was relieved that Mr. Gloom and Doom, who had said a few years ago that this would happen, wasn't saying "I told you so" or freaking out about buying gold now when the price was so high. He knew that she appreciated that he wanted to work together to determine whether to move money around various funds instead of preaching at her.

"No," Lisa said, "I can't think of anything we need to do. It will work out."

"See you tonight at home, dear," Grant said, being the supportive and non-overreacting husband that he was.

Grant got into his car and proceeded to "overreact." He went out to invest in something as valuable as gold; actually, something more valuable than gold. He headed to Cash n' Carry.

He wasn't the only one who had the idea to go to Cash n' Carry. The parking lot was full, but it wasn't a mob scene. It was just a busy shopping day. Most of the world was still oblivious, unaware of what was likely to happen. They were going about their day wondering who would win whatever stupid reality show they watched that night. Grant hated to have such elitist thoughts — he had always thought of himself as a regular guy, a country boy — but he couldn't help but think how much of the population was utterly stupid about all of this. He hated thinking it, but the evidence supported that conclusion. For example, the Cash n' Carry parking lot was not full after all of this news.

It was an interesting cross section of humanity at Cash n' Carry. Some people, like Grant, were well dressed professionals. There were older, middle-aged, and younger people. Lots of kids in tow. Lots of immigrants. It seemed that many immigrants owned restaurants and got their supplies at Cash n' Carry. There were also what appeared to be members of religious sects. Some of the women there, who had about a zillion kids, donned bonnets and wore dresses straight out of the old West. They looked like the people rescued from a polygamist compound or Amish sect that had permission to drive cars to Cash n' Carry. Grant didn't know what religion they were, but they definitely were not the average suburbanites.

All the preppers in the store assumed they were the only ones

214

in a panic stocking up on food. They didn't want to tip off the others about what they were up to. They were trying to leave the impression that it was just another shopping errand, but they weren't acting like it. They had big carts and were throwing fifty pound bags of rice and beans in them without thinking. They didn't have shopping lists.

Neither did Grant. He knew what he needed. He would get more of the foods that met his criteria of requiring only water to cook or being ready to eat, storing for long periods of time, being cheap, and being liked by his family. More pancake mix, pasta, biscuit mix, mashed potato mix, peanut butter, canned fruit, beans, rice, drink mix, and gravy mix.

People were strangely silent in the checkout line. They weren't looking at each other's carts. They just stared ahead, not wanting to pry into other people's business. They were trying to buy all that food anonymously and assumed everyone else was, too. It was like they were buying something embarrassing like lingerie. Grant chuckled to himself. Buying food before everyone else figured out that they should do the same was something to be embarrassed about?

As the name implied, Cash n' Carry only accepted cash and didn't provide help out. That kept costs down. Grant had $320 in the expense-check envelope. He breathed a sigh of relief. Having cash on hand at all times was one of the reasons he kept the cash in the car. Sure, it could get stolen in his car, but it was worth the risk to have a few hundred dollars available when circumstances called for it.

Grant's bill came to $295. He had about three months of basic food for his family for that amount. Grant paid his cash and loaded his bounty in the car.

He stuffed the trunk and the back seat. He wished he had a pickup truck, but Lisa would have flipped out. Oh well, play the hand you're dealt. Instead of getting mad about not having a pickup truck, have a plan and execute it; go to Cash n' Carry when the stock market crashes, load up your food, and take it to your cabin. He was doing far better than a man with a pickup truck who didn't have a plan.

It was 10:00 a.m. on Wednesday as Grant headed out to the cabin. He thought about what average people were doing right then. They were at their white-collar jobs shuffling paper (actually, trading emails). They would be oblivious to all that was happening. They would eat lunch that came from just-in-time-inventory and had been taken to the store by a semi-truck. They would drive home in cars using gasoline that was also delivered by big trucks.

When they got home, they might turn on the network news

that would mention something about some bonds and that FEMA was working hard to help the refugees. They would eat more just-in-time-inventoried food for dinner, probably way more than they needed to eat. They would watch reality shows on TV or surf the internet. They would fall asleep in a safe neighborhood because there was someone to answer any 911 call that might come in.

In a few days, they would hear on the news that "Tea Party" people were upset about some bond rating thing. Quite a few of them would dismiss whatever it was that the "teabaggers" were mad at because they were just ignorant racists. Then they would go about their lives like they always had.

Grant kept driving to the cabin. It was a beautiful drive. The farther away he got from Olympia, the more beautiful it got. The water. The trees. The little farms in Pierce Point. It was a different world than Grasshopperville that he just left. "Grasshooper" referred to the story of the ant and the grasshopper. In the story, the ant works hard all summer gathering food while the grasshopper played; in the winter, the ant is fine, but the grasshopper dies. "Grasshopper" became a term for those who goof off and don't prepare for the inevitable bad times.

Although he trusted his neighbors, the Colsons and Morrells, Grant looked around to make sure they wouldn't see him unload all his food into the storage shed. The Colsons did not appear to be home. The Morrells' truck and car were there, but they weren't stirring.

Stealth time. Grant quietly and quickly unloaded the food into the shed. He wouldn't bother vacuum sealing it now; he just had to get it into the shed. He thought he would be using this food in the next few months, weeks, or even days.

Grant didn't have any rats or other threats to his food in the shed, but he put on his mental list the need to get more thick plastic tubs for the food. He remembered that he had a new, and extremely tough, plastic garbage can in the basement that had never been used. It would be perfect. It stored a tremendous amount of the food; the only thing that didn't fit was the fifty-pound bags of rice and beans.

Grant was in and out of the cabin in ten minutes. He zoomed back to his office. They might start missing him soon. He had a taping of Rebel Radio in a little while and he might be late.

He actually felt guilty about skipping work for the Cash n' Carry run — for about one second. That was that damned normalcy bias striking. Even a committed survivalist like Grant suffered from bouts of normalcy bias. He laughed to himself and thought about how utterly stupid it was to worry about taking a couple hours off for this.

He went to work to earn money to provide for his family. By going to Cash n' Carry and getting about three months of food, Grant was providing for his family, which was the ultimate purpose of working.

Normalcy bias was like fear in combat: It was OK to have it, but not OK to be paralyzed by it.

Driving back to Olympia, Grant kept looking for signs that others were preparing like him. He looked for a full parking lot at the grocery store on the way; it wasn't full. He looked for a full parking lot at the bank because surely people would want to withdraw cash right now; the parking lot looked normal. He was listening to the news station on the car radio. No mention of the bond rating. Lots of talk about the 900 point stock market drop. But, with reassuring comparisons to previous dips in the market. The message from the radio seemed to be: "Nothing to see here. Move along. Go back to work and keep putting your money into the stock market. Lots of good buying opportunities now. Gold? That's what crazy people buy."

Grant's cell phone rang. It was Bill Owens.

"Holy crap, did you hear about the bond rating?" Bill said. "I thought the Mexican refugee thing was big, but this is huge. How are things up there?"

Grant talked for a while about how no one up in Washington State seemed to be fazed by this. He talked about Lisa's non-reaction. It was time to have "the conversation" with Bill.

"Hey, Bill," Grant said, "you know that if you ever need to bug out of Texas you can come up here, but can you keep a secret? I mean a not-even-tell-your-wife secret?"

"Sure," Bill said. "Did you kill a hitchhiker or something?"

They laughed. "Something like that," Grant said. He went on to describe his cabin and the food and guns there.

Bill sounded relieved at Grant's revelation. "Not surprised a bit, Grant. I've been doing the same thing for a couple of years. Sandy is on board. I can store the food in the garage. She's cool with the guns. I was just about to tell you about my preps and invite you down here."

"Preps?" Bill had used a survivalist term. Interesting.

"Bill, did you just say 'preps'?" Grant asked.

"Yeah, it's a term for disaster preparations we use down here," Bill said. "Lots of people in my neighborhood have been stocking up on things for the past year or two. Now we're glad we did. At first we tried to hide it from each other but now we don't. We work together here in the neighborhood. When the Mexicans started flooding in, it was obvious to us that we needed to do things to be more self-reliant.

We have plans to secure the neighborhood if this shit continues, and it probably will. I feel sorry for those poor Mexicans and I would take in a family, but the government needs to control this. You should see what crime is here. Sandy has stopped going into work. So have I. I was going in for a while and carrying a gun. Now it's too risky to leave the house."

Bill continued, "But, looking on the bright side, the state of Texas is standing up to the Feds. The Governor has issued an executive order prohibiting all Texas state employees from assisting the federal government, even with the refugee crisis. That would include me, since I'm Texas Guard and under his command. Since he only has executive order authority over state employees, his order encouraged, but did not order, local government employees to do the same. State and local employees are to concentrate on state efforts to help the Mexicans. He also activated the Texas Guard, and reminded us and the public that he is their commander in chief, not the President."

Oh crap. Governors were in command of their state's National Guard, but they always formally or informally consulted with the federal government before they activated the Guard. Activating the National Guard over the protests of the federal government hadn't happened since... the Civil War.

Bill didn't tell Grant that he was active in the Oath Keepers. He didn't like talking about the possibility of refusing to obey unlawful orders. He hoped that wasn't coming. Bill knew what he would do if he were given an unlawful order, like one to seize Americans' guns. It would cost him his career, maybe his freedom, and possibly his life. Oh well. He had taken an oath to defend the Constitution against all enemies "foreign and domestic." He had not taken an oath to follow the orders of the President or even the Governor of Texas if they were acting unconstitutionally. Everyone had to choose which side they were on, and Bill Owens had made his choice.

Bill continued, "A guy on the cul-de-sac over from me is a cop. He said FEMA was a bunch of idiots. Their inept bureaucracy is getting tons of people killed. The Feds were in a complete panic and started seizing state and local vehicles and even some private ones. There are rumors the Feds are trying to take guns, but I can't believe they would be that stupid."

Oh God, Grant thought. It's happening.

"The San Antonio cops had enough," Bill said. "They are actually going out and repo'ing back vehicles the Feds took. Our sheriff was on TV reminding people that the Texas Constitution guaranteed their right to keep and bear arms and that his deputies would not be taking guns from law-abiding citizens."

Thank God. Grant's theory that plenty of cops would resist unconstitutional orders was panning out so far; at least in Texas.

"On top of running interference with the Feds," Bill said, "the cops are trying to keep up with all the crime. They're dealing with refugees stealing, and then homeowners shooting refugees, on accident or sometimes on purpose. Our home-grown criminals of all races are going on rampages. My neighbor said the Mexican gangs were attacking people in revenge for the treatment of the refugees. He thinks the gangs here are coordinating with their mother ship drug gangs in Mexico. It's a royal mess down here."

This was exactly what Grant had thought would happen, although the strong response from the Governor of Texas surprised him a little. This was getting creepy. He was scared that he could predict what would happen. It might sound cool to know what's going to happen, but it isn't. It's terrifying, especially when what this is what is predicted.

"Have you seen or heard any actual shooting?" Grant asked.

"Nope," Bill said. "Not yet. But there's plenty of shooting on TV, though. Everyone is on edge."

"Now doesn't sound like a great time for us to come down," Grant said.

"Nope," Bill said.

"You can come up here anytime you want," Grant said. "I've got the cabin for you. I might need to use it myself but we would make room for you. Any chance you could get out and get up here?"

"Nope," Bill said. "Travel is impossible now. The roads are choked with people trying to go north. Gasoline is running out. I'm surprised it lasted this long. People are buying up all the food and other supplies. I haven't even tried to go to the gun store, but I imagine those shelves are empty. I've got plenty, though, so I don't need any of that. I think we'll just wait it out in our neighborhood. We have some good old boys here who know how to take care of business."

It was silent for a while. Both men were trying to take it all in. They couldn't believe they were having this conversation.

Finally Bill said, "We'll help anyone we can as long as it's safe. But hungry and scared people, even women and children, will do crazy things to get food. We have to take care of ourselves first and others second. We can't help people if we're dead. And I don't plan on being dead."

There was a noise on Bill's end. "Hey, I gotta go. Roberto says I need to come over to his place." Grant vaguely remembered Bill referring to a neighbor of his named Roberto. "See ya, man. Be safe up there."

"You too," Grant said.

Click.

Chapter 35

Reality Check

Grant felt so alive; more alive than ever. It was a combination of excitement, thrill, fear, restlessness, and a need to do a thousand things at once. He knew this was the beginning of the most important time in his life. The decisions he made now would keep him and his family alive or get them killed. The stakes could not be any higher. He was ready for what he thought was coming, but he knew that things never turned out exactly like it is predicted they will. He knew there would be awful things ahead. He knew.

He needed to get Manda up to speed. She would be invaluable in convincing her mom to do things she didn't want to do.

Grant pulled into the Cedars. What a contrast from his cabin. His neighborhood was a pathetic collection of grasshoppers. Pathetic. After talking to Bill, Grant was envious of Bill's Texas neighborhood. Down there, they were pulling together, prepping openly, and having a neighborhood defense plan. He couldn't see that happening here. One of the reasons he was so thankful to have the cabin was that he knew how vulnerable they were in Cedars. His neighbors were oblivious.

Grant clicked the garage door opener and saw that Lisa was not home. Good. He could talk to Manda without having to whisper.

Cole saw him come in the house and said, "Hi, Dad. How was your day?" Cole was working hard on being conversational with people. He would ask the same handful of questions like that, along with "What does the weather look like outside?" He was doing well. He was working so hard. For Cole, talking and listening to people was the hardest thing in the world, so he had to force himself to be conversational because he wanted to be connected to people. God, Grant loved that little guy, though he was thirteen now and not so little. But he talked like a three year-old so it was still easy to think of him as a little kid.

"I had a bad day, little buddy," Grant said. "But I'm home with you so I'm having a good day now. Thanks for asking. How was your day?"

Cole thought a while. "It was fine, Dad." He was grinning from ear to ear. His dad was home. It was impossible not to love this kid.

"Awesome, little buddy," Grant said as he hugged Cole. "Is your sister home?"

"Why, yes, Dad," Cole said. "She's upstairs."

Grant went up to Manda's room. She was listening to her iPod.

"Hey, Dad, what's up?" Manda asked. She had no idea what had been happening. Grant envied the innocence of being a kid.

"Manda, our little plan might need to be activated," Grant said with as little concern as possible. "Not immediately, but long term." Grant was trying not to scare her.

She slowly pulled the iPod headphones off, looking very serious. She wasn't scared. She looked calm and confident. Like a grown up.

"OK, Dad, what's the situation?" she asked. That was a pretty mature thing for a sixteen year old to say.

Grant described the stock market and, more importantly, the bond rating. She had seen the news about the California and Mexico situations, but thought that was far away. She instantly understood why the bond rating and other crises were a problem. Grant told her about his phone call with Bill Owens.

"I don't expect the refugee problem to be affecting us all the way up here," Grant said. That was downplaying his concerns, but he didn't want to scare her unnecessarily. "The Federal Government is freaking out right now. They are losing control of Texas and probably California, Arizona, and New Mexico. This is a dangerous time because the feds might try to overreact."

Manda was taking it all in. He had never seen her so focused on what he was saying.

"I don't think we need to bug out right now," Grant continued. He didn't really believe that, but he was trying hard not to overreact so he told himself things like that. "Maybe we never need to. But we need to do as much now as possible, in advance, so we can leave on a moment's notice."

"I understand," Manda said. "What can I do to help?" Whoa. Did she just say that? The girl who never picked up her room was asking how she could help the family evacuate? Awesome. Evacuating was way more important than picking up her room.

"Start by getting all the stuff you need — I mean need, not just want — and making a list so you could throw it together quickly,"

Grant said. "Think about what you use every day."

"OK, Dad. I understand," Manda said. She was serious but also seemed relieved that her dad was taking care of her. She knew how hard this was on him, but he was doing whatever it took to protect her and Mom and her little brother.

"If I need to, I'll ask you to come and talk to Mom with me," Grant said. "Can you do that?" Grant knew what the answer would be.

"Of course," Manda said with a big smile. She realized that talking Mom into leaving was what she could do. Manda was proud to have an important role in all of this. "Mom needs to understand how much better off we'll be at the cabin than here."

Wow. Grant couldn't believe how Manda got this but her mom didn't.

She's on board. You did a good job, said the outside thought. He hadn't heard it in quite some time.

Keep doing what you're doing. That was reassuring.

Grant realized he was anxious to get this going. To get the Collapse going. How odd: hurry up and collapse. He was like the eccentric meteorologist who predicts snow in June, gets laughed at, and then sees the snowflakes and gets excited. Grant wanted the snow to come down. Hard.

Then he realized that he really didn't want the Collapse to come soon. He had plenty of things to get done before then. He was very well prepared, but even he could use more time to get everything together and do more. There was always more to do. No, Grant didn't really want the Collapse to come. He just knew it would.

The garage door went up signifying that Lisa was home. Great. Reality check. Time to quit thinking about the end of the world and return to being a supportive suburban husband. This double life thing was getting harder and harder as the Collapse approached.

Chapter 36

The Waitin' is the Hardest Part

Grant thought back to Civil Air Patrol right before they would go on a search for a downed plane. It was a combination of excitement and boredom. They were excited because they were about to do something big and possibly even dangerous. Something thrilling. But it was boring because they had so many tasks before they could go. Checking gear. Making sure their radios had batteries and they had the right frequencies. Having current maps. Making sure they had supplies, like food. Rounding up the search team and coordinating their transportation to the base. Then waiting. Just sitting there. Ready to go, but not going. "Hurry up and wait" they called it. The waiting was difficult because they were delayed from doing what they had been preparing so hard for.

Grant was feeling that same way now. He knew he would be doing many thrilling and dangerous things in the near future. He would be living his life fully in the next few weeks, months, maybe years.

This was what he had been preparing for. Since… well, childhood. Of course, he didn't know when he was a kid that a collapse was coming. But he could see the path of his life and how it led from Forks to Olympia. He grew up hard and had to toughen up. He knew how to live in a rural area; chopping wood, hunting, fishing, canning. Then he forgot all that and became a suburban guy, which was necessary for him to learn how to be a lawyer who could help people fight corruption. Then he married a doctor who would be able to save lots of people. He inherited a cabin in an area where his family could live when the city got too dangerous. He got on a pick-up team of civilian gunfighters. He met a Special Forces Oath Keeper. He got hooked up with a survival podcast and learned how to store food and a million other things. Then he had a front seat to the corruption and collapse of the state. He had inside knowledge on how bad things were. Yes, he had been preparing, knowingly or unknowingly, for this for his whole life. But now he had to wait.

Grant made great use of the time. He knew that the delay, as maddening as it was, actually helped him and his family. He knew that after the Collapse he would look back to before things fell apart and say, "I wish I would have had time to…." The delay was a blessing. It was just so hard to wait.

He focused on the uninteresting parts of prepping, like getting his documents in order. He rounded up the wills, birth certificates, passports, banking and credit records. He scanned them and put them on a thumb drive. He made sure the originals were in a safe deposit box at the bank. He had scanned the documents in case banks closed down for an extended period of time. It seemed reckless to keep the originals of those documents at his house; for all he knew, they would be bugging out of their house with no time to pack the documents. Besides, when everyone was cut off from the originals of their documents, banks and other institutions would just have to get used to copies instead of originals. There would be no other way to do business, if there would be any business to do.

Grant made sure he had at least one key for each lock he would need. He had about five keys to the cabin. He spread them out so that he could always have one. This included hiding one out at the cabin. It was like the can openers in the tubs of food; some critical things are useless without something to open them. He got a few new padlocks and set all their combinations to his family's house number so they could all easily remember it. He had to make duplicates of some keys and he did so. He tested the keys. Surprisingly some of the cabin keys didn't work. He was glad he found that out now instead of later.

He made some extremely accurate directions to the cabin in case Lisa had to come out on her own. Grant always drove when they went out there so maybe Lisa wouldn't know how to get there if she had to on her own. He planned alternate routes to the cabin. This was hard because, given the fact that Pierce Point was on an inlet, there was only one way in and out. But there were a few ways to the nearest town before the one-route-only road to Pierce Point started.

Grant wanted to make sure he had access to as much gasoline as possible. He knew that regular gas stations would run out. He had always noticed those gas-card stations that truckers used. They didn't have any attendants. Truckers needed a special card to use them and were billed directly. They were basically a members-only gas station. Perfect. Fewer people would be able to use them, so there might be more gas there. Grant found out that regular people could sign up for the cards. He got a couple of them for the various gas-card stations in his area and he mapped out where those stations were. They were off the beaten path, which was good.

He got on the Survival Podcast forum and drank in all the information he could. He printed out several helpful threads and web pages linked in the threads. He put a PDF of the military survival manual onto a thumb drive.

He wanted to make sure he got the little things that people forget about but then need when the stores are closed. He found a Survival Podcast forum thread called "The First 100 Things to Disappear in a Crisis." It was created by survivors of the Bosnian civil war. There were things on there he never would have thought of, like safety pins.

The whole time, Grant was glued to the TV. To his surprise, the lowered bond rating hadn't led to an immediate sell off of U.S. bonds and the crash that would result. He realized that he might have overestimated how quickly that would become a problem. Oh well. He was glad there was a little more time.

The Mexican refugee crisis was getting worse. The Mexican government officially collapsed and the drug gangs went on genocidal killing sprees. The estimates were that four million people were crossing the U.S. border. Texas and California, in particular, were totally paralyzed. There had been a lot of crime, but it still wasn't a full-on war. Bill Owens confirmed that during a phone call when they were checking in with each other.

"So how's it going down there, Bill?" Grant asked.

"Kinda dicey," Bill said. "I heard gunshots. Just a couple. They were far away. I had a little run-in at Costco, and had to draw my pistol on a guy. I was getting some bulk foods, like everyone else, and it came down to the last bag of beans. I went for it; I was the first one there. Some dirtbag lunged for it, too. I had to push him out of the way. He started yelling at me. I said some choice words. Store security came zooming in. Apparently they are jumping on things like this. They kicked both of us out of the store."

This was getting crazy, Grant thought. Decent people like Bill were fighting over the last bag of beans.

Bill continued, "I wasn't going to fight this guy over a bag of beans that someone else had already grabbed in the confusion. I was nervous going back to the parking lot because the dirtbag was right behind me heading out of the store. In the parking lot he yelled, 'Hey, you, those beans were mine. Come here and talk to me like a man.' I turned around and he was pulling something out of his sweatshirt pocket. I drew my 1911," that was Bill's .45 pistol, "and put the sights on his chest. I had practiced that a thousand times and it paid off; that was the smoothest draw I can remember. He put his hands up and said he was sorry. I didn't want the cops to come, if there were even any around. They're kind of busy now. So I looked around and no one was around so they didn't see me. I got in my truck and headed to the Sam's Club."

Wow. Bill had to pull a gun on a guy. "It was weird," Bill continued, "Never thought I'd have to do that. I got a feeling I'm going to be doing lots of things I never thought I would be. Glad I didn't have to shoot that guy."

While the TV was downplaying it, Bill confirmed that FEMA continued to completely screw up the relief efforts. People were starting to vandalize FEMA vehicles. Hispanic gangs were targeting FEMA personnel. FEMA workers were prohibited from carrying guns, so many of them quit. The feds had to finally give up on FEMA.

California federalized its National Guard, meaning that the supposedly state-controlled California National Guard was now under federal command. Then the Feds had the regular military join the effort. California was betting the Feds could rescue them.

Arizona joined Texas in basically kicking the Feds out of the state. Grant didn't know what New Mexico was doing. The Arizona and Texas Guards were running the relief efforts and doing a better job than the federal efforts in California. Interestingly, Arizona and Texas were calling their Guard units the "State Guard" instead of "National Guard." Things weren't going well for the Feds. The federal troops were much better than FEMA, but their orders were muddy: Don't shoot anyone, especially refugees, even when they were looting from civilians and civilians were shooting at them. It was like a peacekeeping mission in Lebanon; those never turned out well.

In contrast, the Texas and Arizona State Guards were given more realistic orders: shoot to defend yourself or others. This actually saved lives because looters and trigger-happy civilians knew that if they did anything aggressive they would be shot by the State Guard.

The Feds had just the opposite effect on looters and civilians. The looting went on while the California police, National Guard, and federal troops just watched. It was just like the LA Riots. But bigger. Much, much bigger.

It was weird, though. Even though there was full-on looting in California and the military was deployed, life went on as normal in some ways. People still went to work, although many stayed home.

People still visited Disneyland, but in smaller numbers. Disneyland during a riot! People in California still went out to dinner at trendy restaurants, although there was panic buying at the grocery stores. But the shelves weren't emptied out (at first). People were either oblivious — how was that possible? — or just assumed that the government would get things back to normal soon. The looting was like a snow storm. A hassle and a hindrance, but something that would be over in a while and things would return to normal.

Of course, the government wanted to show that everything was fine and normal in LA so people wouldn't get scared. The mainstream media had stories on how people were still going to the beach and how traffic was so much better now that fewer people were going to work. They even had stories on how the Hollywood stars were still going to premiers of movies. The message was unmistakable: Cool people are not fazed by whatever it is that's going on right now. Relax. Everything is fine.

Grant could not believe that people were not taking this seriously. How could people be so complacent and stupid? They had developed habits over years and years, and not even looting by thousands of starving refugees and gang warfare would break those habits. Life would go on. As long as people had their comfortable routines, everything was fine. Despite all the evidence.

Grant marveled at Americans' ability to shield out stress by doing their routines. It must be because there was something so comforting by being able to say, "Life goes on."

Many Californians secretly thought the violence was in "those" neighborhoods. It didn't affect people in the suburbs or upper income areas. The progressives in California were so tolerant and understanding that they just accepted the rioting. It was not directly affecting them.

Texas was a different story. People were not oblivious there. They were taking it seriously. Many were armed. They bought up all the groceries, gasoline, and ammunition they could. The shelves were bare, but not as many people were freaking out. They had their supplies and would wait until the stores were resupplied. In Eastern Texas, they were used to hurricanes, so this wasn't the end of the world.

Even though most Texans were fairly well prepared, resupply would take much longer than they expected, although it could have been worse. Resupply came via semi-trucks running on diesel and going along safe highways. The State Guard and law enforcement had the highways largely secure, and Texas drilled and refined its own petroleum. Texas refineries were getting a fair amount of fuel to gas stations, and grocery stores were getting the shelves restocked much better than in California. There were problems, of course, but it was not the surreal destruction that was going on in California.

In fact, after a week or so, things in Texas were going OK, overall. It was still a crisis, of course, but it was not the end of the world there.

Grant was getting frequent texts from Bill Owens. It was amazing how well texts worked, even in a crisis. Sometimes cell service for voice traffic would get too busy and shut down, but texting took up much less bandwidth and was not affected. Good to know, Grant thought.

Chapter 37

Annoying Lack of Collapse

Looking at California and Texas, and knowing that Washington State would be more like California, Grant started focusing even harder on his preps. Things were quickening. Events were moving faster.

One of Grant's biggest preparations was his physical conditioning. He had been in good shape since the end of the "Dockers Years." He was strong; stronger than he had ever been. But now, with the Collapse quickly unfolding right before his eyes, he was stepping it up one more notch. He knew, just knew, that soon he'd need to be carrying more, running, and enduring things that never cropped up in his suburban world. Now was the time to get strong enough for what was coming.

Right after the U.S. bond rating news, Grant frequently saw Jim, Jeanie's boyfriend, at the gym. He was getting in great shape, too. Was he a prepper? He had been the first to use the "R" word of "revolution" with Grant, so maybe he was.

One morning at the gym Grant asked him, "You've been here a lot lately. What's the deal?"

"My Guard unit is activating for our annual training," Jim said, "and we might do more than two weeks." The normal thing was for a two-week training period each year.

"I thought your unit did annual trainings in October every year for the annual computer security exercise," Grant said.

"Yep," Jim said. "We're activating early. The brass thinks something might be happening. Maybe we're going down to California." Jim paused and looked around to make sure no one else could hear him. "We're training for civil unrest. It's no secret." Some of the Oath Keepers at Capitol City Guns had told Grant that rumor, too. Jim confirmed it.

He looked a little embarrassed that he was training for civil unrest. Here was Mr. Revolution, but now he was meekly acknowledging that he was going to be part of the military unit presumably cracking down on civil unrest. What had changed?

Grant didn't ask, but as he pieced together bits of information from conversations he'd had with Jim and Jeanie, the answer was that Jim needed the job. With all the cuts in the number of state employees, Jim needed his Department of Revenue job and he needed the Guard job. He had to put his beliefs aside for the paycheck.

That's what happened to so many government employees. Most weren't evil and didn't want to do the things they were doing, but it was their job; their only job. They had to. Perhaps it was the higher-ups who were evil and power hungry. But the worker bees weren't. It was so sad.

"Be safe, my friend," Grant said. "I hope you can do some good out there." Grant was trying to make it easier on Jim.

"Thanks, man," Jim said, appreciating that Grant didn't get on him about shooting Americans.

This was getting crazy, Grant thought; a thought he had several times a day, lately. The Washington National Guard was activating. Quietly, under the guise of the annual training.

This was unfolding exactly as Grant thought it would. He was having that weird feeling again when he couldn't tell if he was in the present or the future.

With all the news and excitement swirling around, he had the strangest urge to call Steve Briggs back in Forks. Grant trusted his instincts more and more. He called Steve.

"Some crazy shit goin' on, huh?" Steve said. That was his country boy way of starting a conversation on current events.

"Yeah," Grant said. "I can't believe people aren't freaking out. But I went to Cash n' Carry yesterday and there weren't that many people in the parking lot. People don't get it. Or maybe I don't. I'm starting to wonder."

"Things are pretty mellow here," Steve said. "People are watching the news and talking about it. But folks are not making a run on the grocery store. Most people have their shit squared away. The welfare shitbags don't, but they're too stupid to watch the news or understand what it means, so they're not going and stocking up on smokes or Doritos. More for the rest of us," he said with a laugh.

That made sense. Rural people were usually less scared about things like this since they didn't depend on as many modern conveniences. Forks was still dependent on Highway 101, which connected it to the rest of the world. But, strangely, remote Forks wasn't as dependent as areas right in the metro area.

"Hey, Steve," Grant wondered, thinking about the auto parts

store where Steve was the manager, "have you seen any shortages of parts at the store?"

"Nope," he said. "So far things seem pretty normal. But, you're right, that's how we'll know if the wheels are coming off. Get it, car parts; the wheels coming off? That's how we'll know when the country is truly falling apart."

"I bet you country boys and girls will do just fine," Grant said.

"Yep," Steve said. "We're already talking about it. People are getting their hunting, fishing, and canning stuff together."

Grant asked Steve how Grant's mom was doing. "Pretty good," Steve said. Grant kept meaning to call her.

"Hey, man, I need to go," Steve said. "I've got a customer here. Take it easy, Grant."

"You too, Steve. Stay safe, brother."

Grant hung up with Steve and couldn't get his mind off the question of why people weren't taking these events as seriously as he was. He kept looking for signs of the Collapse. He would look in parking lots of grocery stores and banks, and look for lines at gas stations.

Nothing.

Don't be impatient. You will need the extra time to get ready.

True. But still. Grant was impatient. The impending Collapse was all he could think about. He went to Capitol City Guns. Surely, those guys would be busy.

They were. People were buying guns. Again. The Capitol City guys could not keep up. It wasn't panic buying or anything; just a full parking lot and a line at the cash register. Some empty shelves. Many people were buying ammo; there was hardly any left, except cases of .40.

"Hey, you guys are busy so I'm just dropping by to say 'hi,'" Grant said to Chip.

Chip looked at Grant and said softly, "It's starting. You know it is." Chip pointed to all the customers and whispered, "So do they."

Grant nodded. "What's selling best?" he asked.

"Pistols," Chip said. "Lots of first-time gun buyers, so they're taking forever to make a purchase, but I'm just glad they're getting guns. We will raise the prices tonight after we close. Just a little. Chip smiled at Grant and said, "You, sir, as an esteemed attorney and a gentleman with shop privileges here, will continue to get things wholesale."

Grant didn't have the heart to tell Chip that he would be

spending his cash on food for the foreseeable future. Besides, he had all the guns and ammo he'd need.

Grant asked, "Need any help?"

"Yeah," Chip said, "you can answer people's questions and get them pointed toward a gun that will work for them. I'll do the paperwork."

"No problem," Grant said. He started helping people with questions about which gun to buy. He spent a couple of hours there, loving every minute of it.

When they had a spare moment, out of earshot of the customers, Grant asked Chip, "You think this is some serious shit?"

"Yep," Chip said. "The Mexico thing is a big problem, but the bond rating is even bigger. We're done for."

"I know," Grant said, "but I must say I'm off on my timing here. I would think people would be making runs on the grocery stores. But they're not. Am I on drugs or what?" He asked.

"Nope," Chip said. "Most people are dumbasses. They won't realize what's happening until it's too late." A customer came within earshot so Chip stopped talking to Grant.

Grant smiled at Chip and said, "Say 'hi' to Ted for me."

Chip knew exactly what Grant meant. He smiled back and said, "Roger that."

Grant was perplexed. Maybe the Collapse wasn't coming. It was unfolding like Grant thought it would, but wasn't happening as quickly as he thought. Maybe there wouldn't be a Collapse. Maybe he was just overreacting.

He left the store and had another weird drive from Capitol City Guns back to his house. It was another period of time for him to transition from thinking about the end of the world to being a suburban guy. Grant hit the garage door button and put the happy face back on.

Lisa asked, "How was your day?"

"Oh, fine," he said, lying. Of course. "How about yours?"

"Pretty typical," she said. Amid all this news of what seemed like the collapse of the United States of America, Lisa managed to have a "pretty typical" day. Grant wished he could be as calm about this as she seemed to be.

"Kids," Lisa asked, "what do you guys want for dinner?"

Grant did not turn on the news. He knew Lisa would change the channel. She didn't want all that doom and gloom to ruin her "pretty typical" day.

Chapter 38

Meant To Be

Grant was pretty worthless at work. He couldn't concentrate on anything. He constantly checked the internet to see the latest news and thought of all the things he needed to do, which usually revolved around buying things like food. He'd sneak out at lunch and hit a drugstore for over the counter medications or hit the Dollar Store for miscellaneous things. He got some vegetable seeds at Home Depot for the vacant lot next to his cabin. He kept wishing he had some handheld radios but didn't know where to get them.

It was Friday, and a shooting session with the Team was planned for the weekend. Grant called Pow.

"Hey, man, with all that's going on, are we still going to the range?" he asked Pow.

"I dunno," Pow said. "I'm kinda thinking about saving some ammo, just in case anything weird happens. We are so well trained now that we just need to maintain skills. We can shoot half as often and maintain them. I'm inclined to say we shouldn't do it this weekend."

Grant felt himself getting sloppy once again by letting people on to the prepping. But he knew he needed the Team to be part of the plan. "Hey, I'd like to show you something this weekend."

"Sure, as long as it's not in your pants," Pow said with a laugh.

"Nope," Grant said. "I only show that to your momma. No, I'd like to show you something that could come in super handy if the shit hits the fan," Grant said.

"Like what?" Pow asked.

"A cabin," Grant said.

"Oh, cool," Pow said. "Who owns it? You?"

"You'll see," Grant said. They made arrangements to meet at an Olympia restaurant that was on the way to the cabin.

Grant was a little nervous about letting Pow know about the cabin. He trusted him, but he was basically showing the leader of several very well armed men a safe place stocked with food, guns, and ammo. Grant couldn't re-take the cabin if the Team turned on him and decided to take it away from him. It seemed very unlikely, but it was still something Grant needed to think about.

Not much had changed in the news. California was still experiencing looting and scattered rioting. Texas was having major problems with all the refugees. Things weren't escalating too much, though. Again, Grant was surprised that this was taking so long.

Sunday came and, after church, Grant met Pow at the restaurant parking lot. On the way out, they talked about the news.

Grant wanted to break it gently to Pow that he was a "survivalist," although Pow was probably one too.

"So, Pow, I've been preparing for this for quite some time," Grant said. "Shooting with you guys is more than just fun; I'm training for when I'll need it."

"Like now," Pow said. "The cops can't stop all this shit. There are going to be meth heads running wild. I hear you about preparing for shit hitting the fan. I've been doing it, too. We all are, Bobby, Scotty, and Wes too."

Whew.

Grant continued, "So, I figure things will get weird in the city. We would be safer out here in the sticks."

"Even an Asian guy?" he said with a laugh.

"Oh, yeah, even an Asian guy," Grant said. "Well, I've got a place for us. The Team could come out and stay. You guys could use a safe place and I could use a team of very well armed and highly trained gun fighters. See where I'm going with this?"

Pow had a big smile. "I saw this coming when you called me and insulted my dear mother. This wasn't hard to figure out. So, I'm in. But, I want to see this place."

They were turning off the highway and onto the road that went to Pierce Point. The only road into Pierce Point had a bridge a 100 yards from the highway that went over a creek. One way in and one way out. Grant thought he'd test out Pow.

"So, what do you notice about this road?" Grant asked.

Pow looked around. "Well, very defensible. Easy to put up a barricade there," he pointed to the bridge. "A natural choke point." Pow pointed up the road from the bridge and said, "And a nice hill there with a clear line of fire to the check point. There's even a little volunteer fire station or whatever right here for some guards. A perfect set up."

Grant was impressed. He had noticed the same things when he

first came out to the cabin. They continued on the road and Grant asked, "What else do you notice?"

Pow looked around and said, "Lots of farms. Lots of chicken coops, cattle, gardens, small tractors, barns, boats. These people know how to get by. They'll be perfect neighbors." Grant couldn't believe his luck. Pow was awesome.

They continued driving and Pow kept pointing out features showing that the residents of Pierce Point were far more self-reliant than those in the city. They went by one house and Pow said, "Ham antenna," meaning a ham, or amateur, radio. "Nice. Comms are key," Pow said, referring to communications. Pow went on to remark on the terrain and how a strategic intersection of two roads could be easily defended.

While Grant was pretty sure he trusted Pow, he still wanted to take some precautions to make sure Pow and the well-armed Team didn't decide they wanted the cabin for themselves. It would be impossible to dislodge them from the cabin, so Grant wanted to make it hard for them to move in without Grant. He took Pow the confusing route to the cabin. He'd never be able to find it again without Grant or directions Grant gave him.

After the twists and turns throughout Pierce Point during the decoy route, they were finally heading toward the water. Once the water was visible, Pow said, "This is beautiful, man."

They left the paved road and headed onto the gravel Over Road where the cabin was. They pulled up to the cabin. Grant pointed to it and Pow said, "Very, very nice. Is this yours? Whoa."

Grant gave him the tour. He didn't show him the food in the storage shed. That was the ultimate secret. Besides, Pow had probably figured it out by now. He was smart guy.

They walked down to the beach. "This is incredible, man. You are a lucky man."

"Yes, I am," Grant said. "And I want the Team to come here if shit hits the fan. Do you think they'll want to?"

"Oh, hell, yes," Pow said. "But where will they stay? Your cabin is nice, but I bet your family will want to stay in there."

Grant had that all thought out, too. He pointed to a yellow cabin about 100 yards from his, down by where the paved road ended and the gravel road began. It was on the road before Grant's cabin, the Colsons', or the Morrells'. "See that. We would liberate that thing."

"'Liberate?' As in, 'steal?'" Pow asked. "That's not my thing, man," Pow said, confused that an honest guy like Grant would suggest such a thing.

"No, that guy hasn't been there in a couple years," Grant said. "He lives in California." Grant pointed to Mark Colson's house. "That guy lives here full-time and has a key to it. If the California owner comes up here, we move you guys to another place, or to my cabin, if necessary. Bottom line, there are lots of unused cabins and RVs here. We house you guys here until someone wants their place back, which might be never. In exchange for borrowing some unused shelter, the community gets a team of gunfighters to take care of security."

Pow was taking all this in. "Are you sure people are OK with this?" he finally asked. "I mean, taking over people's places and being an armed security team?"

"Nope," Grant said. "I have no idea if they are OK with it. But they will be. If not, you guys stay with me."

"What would we eat out here?" Pow asked.

It was time to show him the food. Grant took him to the shed and opened the padlocked door.

Pow's eyes got huge. "Oh, shit, look at all that. You got any stir fry sauce?" Pow laughed his hearty laugh.

Grant showed Pow the adjacent vacant lot and explained the gardening plan. He pointed to the beach and described the clams and oysters, and the fishing in the inlet.

Pow was just taking it all in and nodding. "Nice, nice," he said slowly as he was looking at the cabin and its surroundings.

"So," Grant asked, "you think Scotty, Wes, and Bobby will be glad to come here if their neighborhood is on fire and zombies are running around?"

"Hell, yes," Pow said. "But why didn't you bring them out today?"

"Well, you're the leader of the Team," Grant said. "If you thought this was a stupid idea, it wouldn't have worked. Besides, I don't want to tell too many well-armed men about my little hideout, so I was keeping it on the down-low." Grant knew Pow was a devout Christian and member of a Korean church. "Will you promise me — swear on the Bible — that you won't tell anyone about this place. That you'll only tell the Team if, and when, it's time to bug out here. I'm serious, Bill." Grant had never called Pow by his real name, "I'm trusting you with my life, here."

Pow said, "Hell, yes, man. You've trusted me with your life during movement drills with live ammo. I've trusted you with my life doing the same. I really appreciate it. I feel much better knowing that we have a place to come and it is one that's got so much stuff. Thank you, man." Pow was getting a little emotional.

So was Grant. "No, thank you, man. This great cabin and all this food won't mean much if some zombies try to steal it. Between the five of us on the Team, we can have one or two guards up at all times. It's like we were supposed to meet each other."

Pow looked very serious and said, "Yeah. I was just thinkin' that." Changing the subject before things got too emotional, he said, "Hey, Grant, you got any beer in your fridge?"

"Sure do." They had a great afternoon, talking about all the things they could do out at the cabin if the world ask they knew it ended.

On way back to Olympia, they were still talking about ways to secure their area, gather food, and communications. Pow asked, "What about medical? The hospitals will be closed or whatever."

Grant smiled. "Have I ever told you what my wife does?"

"No," Pow said.

"She's an ER doc," Grant said.

"No way," Pow said. He thought Grant was joking.

"I ain't shittin' you," Grant said, smiling. Having an ER doctor out there was the frosting on the cake.

"Wow," Pow said. "This set up was meant to be. Meant to be, my brother." Pow stared out the window.

"Yep," Grant said. "Meant to be."

Chapter 39

The Unraveling

Grant was still looking for signs that people were starting to comprehend what was happening. He wasn't seeing many. Then something happened that surprised him.

Government started to make cuts. Real cuts, not the "reorganizations" of the past where promises were made to cut, but the total number of government employees and spending actually went up. These cuts were real. The Governor ordered a 10% across the board cut in most state programs. The unions and all the people with their hands out, from welfare recipients to the corporations, went ballistic. It was fun to watch.

None of the higher-up state employees in Grant's neighborhood were getting laid off. The Baby Boomers about to retire kept their jobs while the younger workers making much less were largely the ones losing their state jobs.

Local governments were cutting even more than the state. The City of Olympia, which had one of the highest ratios of government employees to residents in the country, cut a staggering 20% of their workforce. It was unbelievable. A few years earlier, as a "stimulus" project, the city had built a $10 million city hall and now it was largely empty because the city couldn't afford to hire any workers to fill the space. Classic government: spend like drunken sailors when the money is pouring in, and then drastically cut services when the money dries up.

The part of the city's cuts that affected people the most were the layoffs in the police department. Not only were there 20% fewer patrolmen, but the fuel budget was severely cut. Those fewer patrolmen could drive around less. It became rare to see a police car anywhere. The criminals figured this out very quickly. Investigation of crimes that were hard to solve, such as an attack by a stranger or a burglary, were going by the wayside. White collar crime was no longer investigated, at all. Neither were DUIs. Crimes where someone knew who did it, like theft by former friends, were still being investigated.

They were half-assed investigations, however.

Of course, with the huge cuts at the Prosecutor's Office, fewer and fewer cases were being prosecuted. Plea bargains were the answer, and the deals for criminals kept getting sweeter and sweeter. Predictably, the cops basically quit arresting people for property and drug crimes. There were only enough police and prosecutors to take care of easy-to-solve violent crimes. Many people who had never called the police to report a crime were shocked to learn that they needed to fill out a police report on the city's website and that was it. No police officer would show up to talk to them. People were told to fill out a police report online; that was usually as far as the "investigation" went.

People like Grant, who lived in safe neighborhoods, started to hear about their friends getting burglarized, and even robbed. One of the support staff at WAB had a burglar come into her house late at night. Luckily, she had a gun and scared him out. He might not have only been looking to burglarize her.

Grant started to notice that petty criminals were hanging out together. It used to be common to see one or two dirtbags; now, they seemed to travel in groups. Lately, five or ten "youths" would mill about downtown by the WAB offices looking like they were ready to cause trouble. It would be a stretch to call them a "gang," but they were the beginnings of gangs. "Gang seedlings" Grant called them. They were unemployed punks hanging out together and working together to steal and do worse. In the past, when Grant saw them they would disburse because they didn't want the attention. But as time went on, they didn't do that as much. They would stand there and stare as if to say, "Whatcha looking at, dickhead?"

Grant had a solution. Carry a gun. He had his concealed weapons permit, so he could. Although he liked his full-sized Glock 22 in .40, it was a little large for concealed carry. So he got a compact Glock in .40, a Glock model 27. Grant knew how to operate the Glock 27 because it was just a smaller version of the Glock 22 he had mastered. It was perfect. He carried two spare 10-round magazines because, with increasingly large packs of criminals, Grant knew that he would likely have to fight off a group of them.

When he couldn't wear a Glock 27, he would slip his 380 auto LCP in a pants pocket. He was armed nearly all the time, even at work. No one knew. He didn't advertise that he was carrying; he didn't want people to think he was weird or, when they needed protection, come flocking to him. He wanted to just lay low and protect himself and his family.

He had to hide his gun from Lisa, of course. He kept it in the car, in a locked console that was legal under Washington law.

Grant constantly worried about Lisa being out and about with all the crime going on. She was a petite and beautiful woman. That thought was awful.

He tried once to suggest that she get consider carrying a gun. She rolled her eyes and walked out of the room. That hurt. All he was trying to do was suggest a practical way to protect his wife. But, decades of Lisa's upbringing that guns are weird and unnecessary was too strong to change. This was despite all the stories of people she knew who had become victims of crime. Carrying a gun was just… something a normal person didn't do.

Grant tried a second time to convince her. His birthday was coming up and she asked him, "What would you like for your birthday?"

"I'd like something that doesn't cost anything and makes me very happy," he said with a smile.

"You already get too much sex," she said with a grin.

"Well, you'll need to get your hands dirty for what I have in mind," he said with that same bedroom smile.

"You sicko," she replied.

"I mean getting some ink on your fingers when you get your fingerprints taken for your concealed weapons permit," Grant said. "I am really, really concerned for your safety, dear. Seriously. All joking aside. I'm worried about you. Please do this for me. It's my birthday."

"What's your second choice?" She asked.

That was it. No more talk of her getting a concealed weapons permit. A few days later, one of her friends she went running with was attacked by some teenagers in the parking lot at work. Grant didn't even bother to say anything resembling "I told you so." It was a lost cause. Grant hoped — actually, prayed — for the best.

At the same time criminals were learning that they could practically get away with anything, the economy started sucking even more. Why even attempt to have a legitimate job? There weren't any. Crime paid; literally.

Grant was at the grocery store with Manda and Cole one Saturday. All the prices were way higher. It happened suddenly. Cole's favorite pancakes had been $2.79, and now they were $4.15. That kind of price increase was typical for other foods. Gas was going up, too, almost one dollar per gallon at a time. Suddenly, there were shortages of medical supplies and prescription drugs. A significant portion of the population was on at least one prescription drug. They had never been told by a pharmacist, "We're out of that." They couldn't believe it. Didn't their prescriptions just appear at the store and someone else paid for them?

Police check points were springing up. They police asked people to "voluntarily" allow them to search their vehicles; most did.

In Olympia, there were increasing numbers of traffic jams from all the protests due to all the budget cuts and high prices.

People were starting to figure out that things weren't going so well. About time.

Chapter 40

We Have a Fight on Our Hands

Rebel Radio was going strong. There was so much to talk about, like the fact that massive government budget cuts were suddenly needed, for one. How did this situation get so out of control that these huge cuts, like letting criminals out of prison, were necessary in the first place? For the first time, people were actually asking this question. Rebel Radio had the answers.

The podcast was growing by leaps and bounds. Over 5,000 people regularly downloaded the weekly broadcast. Bloggers were talking about Rebel Radio. Conservative and libertarian bloggers loved it, and progressive bloggers demonized it. Progressives in Washington State made Rebel Radio public enemy number one. There was speculation about the identity of the "Rebels" as Grant and the other podcasters were called. People in government were figuring out it was the WAB guys.

One of the government people most concerned by Rebel Radio was Rick Menlow. He hated the fact that one of his former employees was thought to be one of the Rebels. He also hated the fact that the podcast seemed to have inside information about the lack of reform coming from the State Auditor's Office.

This pissed him off because his campaign for Governor was in full swing. He was running as a "moderate Republican" and really needed the establishment to like him. His trusted campaign adviser was Jeanie.

Grant kept in regular contact with her. He wanted to gather intelligence on what the state agencies were doing. She wouldn't tell him anything too specific, just the general situation in the Auditor's Office. She didn't want to get in trouble because she needed her job, just like everyone else did. She also hated what Menlow was doing. He was betraying people like her and it was sweet revenge to whisper gossip to Rebel Radio.

One day, Grant was talking to Jeanie about Menlow's run for Governor. "How in the world does a Republican think he could win in this state?" Grant asked.

"He's counting on the budget disaster to get him into office," Jeanie said. "The worse things get, the better for him so he can run on 'change.'"

"But the worse things get, like all the government employee layoffs, the more of a government 'safety net' people will want," Grant said. "So they won't vote for a government-cutting Republican."

Jeanie laughed. "Who said anything about Menlow being a 'government-cutting Republican?' He will be a 'new' Republican who will run government more efficiently, saving money that can be spent to help people." Her voice was dripping with sarcasm, but she was serious.

"So he'll spend just as much money, but be the 'change' people want?" Grant asked.

"Yep," Jeanie said. "It just might work. Especially if we get a tape of the current Governor running over a little kid in an intersection." It was important to remember that Menlow got into office by accident.

Menlow's campaign strategy was the topic of the next Rebel Radio. Menlow was furious. He didn't suspect Jeanie as the source because he had been bragging to so many Republican legislators and others about his brilliant strategy.

WAB started to pay a price for Rebel Radio. WAB was a tax-exempt trade association, but the IRS selected WAB for a "random" audit. They started coming up with "interpretations" of the tax regulations, and hinting that WAB might owe millions in taxes for its "for-profit" work. What "for-profit" work? They were a typical trade association; they didn't make a "profit."

The state Department of Revenue decided to do a "random" audit, too. The state unemployment insurance agency piled on, too, looking for past unpaid unemployment insurance premiums that should have been paid. Even with their creative "interpretations," DOR and the unemployment agency did not find any violations. When they reported that to the Governor, it just made her angrier. They had to find a way to shut down WAB.

Nancy Ringman's phone rang; it was the Governor.

"Yes, Governor," Nancy said. She listened to the Governor's short description of the WAB problem.

"I share your concerns about WAB, Governor," Nancy said. "I will personally look into whether they might be committing any campaign finance violations. A hate group like WAB must be violating some campaign law. I will keep you updated on my progress."

Nancy put down the phone and felt warm all over. "OK, Grant Matson," she said to herself. "Payback time."

Nancy Ringman was a bully. She wore business attire and had a peace sticker on her Subaru, but she was a bully. Grant had been fighting bullies like her his whole life. He would fight them even more in the near future.

A few days later, a process server came to WAB. The Campaign Finance Commission, headed by Nancy Ringman, filed a suit asking for a $10 million fine and scheduled a court hearing for later that same day to get a court order to seize WAB's bank account. That was necessary, the court papers said, because WAB was a "continuing criminal enterprise" violating the campaign finance laws and using the money in its bank account to do so. CFC needed to have control of WAB's bank account to "prevent further violations." After going home to change into a suit, Grant ran off to court and tried to reason with the judge.

The judges in the county where the state capitol was located were friendly toward government. The judge who received the request to seize WAB's bank account was, like Nancy Ringman, a good friend of the Governor. The judge signed the court order allowing the seizure of the bank account. CFC was ordered to continue paying the salaries of WAB staff unless it found a reason not to. The financial lives of WAB staff were held in the hands of a hostile Nancy Ringman. It happened so quickly.

Ted Foster, the head of WAB, was unfazed. "Well, gentlemen, looks like we have a fight on our hands." He had halfway expected something like this, given how hard WAB was hitting the government. He was surprised that the bank accounts had been seized, however. "Rebel Radio stays on the air. We fight on." Ben, Brian, and Grant were relieved.

It felt like a war had begun. Grant had never been in a war, but assumed this was what it felt like. He rallied around his guys. There was a huge and evil threat. Things looked bleak. But Grant knew who would win in the end. Just not how.

Chapter 41

Tough on Crime

The CFC suit and bank account seizure actually wasn't as bad as WAB thought at first. Their paychecks kept coming. It would take CFC months of gathering all of WAB's financial records to see that WAB hadn't done anything wrong. If anything, WAB was overly compliant with the campaign finance laws because they knew something like this might happen. In fact, Nancy Ringman was actually worried that she couldn't find any violations. The Governor would be pissed.

The Legislature was in session, which was never a good thing. How would they address the budget deficit? Raise taxes, of course. The necessary increases were staggering. A 66% increase of the property tax, a 250% increase of the corporate tax, and a 50% increase in the sales tax. The Governor knew that she must do this to try to bring in money. She also knew that the more she raised taxes, the less business activity there would be, and the less tax revenue. She decided to go down in state history as a "leader" who made "tough choices." She would do it and not run for another term. Besides, who would want to be Governor with all these messes?

Rick Menlow, that's who. When Menlow got wind of the Governor's proposed massive tax hikes, he knew that she could not possibly be attempting to run for another term. And no Democrat could get elected when their party had just raised taxes like that. Menlow knew he would be the next Governor.

Menlow felt a surge of adrenaline. Then he felt... it was hard to describe... a darkness. A happy darkness. He felt like the darkness was saying that he was getting something he wanted, but that the darkness would be back to tell him what he needed to do in return.

The economy was the worst anyone had ever seen. People were scared. It seemed like everyone was out of work. People started to use the "D" word of "depression." The term "D2," for Second Great Depression, was starting to be used. Up until this point, everyone on TV had been referring to the economic situation as a "recession." This wasn't any little "recession."

Crime was getting worse. It had grown slowly when the police quit patrolling. Now it was everywhere. Not a complete breakdown of law and order, just rampant crime. It was like Detroit. In fact, people started referring to the slowly unfolding Collapse as the "Detroit-ification" of America.

Amid the virtual bankruptcy of Washington State, the Legislature decided to go to the easy plays from their political play book: crack down on crime. It was far more popular than reducing the size of government spending. Democrats loved "tough on crime" legislation because it helped them get over their 1960s image as being soft on crime. Republicans loved "tough on crime" legislation because... well, they were Republicans. The Governor wanted to appear in control of the whole mess so she could call for tougher and tougher measures.

Of course, increasing prison terms for crimes that were going uninvestigated and unprosecuted wouldn't do much. Besides, increasing prison sentences would make the state's financial crisis worse because it meant spending more for prisons. The state was being forced to release prisoners because it couldn't afford to keep them. So no one, not even the mind numbed zombie voters, would go for increasing prison sentences. The state needed to do something else to show they were cracking down on crime.

The Legislature passed a package of "temporary" laws to make it easy for the police to search people at the new checkpoints and to enter homes without a warrant. The checkpoints were usually a police car or two at a key intersection stopping traffic and asking people for their ID. The police didn't search every car; they didn't have the resources for that. The main reasons the ineffective checkpoints were set up were to make citizens feel safe and to show them that the authorities were in charge.

This wasn't "martial law"; it was an expansion of the powers the civilian police already had. A really big expansion. Most of the voters ate it up. "Something needs to be done," they said.

The Legislature attempted to pass some strict gun control laws, but didn't have the votes. People in Washington State, while progressive as a whole, still wanted guns. They saw the packs of punks milling around their neighborhoods. They might tell their progressive friends that they supported gun control, but they were the ones flooding places like Capitol City Guns. That surprised Grant. He figured the state was so far gone that gun control would pass easily, especially in a crime wave. He was glad to be wrong about that.

One small provision of the new "tough on crime" law that went largely unnoticed was a huge expansion of the civil forfeiture law. This law allowed the police to seize (without a warrant) anything of value involved in a crime or suspected crime. For example, if a car were suspected of being used by a criminal, the police could seize it, send the owner listed on the registration a certified letter, wait ten days, and then sell it, and keep the money. That last part was the key.

The police had a profit motive to grab as much stuff as they could; guns, houses, boats. Of course, the overworked police who couldn't investigate crimes had plenty of time to send out certified mail letters to owners and to sell their bounty. It was a great way to fund police departments without raising taxes. It was also government-sanctioned theft. But it only affected criminals. Right?

No; it affected anyone unlikely enough to have their property stolen first by a criminal and then by the police. For example, when a criminal stole a car, used it to rob someone, and then got caught, the car — stolen from an innocent victim — was sold after ten days. The law abiding owner who had her car stolen was now the victim; the government had taken her car, but if she didn't get the letter within ten days and go through the process of proving she wasn't a criminal, then they got to keep the proceeds. The innocent victim had to prove her innocence. Civil forfeiture was a civil, not criminal, law so the burden of proof could be on the citizen to prove innocence. Many innocent crime victims were having their things stolen by government. There were more and more stories to describe on Rebel Radio, just like there were more and more pissed off people who used to trust government and now hated it. Things were getting out of hand, quickly.

Grant went into Capitol City Guns to get a reality check. Hanging out with lawyers and lobbyists was not reality. Gun store guys; that's reality. Special Forces Ted was there with Chip and a Sheriff's deputy. Grant avoided talking to them because they might be talking business. Chip motioned for Grant to come over. The deputy looked a little nervous about having Grant join the conversation.

Chip introduced Grant to the deputy. "Jeff, this is Grant. He's a lawyer and has shop privileges here, so he's cool. I trust Grant with my life. So tell him what you were telling us."

The deputy looked a little nervous but said, "Some of us are a little concerned at all the stuff that's happening. That civil forfeiture thing is a frickin' racket. My guys…"

Ted asked, "Oath Keepers?"

"Yeah, Oath Keepers," Jeff said. "We are starting to wonder when this shit crosses the line and violates our oaths. Any thoughts from the lawyer?" Jeff asked Grant.

Grant thought. "I think the civil forfeiture laws are unconstitutional, but I don't think it's to the level of an unlawful order. You're not being ordered to round people up or take all lawful firearms. You could ask to be reassigned so you don't have anything to do with the forfeitures."

Jeff nodded. "Yeah, that's what I thought."

They were all quiet for a few seconds.

Jeff said, "Here's what bugs me the most. The majority of my fellow deputies don't seem to be bothered by this 'crime wave' and the crackdown. They are kind of excited to be out fighting it. They feel like they are more needed than ever because there are so many crimes out there. They're not seeing the bigger picture. I'm kinda concerned."

More silence. Shit, this was not good. Grant had always counted on Oath Keepers to prevent his kind of thing. It looked like it wasn't working. This might be even worse than he thought.

He looked at his watch and realized he needed to take off. He said goodbye to the guys and headed home. It was another one of those drives from Capitol City to his home where he had things to wrestle with, like the police and military deciding to fight the government, or not, as today seemed to indicate.

He could think about that the entire drive, but when he hit that garage door opener, it would be all about doing homework with the kids and going to ballet lessons. These two worlds were getting farther and farther apart. And the real world of nastiness was becoming more and more apparent and less theoretical. It was scaring the hell out of Grant.

What really scared Grant, though, was what was happening when he walked into his house. Lisa was sitting on the couch with Cole.

"OK, Cole," she said, "what do you do if a stranger comes in our house and Mom or Dad aren't here?"

Cole thought. "Call 911?"

"That's right," Lisa said. "Good. Call 911 and the police will come and help you." Lisa saw Grant and smiled at him. She was putting her faith in the government to protect them. Grant was not. This rift between them was getting bigger.

Grant looked at Cole. He was the sweetest boy in the world. But he couldn't talk too much or understand people. Oh, God. What will happen to Cole when all of this hits? Grant was dealing head-on with the collapse of the United States. That didn't scare him too much since he had prepared. He was calmly planning on it. But the thought of Cole by himself in a very dangerous world terrified him.

Chapter 42

Lawyers, Guns and Money

The worse things got, the more Grant prepped. It was an emotional crutch. Yes, Grant admitted, it was an emotional crutch. After his conversation with the police about how they are going along with legalized theft, he found comfort in building up his food storage and self-defense capabilities. If that's an "emotional crutch" then Grant was proud to be guilty of it. Prepping sure beat the other form of dealing with the situation, which was the form most people were using: pretending nothing was wrong.

Most people, even his conservative WAB friends, were trying to convince themselves that things were going to be OK. Tom did not talk about it much. In fact, he avoided the topic altogether.

During one conversation, Grant was making the point with Tom that things were getting worse. They were in Tom's car and the Warren Zevon song "Lawyers Guns and Money" came on, which is about a guy getting out of various jams with lawyers, guns, and money.

Grant tried to make the point to Tom about things getting worse by saying, "You know, at first we tried using money to make donations and elect good people. Didn't work. Now we need lawyers to fend off things like the CFC charges and the IRS. That may not work. I think it'll take guns, next."

Tom was silent. It appeared that he either didn't understand or didn't want to hear it. Grant had no idea why Tom wasn't reacting. It was weird because Tom was such a fighter but he couldn't conceive of the likelihood this fight going beyond the political realm. Even a fighter like Tom had normalcy bias. Tom changed the subject for the rest of the ride.

Brian was in outright denial. He would talk to Grant about how bad things were getting and then say, "This is no time to overreact. Things always seem worse than they usually are." It was like he was trying to convince himself into believing it. Grant worried about how Brian would react when the shit hit the fan.

Ben was handling it better. He realized that things were not normal. He seemed to understand that something big was developing, and he would be a part of it. He and Grant talked about it one day.

"Hey, Grant, you own some guns," Ben said. "Are you freaked out about what's happening?"

"Yes." That's about all Grant would say. He fully planned on including Ben, Brian, Tom, and their families in his survival plans, but now was not the time to chitchat about it.

"I can tell something is coming," Ben said. "Something bad. Guys like you and I will be the first to be rounded up," he said with a half-smile. But he was also half serious. "I can't bring myself to start stockpiling food and getting a gas mask." He said that last part with another smile. The WAB guys, while they didn't know the full extent of Grant's preps, figured Grant might be preparing and often teased him about being a "survivalist" and running around in a gas mask.

Ben paused and looked at Grant in the eye. "I think I'll be OK even when things get crazy. I don't know why, I just do." Ben seemed genuine; he wasn't just convincing himself of something to believe like Brian was.

"Let's hope so, my brother," Grant said. Maybe Ben was prepping, too, and didn't want to tell Grant. There was something about what he was saying that convinced Grant that Ben would, indeed, be OK.

We'll see, Grant thought. We'll see.

Grant's refuge from all this stress and worrying was the cabin. Everything was calm there. It was quiet. It was beautiful. Every time he went out there, he was on vacation. Even if it was for an hour in the middle of the day. It was a vacation from the world.

Grant loved the smell of the cabin. It smelled like fresh Christmas trees and the ocean, which made sense because it was surrounded by evergreen trees and the ocean. Just smelling the cabin calmed Grant and relaxed him to the point that it was almost impossible to get mad.

Lisa wondered sometimes why Grant was in such a good mood around the house. What she didn't know is that earlier that day he had run out to the cabin for a short time. He wouldn't tell her.

Lisa was still rather cold toward the cabin; it was "his thing," not hers. The maintenance and utilities were costing a fair amount of money. Regardless, it seemed like she had just decided that she wouldn't like the place. She didn't hate it and didn't try to stop Grant from going there; she just didn't like it. Grant didn't know why. He thought that perhaps it was because his worthless parents, both of whom Lisa really disliked, had just handed him something. She also knew that Grant loved the cabin more than anything else except her and the kids. She was competing with a building out in Hickville. She was a beautiful doctor; why couldn't that be good enough for him? Why did he need a stupid old cabin to feel great? He had her. Wasn't that enough?

When he was out there for more than a little while, he would drop by the Colsons and Morrells and visit. Strengthening his relationship with these neighbors was as important as any other prep; maybe more so. He would explore the woods around the beach, and looked for sources of water and defensible terrain. He just watched the wildlife. There were amazing birds out there. There were harbor seals in the inlet and fish jumping. Fox roamed around the area. Eagles flew by, sometimes grabbing a fish out of the water. It was amazing.

It was now spring, and everything was blooming. There was something terribly dreary about a winter of cloudiness and rain in Washington State. Residents of Washington must endure rain from about Thanksgiving to St. Patrick's Day. However, when it stops raining and the sun comes out, the place is glorious.

Grant looked around the cabin, which was surrounded by spring blooms. He kept thinking that this spring was going to be the beginning of something more than just a growing season for plants.

He couldn't put his finger on it, but it felt like the beginning of something big. Then, when he was down on the beach just looking at the water, the outside thought said something jarring.

It will be big. Keep preparing. You don't have enough.

Grant heard that loud and clear.

He would step up his Costco food runs. Whenever he went to Costco alone for weekend errands, he would "accidently" put some oatmeal packets, pancake mix, or other bulk foods in the cart. He would put these items in the trunk of his Tacura for the weekly run out to the cabin. Lisa never looked in his trunk. When he had enough items out in the shed from the recent runs, he would vacuum seal them. His six month food supply had slowly grown to about eight months. His shed was getting filled up. Good.

- End Book One -

19702556R00143

Made in the USA
Lexington, KY
05 January 2013